"You're a better hostage than I deserve," Dillon told her.

"So that's your way of saying thanks?"

"No. My way of saying thanks will be to walk away from here and never look back. To leave you the way I found you—unharmed. Safe. Too trusting, but out of danger." Damned if he wasn't sure he could do it. Two days ago, all he'd wanted was shelter from the rain, heat to ward off the cold and a little precious rest to deal with his injuries. Today...today he wanted Ashley.

And he couldn't have her. She wasn't the sort of woman a man could seduce, then forget, wasn't the sort a man walked away from.

"You know, you could stay a while," she suggested quietly.

"Don't say that." *Don't tempt me.*

Dear Reader,

We've got six drop-dead-gorgeous and utterly irresistible heroes for you this month, starting with Marilyn Pappano's latest contribution to our HEARTBREAKERS program. Dillon Boone, in *Survive the Night*, is a man on the run—right into Ashley Benedict's arms. The only problem is, will they survive long enough to fulfill their promises of forever?

Our ROMANTIC TRADITIONS title is Judith Duncan's *Driven to Distraction*, a sexy take on the younger man/older woman theme. I promise you that Tony Parnelli will drive right into your heart. *A Cowboy's Heart*, Doreen Roberts' newest, features a one-time rodeo rider who's just come face-to-face with a woman—and a secret—from his past. Kay David's *Baby of the Bride* is a marriage-of-convenience story with an adorable little girl at its center—and a groom you'll fall for in a big, bad way. *Blackwood's Woman*, by Beverly Barton, is the last in her miniseries, THE PROTECTORS. And in J.T. Blackwood she's created yet another hero to remember. Finally, Margaret Watson returns with her second book, *An Honorable Man*. Watch as hero Luke McKinley is forced to confront the one woman he would like never to see again—the one woman who is fated to be his.

Enjoy them all, and come back next month for more great romantic reading—here in Silhouette Intimate Moments.

Yours,

Leslie Wainger
Senior Editor and Editorial Coordinator

Please address questions and book requests to:
Silhouette Reader Service
U.S.: 3010 Walden Ave., P.O. Box 1325, Buffalo, NY 14269
Canadian: P.O. Box 609, Fort Erie, Ont. L2A 5X3

Marilyn Pappano

SURVIVE THE NIGHT

Silhouette®
INTIMATE™MOMENTS®
Published by Silhouette Books
America's Publisher of Contemporary Romance

SILHOUETTE BOOKS

ISBN 0-373-07703-3

SURVIVE THE NIGHT

Copyright © 1996 by Marilyn Pappano

This edition published by arrangement with Harlequin Books S.A.

Printed in U.S.A.

Books by Marilyn Pappano

MARILYN PAPPANO

has been writing as long as she can remember, just for the fun of it, but a few years ago she decided to take her lifelong hobby seriously. She was encouraging a friend to write a romance novel and ended up writing one herself. It was accepted, and she plans to continue as an author for a long time. When she's not involved in writing, she enjoys camping, quilting, sewing and, most of all, reading. Not surprisingly, her favorite books are romance novels.

Her husband is in the Navy, and in the course of her marriage she has lived all over the U.S. Currently, she lives in Oklahoma with her husband and son.

Prologue

The first thought in Dillon Boone's mind when the car stopped its violent side-over-side roll at the bottom of the ravine was that he had to escape. Maybe the men on the roadway up above would assume that the crash had killed him; maybe they wouldn't bother making their way down the steep, rocky slope and would instead leave the scene as quickly as possible to avoid detection, but he doubted it. Not when they'd chosen the spot for their attack so carefully. Not when they had ignored the deputy with him. Not when they had apparently decided that killing him would be worth killing a cop.

The cruiser lay upside down now, its wheels still spinning, one side lodged against a barrier of fallen trees, rocks and other debris that darkened the interior and made escape from the passenger side impossible. Another small tree blocked the rear door on the driver's side, and a solid steel-mesh screen prevented him from climbing into the front seat and exiting the driver's door, which had come open and broken off in the wild ride. His only chance was to kick out the window, already marked with a web of cracks, and wriggle through the small space. The way the roof was compressed, he wasn't sure he could make it. He wasn't sure he had the time. He wasn't sure he could endure the attempt.

But he had no choice. It was either try... or wait here to die. Damned if he was going to make it easy for the bastards. They still might succeed, but they were going to have to work for it.

Turning onto his back, he raised his feet, drew a breath, then slammed them hard against the glass. Jolts of pain traveled up his legs, becoming knife-sharp and hot as they moved through his ribs. If his ribs weren't already cracked, the shock wave just might finish the job, he thought with a grimace; then, pushing the pain to the back of his mind, he kicked again. This time the weakened glass popped out, falling without sound to the wet, mossy ground outside. He twisted around, working his way out headfirst, swearing silently, viciously, to keep the pain under control.

For one precious moment he simply lay there, barely able to breathe, feeling the mist soak through his clothes and trickle down his neck, then he forced himself to his knees, forced himself to look above for signs of danger. He could see the ragged scar of downed saplings, scraped rock and disturbed earth where the car had tumbled its way to the bottom, but from here, he couldn't see the roadway where the men had been waiting for them. He couldn't see the black van that had been pulled across the lanes on a hairpin curve, leaving the deputy nowhere to go but down. He couldn't see the three men, two of them strangers, the third vaguely familiar, who had opened fire on them as they'd skidded across the blacktop and, finally, over the side.

But they were still there. He could hear voices, low, the words indistinct, the tones threatening. They were coming after him, and they intended to kill him.

As he summoned the strength to get to his feet, his gaze settled on the deputy in the front seat. His name was Coughlin, and he was about Dillon's age and probably twice his size—beefy and muscular. His seat belt still held him in place and had likely saved his life when the door had snapped off under the car's weight. He was unconscious, his breathing labored, his green uniform shirt stained with blood. If he left the deputy here alone, the man might die, Dillon acknowledged. It wasn't likely that the men responsible for his condition would summon help for him, and passersby probably wouldn't notice the skid marks or even see the damaged hillside unless they were out of their cars looking.

But if he stayed, he couldn't help Coughlin.

If he stayed, all he could do was die with him.

From overhead came the squeal of tires, then the slamming of car doors. Maybe help had arrived . . . but for him and the deputy? Or the men trying to kill him?

"Wow, look at that!" A child's voice drifted down into the ravine. "Did someone have a wreck? Is there a car down there? Jeez, do you think they're okay?"

Another one, this one a girl's, maybe a few years older, joined in. "My mom's calling the sheriff from her car phone. They'll be here any time now. Are you guys hurt?"

Maybe Coughlin would be all right, after all, Dillon thought. Surely Russell's men wouldn't try to finish the job with two curious children and their Good Samaritan mother standing by, and there was no way they would stay around and wait for the sheriff to arrive. Any minute now they would return to the van and drive away, and more than likely, neither the kids nor their mother would be able to provide a tag number or even a decent description of them or their van.

Reaching inside the car, he removed the deputy's pistol from its holster and tucked it into the waistband of his jeans. He took a moment to lean past the deputy, close enough to hear his uneven breathing and pull the keys from the ignition. If he was going to survive, he needed the small key dangling next to the car keys, the key that would open the handcuffs fastened around his wrists. Sliding the keys into his pocket, he rose to his feet and made his way awkwardly around the car and over the pile of debris. He headed deeper into the mountains. The handcuffs could be dealt with later, but his first priority was getting out of there alive.

His second was staying that way.

Chapter 1

With a glance at the clock, Ashley Benedict removed the last of the reeds from the tub filled with gallons of strong tea, checked the color against the last batch she had dyed, then began hanging them from the line suspended the entire length of her workshop. By tomorrow morning they would be dry, and she could begin making the oversize market basket Seth was giving his mother for her birthday. Mrs. Benedict would love the basket, would love that her son had gone to the trouble to have something specially made for her, would love that he'd listened all those times she had complained about keeping her knitting yarns neat and convenient, but she wouldn't be at all happy with the idea that the basket had been made by her former daughter-in-law. Although she hadn't minded Ashley and Seth's friendship when they were growing up, she had seriously disapproved of their marriage.

That was all right, though, Ashley mused as she hung the last of the pliable strips. Marriage to Seth had been a mistake from the beginning, and for the past four years, it had been over and done with. Now they were just friends, which was all they ever should have been.

Reaching for a towel on the worktable, she dried her hands, then opened a jar filled with pale pink cream and scooped some onto her hands. Her own concoction, the lotion was satiny, cool and smelled of roses. It kept her skin soft, and the aloe it contained helped heal the scrapes and cuts that were a hazard of her work.

While she rubbed it in, she leaned against the sturdy table and stared out the window. It was a little after five on a dreary March afternoon. Yesterday had been beautiful, with temperatures in the seventies and a definite hint of spring in the air. Even this morning the sun had been shining brightly, warming the air, filling the workshop with its light and heat, and she had allowed herself to wonder if winter truly was past. Then the sun had disappeared, the temperature had dropped a good twenty-five degrees and the rain had started. It had been a good day to snuggle beneath a quilt in front of a roaring fire, to drowse away the hours and weave nothing more than dreams.

It had also been a good day for weaving baskets and blankets, for mixing potpourris and herbal concoctions, for making soap or baking bread or any of the other hundred and one chores that kept her in food, clothing and money.

With a soft sigh, she shut off the lights and stepped outside, pulling the door firmly shut behind her. The only locks were hook and eye, one on the inside, one on the outside, to secure the workshop against the door blowing open, not against intruders. She never had intruders up here. Surrounded by parkland on three sides, more than five miles from her nearest neighbor and ten miles beyond that to the nearest town, she was too far off the beaten path for wanderers or drifters. Seth came by at least once a week to check on her, and she had occasional business-related visitors, but no one else ventured so far. Her friends were hours away in Raleigh and Durham, and her parents and sisters lived on the California coast, selling pottery by the sea. She was alone.

And she liked it that way.

She had taken her first steps from the workshop's sheltering stoop when movement in the clearing caught her attention. A man was coming around from behind where her van was parked, his head bent low against the rain and the piercing wind. It took only a second's glance to tag him a stranger, only a second longer to identify him as an outsider. No local would be out in weather like this wearing nothing but jeans, sneakers and a stained T-shirt. Even though the sun had been shining this morning and the temperature had been on the mild side, no one who had lived more than a season in these North Carolina mountains would make the mistake of wandering far from home without a jacket.

Maybe he was a hiker who'd lost his way in the park...but no serious hiker would take to the rugged trails around here in worn tennis shoes. Even a novice on a day hike knew to wear sturdy boots with ridged soles.

She felt a moment's uneasiness brought on by his presence, but she shook it off. Living the way she did, isolated and with no one but herself to depend on, she couldn't afford to let every unusual occurrence frighten her. She couldn't acquaint herself with easy fear, or she would start thinking that every bump in the night was the bogeyman come to get her. When that happened, she would have to give up her solitude, her peace and her easy way of living and move into town.

Besides, this wasn't such an unusual occurrence. She'd had unexpected visitors before, and all they had ever wanted was a little neighborly assistance. This man wasn't likely to be any different. In fact, she was pretty sure she had seen him before, probably in town. He didn't live nearby—she knew all her neighbors—but maybe he was visiting one of them. Maybe he was a relative of one.

"Can I help you?" she asked, folding her arms across her chest, wishing she'd grabbed the jacket she kept in the workshop, wishing she hadn't planned on a quick dash across the clearing when she'd walked right past it.

His head came up, and his steps slowed. Coming to a stop a half-dozen feet away, for a moment he simply watched her in the thin light. He looked tired and battered, with a few raw scrapes and bruises that darkened his face, and he was obviously weakened. However long he'd been out in the cold rain, it had been too long. He was suffering, probably a little from shock and a lot from exposure.

"My car..." His voice was raspy and rough, perfectly matching the appearance he presented. "I hit a slick spot and ran off the road back there. Do you have a phone?"

At least that explained his face, the awkward way he stood and moved and his lack of warm clothing, she thought as she shook her head. "Sorry, I don't."

"Is your husband around? Maybe he could help...."

She smiled. "I don't have one of those, either. But I can give you a ride into town or down to the Parmenters' place about five miles down the road. They have a telephone, and they would be happy to let you use it. Wait here, and I'll get my keys." Still hugging herself for warmth, she hurried across the clearing, taking the half-dozen stairs to the porch in three steps. Under the shelter of the porch roof, she opened the unlocked door, switched the lights on and went inside and to her purse on the kitchen table. She was digging through it when the floorboard right in front of the door creaked and the man stepped into the open doorway.

The uneasiness she'd felt briefly outside reappeared. *Wait here,* she had said. Instructions couldn't get any simpler. So why had he followed her? Why was he standing there blocking the door, making the hair on the back of her neck stand on end, making her feel very unsafe?

Her fingers closed around her car keys, but she continued to dig through the deep shoulder bag. "I keep telling myself I should get a smaller purse. I'm forever losing things in here," she said, hearing the beginnings of fear in her voice, hoping he didn't recognize it as that. "What's your name?"

He was looking around the cabin, paying it far more attention than it deserved. Was she about to be robbed? Ashley wondered, the thought sending chills down her spine. Surely not. Even the most inept thief could find a better target than this primitive little cabin with her inexpensive furniture, aged appliances and minimal personal belongings.

After a long, still moment his gaze settled on her. "What does it matter?"

"Just trying to be friendly." She tried for a casual shrug. "I thought maybe I'd seen you before."

"Where would you have seen me?"

"In town. In Catlin."

He shook his head. "I never met you there."

No, she knew that. She never would have forgotten such a handsome face... or such an unsettling manner. But she *had* seen him. She was sure of it. Maybe in a store, maybe on the street, maybe even in a photograph or...

A photograph. Yes, that was it. A grainy black-and-white photograph underneath a red heading: Have You Seen This Man? For a few months last year those flyers had been prominently displayed in every business in town. Bill Armstrong, president of Catlin's only bank, had paid for the printing and had distributed them himself. It was a waste of time, Seth had confided in her. After weeks of investigation and intensive searches, there was one place the Catlin County Sheriff's Department was sure the man wasn't: in Catlin County.

Neither was the four hundred fifty thousand dollars he'd stolen from Armstrong's bank.

The caption underneath the photo and the lines directly following it came clearly to mind: Dillon Boone. Wanted for bank robbery. If you have any information regarding his whereabouts, please contact the Catlin County Sheriff's Department. Reward.

It was Dillon Boone. Dear God, what was he doing back here in Catlin County, where everyone knew his name, where practically everyone knew his face?

He stood absolutely motionless, watching her watch him. He knew, she saw—knew that she had remembered. He read it in the shock that had turned her face pale, in the trembling that swept over her as if she'd just stepped into a frigid wind.

Slowly he stepped inside the cabin, then closed and locked the door behind him. He moved stiffly, as if each motion were painful. He was badly hurt, she realized. In addition to the cuts and bruises on his face and arms, she would guess from the way he was breathing that he had a few broken ribs, and that rusty stain spreading across his shirt she recognized now as blood that might have come from something as innocent as a cut or as sinister as a gunshot wound. Toss in his inadequate clothing, the rain and the chill—the temperature outside was hovering in the high forties now, she estimated, with a stiff breeze out of the west—and he was in seriously bad shape.

Watching him, Ashley ran through a mental checklist of anything in the cabin that might be used as a weapon against a man in an obviously weakened state: the butcher knife and the rolling pin in the kitchen, the scissors in the sewing basket at the end of the sofa, next to the door the solid length of hickory that she took on her walks into the woods and the logs stacked next to the hearth. Most of the logs were too short and fat to be of any use, but there was an occasional slender piece that could do some damage if she got close enough. It wasn't much of an arsenal, she admitted grimly. Not that it mattered much. The mere idea of stabbing someone with a butcher knife or scissors or of swinging that hickory stick or a sturdy length of firewood against unprotected flesh was enough to make her cringe.

Get a gun, Seth had counseled when she'd moved up here, but she had protested. It was a less intimate means of defense, true—it could be used with the safety of distance between shooter and target—but it was also such a final one. She couldn't risk killing someone to protect her property; she wasn't sure she could do it even to protect herself. If she tried and couldn't, she would simply wind up giving a possibly unarmed intruder a weapon to use against her and any other poor unfortunate who crossed his path in the future.

But Dillon Boone wasn't unarmed. When he faced her again, he was holding a gun in his left hand—holding it as if he were comfortable with it, as if he were comfortable with the idea of using it. "Put the purse down and move over there," he instructed, waving the gun toward the braided rug in front of the fireplace.

Withdrawing her hand, she let the keys drop to the table, then backed away as he'd directed.

"Do you live here alone?"

She considered lying, but she had already been foolish enough to tell him that she wasn't married—*and* that she had no phone she could use to call for help. She had already let him into her house, where the only jackets that hung on the coatrack next to him were obviously hers, where the only shoes lined up next to the bed in the corner were women's shoes, where the only items scattered across the dresser top were perfume bottles and a lacy, flowery fabric box filled with earrings. Biting her lip, she nodded.

"What's your name?"

"Ashley."

"You know my name."

"A person can't live within fifty miles of Catlin and not know who you are." Softly she added, "Especially a person with money in the First American Bank and Trust."

"And did *you* have money in the First American Bank and Trust?"

"I don't have money, period. So if you're planning to rob me..."

He made an impatient gesture that caused him to sway unsteadily. Taking a few steps forward, he leaned against the table for support, the gun hitting the wood with a hollow thunk. The exertion made his voice thinner, his breathing raspier. "I don't want your money or your van or anything else. I just need a place to rest. As soon as I can, I'll be on my way."

She wanted to believe him, wanted to believe that he would stay, get warm, get dry, maybe eat and sleep a little and then be gone. She wanted to believe that he wasn't going to steal anything, that he wasn't going to hurt her. But Dillon Boone was a bank robber, a fugitive on the run from the law for nearly a year, living in the shadows, desperate to avoid jail. He was a criminal who had forced his way into her house and was now holding her hostage. How could she believe *anything* he said?

His gaze moved past her to the fireplace behind her. The ashes were cold. The morning had held such promise that she hadn't bothered with the fire when she awoke; she had let the embers from last night's fire burn themselves out. It wouldn't take much to coax a flame from the kindling stored in the rough-woven basket on the hearth, wouldn't take long for the well-seasoned hickory logs to blaze into the bone-warming sort of heat that he obviously needed— that *she* was starting to need. Still, she didn't offer to build a fire. She remained silent, watching him warily.

After a moment he redirected his glance toward the kitchen, where a pot of stew was simmering on the back burner. He was cold, but he didn't ask her to build a fire. He was hungry, but he didn't ask to share her food. Instead, he said, "Your clothes are wet. Go change."

With a shiver, she realized that he was right. The rain had been blowing with enough force that those brief moments she'd spent in it had been enough to turn her faded jeans dark, enough to streak her shirt and to dampen her canvas shoes.

She made her way around the foot of the bed to the small armoire that served as her closet. There she pulled out a heavy chambray skirt and a navy blue sweater, then, eyeing him cautiously, she started toward the bathroom. He was still standing next to the table, his head bowed, his hands spread wide to support him. He looked miserable and just barely able to stay on his feet. If she could make it into the bathroom, she could lock the door; she could open the window, pry the screen off and climb out in no time. Before he even realized that she was taking too long, she would have retrieved the jacket she kept in the workshop and would be halfway down the driveway to the road. She would be cold and wet, but she was in good shape. She could easily make it to the Parmenters'.

If she could make it into the bathroom.

She was halfway there when a creaking board brought his head up. He shoved himself away from the table and once more brought the gun up. "Out here," he commanded, closing the distance between them more quickly than she would have thought him capable of. "You change right here."

Seeing her chance to escape slipping away, she faced him, only inches between them, intending to inform him that there was no way she was changing clothes in front of him. But when she opened her mouth, no words came out. Her voice failed to materialize; her brain failed to give the command.

Dillon Boone, so the talk went in town, was a dangerous man, but Ashley had never quite believed it. He had worked in Catlin for several weeks before the robbery, and the people who had met him had liked him well enough. Seth had met him and hadn't found him worthy of suspicion or scrutiny. His crime hadn't been violent; no one had been hurt. The bank's money had been insured. He had used his brains instead of brutality, had used his inside knowledge of the bank's security system—which he had helped install—rather than a weapon, hostages or threats.

But now, in an instant of eye contact, she had become a believer. Standing there, face-to-face, looking into those empty eyes that were colder than the iciest winter wind, she *knew* he was dangerous. Just that look made her heart rate increase, made her breathing grow quick and unsteady, made her muscles quiver. Just that look made her realize what a precarious position she was in. Just that look put the fear of God into her.

A sensation feeling distastefully like defeat—acceptance, resignation—swept over her. It was Boone's lucky day. She was a reasonable woman. She wasn't going to fight him. She wasn't going to anger him. She wasn't going to give him a reason to hurt her. She intended to follow his every order, to see to his every need, to fulfill his every wish. She intended to be the best little hostage any fugitive could wish for.

And she intended to come out of this alive.

* * *

How quickly the woman could change, Dillon thought bitterly. Her expression when she had faced him had been mutinous. She hadn't liked the idea that he was giving orders, hadn't liked that he was going to make her undress in front of him. Most of all, she hadn't liked that she wasn't going to be allowed to lock herself in the bathroom, with its two big windows offering a chance to escape.

But she had taken one look at him, one really good face-to-face, up-close-and-personal look at him, and it had scared her in a way that his sudden appearance outside, his barging into her cabin and his gun hadn't. What was it she'd seen that had frightened her? What was it that made him capable of terrorizing an innocent woman with no more than a look?

Tearing her gaze away, she turned and laid the clothes she carried on the hearth. He retreated once more to the table, giving her plenty of room. He'd told the truth when he'd said that he didn't want anything from her. If he'd had his way, the cabin would have been empty and he wouldn't have been forced to take a hostage. The less contact he had with anyone, the better.

The less contact he had with a *woman,* the better, he amended as she turned her back to him and began removing her T-shirt. Her skin, as it was revealed, was smooth, pale, probably soft, probably sweet smelling. She was naked underneath the shirt, he realized as she drew it over her shoulders, then up over her head. That long expanse of bare skin somehow seemed vulnerable, made *her* seem vulnerable...which, of course, she was. She was his prisoner, his hostage. She had to respond to his whims, had to do whatever he commanded.

He wished he could command her to disappear. He wished he could remove her from this place and time, wished he could remove himself from her life. Of course, he couldn't. For now they were stuck with each other.

Raising her arms over her head, she pulled the sweater on. The movement gave him just a glimpse of the soft swell of her breast, fuller than a man might have imagined, swaying unrestrained as she tugged the sweater down. When the ribbed hem was in place somewhere high on her thigh and she began working her jeans off, he swallowed hard and looked away, muttering a silent curse.

He had never known such misery as he'd felt today. His clothing had been soaked within minutes of leaving the wrecked patrol car, and the temperature had gone into a steady downhill slide. Around midafternoon he had considered making a shelter of some sort, but he knew that, without heat and dry clothes, he would never survive the night. Sheer desperation had kept him moving, and sheer luck had brought him here. He had been stumbling through the woods for hours, thinking numbly that death couldn't be worse than what he was already enduring, when he had smelled the woodsmoke coming from her workshop. He had forced his way through thick undergrowth to the clearing, praying that he would find no more than a place to get out of the rain, a place to recuperate just a little, a place where he could be alone, as he'd been his entire life. He hadn't asked for this. He didn't *want* this. God help him, he couldn't deal with this.

Forcing himself to concentrate, he gave the cabin another slow, searching look. It was one big room divided into distinct areas. There was a kitchen in one corner with appliances older than their owner. Through an open door just beyond the kitchen, he could see the bathroom with its windows and a big claw-foot tub, the absence of a shower curtain indicating the absence of a shower. In the opposite corner was the sleeping area with a bed, dresser and night table. The center of the cabin was her living room, with a sofa, two chairs and the big stone fireplace. The *cold* stone fireplace.

There was no television. No telephone. No stereo. No microwave. No dishwasher. No washer and dryer. Who lived out in the middle of nowhere like this without any conveniences beyond electricity and running water, a refrigerator and a stove? What kind of person—what kind of *woman*—thought that was a sensible way to live? Hadn't she ever realized that her isolation placed her in danger?

Hadn't she known there were people in this world who would take advantage of it? Mean people, desperate people. People like *him*.

The acknowledgment made him feel sick. So this was how low he had sunk. This was what his old friend Russell had brought him to. As of today, he deserved undeniably every derisive and scornful insult he'd ever been given.

"I—I have a pair of sweatpants...."

Slowly he shifted his attention back to her. She was dressed now in a pale blue skirt that reached practically to her ankles and that sweater, its sleeves long enough to warm her hands, its weave heavy and nubby, its fit big and loose...but not loose enough to make him forget that she was naked underneath.

"Th-they belong to Seth, my ex-husband." Her voice was softer, less steady, more frightened. "H-he left them when he did some work out here. You can wear them while your clothes dry."

Dry clothes. Damned if that didn't sound good...and damned if even the idea wasn't enough to make him feel weak. With the hand that still clutched the gun, he gave her silent permission to return to the armoire. "He come out here often?"

"Usually every Saturday."

Today was Tuesday. He would be long gone before Saturday rolled around. He intended to get some rest, spend a night—maybe two—and then he was going to head west. Last time he had stopped running in his hometown of Atlanta, but this time, he vowed, he wouldn't stop until he was hell and gone from Catlin, North Carolina. Maybe he would head for Mexico, or maybe Canada. At least he spoke their language.

Whatever his final destination, he was never coming back to North Carolina. He was never going to let them take him to trial.

God help him, he was never going to spend another night in jail.

After a moment she returned with a pair of gray sweatpants. Loath to approach him, she laid them across the arm of the sofa, then took a few steps safely away. Hiding a grimace of pain, he crossed to the sofa and picked them up. They were soft and well-worn, the fleece incredibly warm around his frozen fingers as he measured their waist against his own. It was a pretty good fit, maybe an inch or two looser than he preferred, but the drawstring that ran through the elastic waist would take care of that. They were going to feel good . . . *if* he could manage to get them on. *If* he could bully her into helping him undress. *If* he could frighten her into coming that close.

Gripping the sweats as if someone might try to rip them from him, he raised his head to look at her. "I—I can't. . . ." His face grew warm with embarrassment. He was thirty-four years old, on the run and trying to hold a hostage, and he was so helpless that he couldn't undress himself. He couldn't even kick off his shoes.

She stared back, her blue eyes rounded, her blond hair frizzing a little as it dried. She was afraid to help him, afraid to come close enough to touch him. No matter how much he might hate it, he *needed* her fear. He was in no condition to stop her if she tried to escape. Except for its ability to frighten her, the pistol was worthless; it was for damned sure he would never use it. He hadn't been in the greatest shape when the deputy had picked him up at the Sylvan County Jail this morning for transfer to Catlin, and the gunshot wound, the car crash, the new injuries and seven hours in the cold and rain had left him pretty useless. If she decided to walk away from him right now, to turn her back and leave, he couldn't stop her. He couldn't go after her. He couldn't make her stay.

Part of him wished she *would* go. All he wanted was a fire, some food and a night's rest, wrapped in one of her quilts and huddled on the stone hearth, as close to the flames as he could get without being singed. He *didn't* want a hostage. He didn't want any more regrets, any more guilt, any more complications.

He smiled grimly. His life, from the moment of his conception, had been nothing *but* complications. There had been the mother who had never wanted him and the father who had always denied him, the kids who had made fun of him and the adults who had looked down on him. And his failures . . . He'd failed at everything he'd ever tried—his jobs, his relationships, his affairs. It was a failed relationship that had brought him here. Nearly eleven months ago the best friend he'd ever had had set him up. Just this morning the same friend had tried to have him killed.

He wondered how much it cost to buy such a betrayal. How much of that four hundred fifty thousand dollars had Russell required to ease his conscience?

The woman took a reluctant step toward him. "Sit down," she requested, her voice little more than a whisper, and he did, sinking heavily onto the nearest chair. The muscles in his legs, relieved of his weight for the first time all day, cramped, then eased and grew warm. He hadn't realized how exhausted he was, hadn't let himself feel the fatigue that now coursed through him.

The woman. *Ashley.* He silently tried her name and liked it—liked its softness, its gentleness—and because he *did* like it, he didn't use it.

She knelt in front of him and reached for his foot. The muddy laces were soaked and didn't want to release their loops. He watched as, with trembling hands, she tugged the laces free, removed one shoe and dripping sock and then repeated the process with the other.

Setting the shoes aside, she reached for the hem of his T-shirt. She had to lean closer to him, close enough that her trembling increased, close enough that he could identify the faint fragrances—roses and sweet honeysuckle—that clung to her hair and skin. Closing his eyes so he wouldn't have to watch, he gritted his teeth as she began tugging, sending agonizing little waves of pain through his entire body, until finally he groaned aloud and she stopped.

Her fingers, soft and warm, gently probed his rib cage. "I think you've cracked some ribs."

Feeling queasy from the pain, he didn't respond.

"I can tape them for you, but most people find it doesn't help."

"Don't bother."

"I'll have to cut your shirt off. I don't have any of Seth's shirts here."

"Fine." If worse came to worst, when he was finally able to leave, he could take that sweater she was wearing. It was big enough to make, at worst, a snug fit on him, and it would keep him warm and, until the scent of her faded from its fibers, it would remind him of her, standing in front of the fireplace, arms upraised, naked to the waist, pulling it over her head. It was safe to indulge in such thoughts, since nothing would ever come of them. Right now he hurt too badly to even contemplate intimacy ever again, and when he left here, when he was trying to make it out of the South, staying alive and uncaught would require all his energies.

Using scissors from a nearby lidded basket, she began cutting away his shirt. When she was finished, she dropped the tattered pieces on the floor with his shoes, then, with a reluctance he could feel deep in his bones, she reached for the button at the waistband of his jeans. Wrapping his fingers around her wrist, he lifted her hand away. "Build a fire, would you?" he asked, his voice shakier than he would have liked. "I'll do this."

Relief easing the tautness of her features, she got to her feet, placed a pile of kindling on the grate over a small waxy glob, then set a match to the starter. The pieces caught fire almost immediately, as did the narrow lengths of old, seasoned wood she laid over them. She gave them a minute or two to burn before adding longer, thicker cuts. When the sap was crackling and the flames were curling over and around the top log, she dusted her hands and sat back on her heels. She didn't look over her shoulder at him. She didn't check to see what progress he'd made. She simply sat there and stared into the flames.

Dillon wasn't sure he could finish the job she'd started. Every breath was agony, and moving, bending, tugging and wriggling were all going to hurt like hell. But what were his alternatives? Spending the night in clammy, wet jeans? He would never get warm enough to rest. Letting her undress him? He would never get *relaxed* enough to rest.

Sliding the gun deep between the seat cushion and the side of the chair, he forced himself to his feet. He unfastened his jeans, then began working the tight, wet fabric down his hips, his body protesting every movement. His breathing grew heavy and labored as pain swept over him, bringing with it fiery heat. By the time he'd stripped, then stepped into the sweats she'd given him, his face was flushed and damp, his stomach was churning and his muscles were quivering uncontrollably.

Taking breaths too deep to be painless but too shallow to fill his lungs, he removed an item from his jeans pocket, then made his way carefully to the bed. It was neatly made and turned back, a pink blanket sandwiched between white sheets and a pastel-hued quilt. He stacked the pillows against the headboard, then lowered himself to the mattress, groaning aloud as he settled in. "Do you have a first-aid kit?"

Still kneeling in front of the fire, she nodded without looking at him.

"Do you have any objection to using it on me?"

She was still for so long that he knew she wanted to refuse. The only concern she had for his injuries was that they weren't serious enough. She would have preferred it if he had been hurt too badly to escape the deputy's custody, if the gunshot wound had been a few inches lower and a few inches to the left, if one of the bumps on his head had been hard enough to leave him unconscious. She certainly wouldn't choose, of her own free will, to take care of him.

Well, *he* certainly wasn't choosing, of his own free will, to be taken care of. The last thing he needed—besides jail—was her closeness. Her nursing. Her touch. But he had no choice. The longer he stayed in Catlin County, the greater the risk of discovery. He couldn't leave until he was in at least a little better shape, and she was his best—his only—chance at getting better.

Finally she got to her feet and went to the kitchen, filling a basin with water, collecting towels from a cabinet. She set them on the night table, then left again, this time getting a basket from the hook where it hung near the bathroom door. He saw when she returned that it was filled with bottles and jars, with sterile dressings, scissors and tape.

As she sat down on the bed beside him, he tilted his head back and focused his gaze on the ceiling and the massive beams that crossed it. A half-dozen baskets hung from one beam; a variety of flowers and stalks with dull green leaves were hung upside down to dry from another.

God, he was tired. He had never wanted sleep as badly as he wanted it now, had never needed oblivion the way he needed it now. His body was about to give out on him. Unless what she had in mind for him was particularly excruciating, he had no doubt that being in her bed, underneath her covers, leaning back against her pillows, would soon put him to sleep for the rest of the night.

And then she would be free to go. Free to summon help. Free to lead the sheriff and his deputies straight to him.

He couldn't let that happen. He knew how to stop her—was prepared to stop her—but he found the idea distasteful. He knew all too well how violently *he* hated being handcuffed and utterly helpless. He knew how vulnerable those thin steel bracelets made a man feel. He couldn't even imagine how threatening they would feel to *her*.

He had no choice, but at least he could delay it. He could let her doctor his injuries, could let her get something to eat. He could put it off as long as possible, but the woman—Ashley, he reminded himself. Her name was Ashley, and she was going to have one hell of a miserable night.

For once, Ashley thought, Dillon Boone had gotten lucky. Seth considered her interest in herbs more than a little odd, but there were plenty of people in the surrounding mountains who considered her something of a healer. She knew practically every plant that grew in the region, knew its healing properties and its harmful ones. She knew what could prevent infection, what could aid healing, ease pain and soothe discomforts. She knew what was harmless, knew what would help and what would hurt.

Unfortunately she had nothing accessible right now that might hurt the man who'd made himself comfortable in her bed.

The thought brought her a flush of guilt. Even if she had some deadly herb available to her, she wouldn't make use of it. Boone was suffering enough. She could never do anything to add to that.

Dipping a cloth in the crockery bowl filled with warm water, she began bathing dirt and blood from his face and arms. None of his injuries there was serious—scrapes, bruises, some minor lacerations, a split lip. He sat motionless for her ministrations, still as a statue, not looking at her. It was as if he found the situation too personal, too intimate to acknowledge; the only way to endure it was stiffly, impassively.

Funny. The man was a fugitive. He had forced his way in here, had used his gun and his absolute soullessness to frighten her into helping him and yet he didn't *want* her help. He hadn't wanted to ask for the fire whose warmth he badly needed. He had refused to ask for food. Instead of worrying about exchanging his own soaking clothes for something dry, he had suggested that *she* get out of her wet clothes. Even now he didn't want her to touch him. He didn't want her to come close to him. Very odd.

Needing to break the uneasy silence between them, she asked the first question that came to mind and found that her voice was steady for the first time in too long. "Why did you come back to Catlin County?"

"Believe me, it wasn't by choice." As if sensing that she found the answer lacking, he scowled a little and continued. "I caught the attention of a deputy with a good memory for old Wanted bulletins."

"Then you were in custody when you came back." He offered no response, but she didn't need one. So he had been arrested, but had somehow escaped. Now he was not only a fugitive, but an escaped fugitive. Now he faced additional charges—as if the original charge hadn't been serious enough. Now he was likely more desperate than ever to get away.

Rinsing the cloth, she moved to his chest. His skin was icy cold, and he was shaking, as much from the cold as from his injuries. There were plenty of those: more cuts and scrapes, a number of bruises—some recent, the others older and healing—and a furrow cut across the top of his right shoulder. Anything from a cut to a gunshot wound, she had thought earlier, and she had been right on the last guess. The bullet had penetrated from the back, entering at a downward angle and scooping a deep V out of the flesh in its path. If the angle had been a few degrees sharper, the injury would have been much more serious, a through-and-through wound that would have required threading a gauze wick through his shoulder. It would have been much more painful, much slower to heal and much more susceptible to infection.

The nature of his injuries disturbed her. The split lip and the bruising around his right eye seemed indicative of being on the losing end in a fight. Of course, maybe he had struggled with the deputy before he'd escaped, but she knew all of Seth's deputies. There wasn't one of them who didn't dwarf Boone in size, who couldn't break him in half without even breaking a sweat. And there was the gunshot wound. Obviously he'd been shot from behind. Granted, he *was* a fugitive, but to shoot a man in the back seemed cold, almost vicious. Surely there had been other ways to stop him.

But maybe not. After all, he *had* escaped, even with getting shot in the back.

"Who shot you?" she asked as she laid the basin on the floor and put the basket in its place.

Finally he looked at her, his scowl deeper, his eyes emptier. She'd never seen eyes so intensely brown—or so utterly blank—before. "Does it matter?"

"Was it Sheriff Benedict or one of his deputies?" Seth was an expert shot. If he had shot a fleeing prisoner, it was pure luck that Boone had survived to tell the tale.

"No."

"Then you weren't in Catlin County's custody when you escaped."

"Yes, I was."

His answers confused her. She had assumed that he'd been captured elsewhere—that he was too bright to come back to the county on his own—and was being transported to the Catlin County Jail when he escaped. She knew from conversations with Seth that if Boone had been caught in another jurisdiction, it was up to Catlin County to go after him and bring him back, and the man had just confirmed that he'd been in their custody. So if he'd been under escort by a Catlin County deputy but it wasn't a Catlin County deputy who'd shot him, then who had? A dutiful citizen, perhaps? Had someone witnessed his escape? Had he stumbled onto someone else's property before he'd made his way here?

Selecting a bottle of antiseptic from the basket, she dampened a thick gauze pad, then began cleansing his open injuries. "You *were* shot when you escaped," she stated, just to clarify things, but she couldn't keep a faint questioning tone from her voice.

"No," he answered softly. "I was shot *before* I escaped."

The implications of that sent a shiver up her spine. Shooting a prisoner to stop an escape was one thing. Shooting him when he was doing nothing, when he was basically helpless and at his escort's mercy... That was criminal.

That was attempted murder.

If it was true.

Finishing with the rest of his injuries, she turned her attention to the gunshot wound. He watched as she blotted the blood, bathed the wound with antiseptic, coated it with ointment and covered it loosely with a sterile dressing. It was nasty and painful, but there was nothing else she could do for it. The tissue was destroyed, leaving too wide a gap to bring the edges of the skin together and suture. In a few days' time it would start to heal, the tissue granulating in from side to side and bottom to top. Tomorrow she would find a square of fabric to fashion a sling from, and, barring complications, within a week to ten days the wound would be healed enough to allow him some use of his arm again. Another two to three weeks after that, and nothing would remain but the scar.

He was waiting for her to ask more questions, waiting to see whether she would believe him. Finally done, she folded her hands in her lap and quietly asked, "What happened?"

"Does it matter?" he asked again, closing his eyes, wearily letting his head roll back.

"Yes."

"Why?"

"It just does. Where were you arrested?"

"Sylvan County."

That explained his more minor injuries, Ashley thought, her expression turning somber. Sylvan County was right across the Tennessee state line from Catlin County. There were a lot of ties between the two counties; they had a lot of things in common. Fair and humane treatment of prisoners by their sheriffs' departments, though, wasn't one of them. People who ended up in Sylvan County's custody seemed to fall a lot, to suffer a lot of mysterious injuries while locked alone in cells bare of everything but cots and toilets. There had been a number of complaints filed and investigations conducted, but few, if any, changes. Seth hated picking up prisoners there almost as much as he hated transferring his own prisoners there. As pleased as he must have been to hear that Catlin's one and only bank robber had been arrested, he also must have been dismayed to find out by whom.

"How long were you there?"

"Three days, four nights."

Three days was about the right age for the oldest of his bruises. "Who picked you up to take you to Catlin?"

"A deputy named Coughlin."

"I know Tom Coughlin. He never would have shot you unless he had absolutely no other choice, and he never would have stood by and let someone else shoot you."

After a long, still moment he opened his eyes just a bit and looked at her. "I told you it wasn't a Catlin County deputy.'' He started to heave a sigh, but winced and blew his breath out gently instead. ''We were ambushed on our way to Catlin. We came around a curve, and there was a black van and three men blocking the road. They opened fire, Coughlin swerved and we went over the side and down into a ravine.''

She stared at him in dismay. ''Was Tom hurt?''

''He'd been shot.''

''And you left him there?'' Her voice rose a few notes. ''You just walked off and *left* him?''

''Some people came—a woman and her kids. I could hear them talking from down below. They called the sheriff from their car phone. They got help for him.'' His dark eyes turned even darker. ''Damned right I walked off and left him. Those men were trying to kill *me,* not the deputy. He was unconscious. He was of no use to me, and there was no way in hell I was going to wait around for them to finish the job. I took his gun, and I took off.''

''Why would anyone want to kill you? What you did was wrong, but it's not worth dying for.''

''No,'' he agreed. ''But to a couple of people out there...'' Grimness settled over his features. ''It's worth killing for.''

Chapter 2

She was staring at him. Dillon knew it without looking. He could *feel* the weight of her wary blue gaze. She was looking at him and trying to figure out whether or not to believe anything he'd just said.

He knew what her decision would be: that he was unreliable. Untrustworthy. That anything he said was more than likely a lie. That naturally he would try to put himself in the best light and so he would claim that he'd been forced to escape from custody in order to save his own life.

He didn't give a damn whether she believed him. He was used to not being believed, to not being trusted. Since the time he was nine years old and had gotten the devil beaten out of him by Alex Waters and no one had believed his side of the story, he had known that he would always need proof. Well, he didn't have any proof to give this woman, and he wasn't sure he would offer it if he did. He was tired of always having to provide verification. He was tired of never being believed on nothing more than his say-so.

He was just tired, period.

Beside him the mattress shifted as she moved to stand up. Moving far too quickly for the comfort of his shoulder and ribs, he caught her wrist. He felt her tremble beneath his fingers, but he didn't release her. Instead, he pulled her back down and held her there.

"I was just going to put these things away," she said, her voice unsteady once again and tinged with fear, "then fix dinner. You could use some food."

After a moment he let go, and she rose to her feet. Before she walked away, though, she hesitated, then bent to draw the covers up to his shoulders, tucking the edges between his back and the pillow to hold them in place. It was a little gesture. It didn't mean a thing. No one else would have even noticed.

But *he* did. He noticed it and appreciated it like hell, and it made him feel even guiltier about his plans for her and the steel handcuffs he'd hidden beneath the covers and out of her sight.

Settling back against the pillows, he watched as she returned the basket to its hook, then emptied the heavy bowl in the sink. She washed her hands, took down dishes from the cabinet and cut thick slices of homemade bread all with the same easy, familiar movements. These were tasks she had performed hundreds of times, mindless jobs that she did without thought. So what *was* on her mind? he wondered. Maybe she was sending silent prayers to God for her safety. Maybe she was asking why *she'd* had the bad luck to get trapped with an escaping bank robber, or maybe she was planning an escape of her own. Maybe she was cursing the day he'd set foot in Catlin or regretting the day she'd decided to make her home all alone at the top of an isolated mountain.

He didn't blame her for that decision, even if, thanks to him, it hadn't turned out to be a great one. For all his negative feelings regarding the area, he had to admit that Catlin County was the most beautiful place he'd ever seen. He fully understood the desire to make a home there, especially all the way out here, where she had no neighbors, no intrusions and very little contact with the everyday world. If it weren't for the small matter of money to pay the bills, he could be perfectly happy living off away from other people like this.

He had never had much skill in the art of getting along with others.

But he was a man, fully capable—most of the time—of taking care of himself. The very virtue of being female made her less physically capable, more vulnerable, more at risk. If she wanted to live like this, she should at least have a gun to protect herself and a telephone to call for help. What she really needed—with no apology for the chauvinism—was a man to do the protecting for her. If he'd seen any sign of a man around, Dillon would have kept on going. If she'd answered affirmatively when he'd mentioned a husband, he probably would have stolen that beat-up old van of hers and tended his wounds himself once he got someplace safe. He wouldn't have followed her into the house. He wouldn't have taken her hostage. He sure as hell wouldn't be lying in her bed, watching her fix dinner as if he were a guest.

Wearily he slid a little lower beneath the covers. His shivers were slowing, his misery slowly easing. Powerful heat from the fireplace radiated into the room, and the heavy blanket and quilt she'd tucked around him were trapping the heat and keeping it comfortingly close to his body. After hours in cold, wet shoes, his feet were thawing; he could wiggle his toes and actually feel them respond. He was starting to feel human again—except for the hunger. And the pain. And the grim future facing him.

Her bare feet making little noise on the floor, she came across the room to the bed, bringing with her a tray fashioned from twigs and lengths of narrow rope. He assumed she had made the tray herself; in the long minutes that he'd stood beside the van and watched her through the workshop windows, he'd noticed a table full of similar items. That must be how she supported herself—with baskets and twigs, with the weaving loom and the quilting frame that filled half the workshop, with the soaps and the candles and the flowers drying overhead. She was never going to get rich, but if it paid the bills and made her happy, what else mattered?

She set the tray across his lap, and he studied it for a moment. It was well made, the legs sturdy and level, the twigs that formed the top smooth, uniform in size and tightly lashed. It held a cloth napkin in faded red gingham, a soup spoon, a salt shaker filled with some seasoning that wasn't salt and a pottery mug filled with a fragrant, steaming liquid.

"What is that?"

"Chamomile tea. It'll make you feel better."

He looked at it suspiciously. It hadn't escaped his notice that she was into herbs. There were pots of them on the windowsills all around the room, there were bunches hanging overhead, and the antiseptic and ointment she'd used on his injuries hadn't come out of any commercially prepared tube or bottle. Anyone who knew the good about herbs had to also be aware of the bad. Maybe the pale brew in the cup was no more harmful than the iced tea served by the gallons in restaurants all across the South. Maybe it *would* make him feel better... or maybe it would put him to sleep. Maybe it was beneficial.

Or maybe it was poison.

"Oh, for heaven's sake..." Picking up the mug, she blew gently across the surface, then took a drink, followed immediately by another. Then she put the cup down again, took a step back, folded her arms and watched him.

Working his left arm free of the covers, he reluctantly picked up the mug and sniffed. The fragrance reminded him that he'd had nothing to eat or drink since the breakfast of soggy cereal, dry toast and weak coffee a Sylvan County deputy had served him shortly after dawn and that he'd eaten none too well the three days before that. For a short time out there in the woods, ignoring the emptiness in his stomach had been even harder than ignoring the pain in every part of his body. Then the thirst had kicked in, and the hunger had been immediately forgotten. All that water around, and not a drop to drink. A couple of times he had been convinced that he would gladly give up food forever in exchange for a cup of hot coffee.

He tasted the tea and found it warm on his tongue and sweetened with honey. It wasn't coffee, but it was good, and she was right. Even that one small drink made him feel better. It made him feel a degree or two warmer and a degree or two more human.

At last she turned away, making another trip to the kitchen while he finished the tea. She brought back a basket—the gingham napkin inside wrapped around warm slices of bread—and a pottery plate holding a bowl filled with vegetable stew and set both on the bed tray.

When she sat down once again on the edge of the mattress, he scowled at her. "What are you doing?"

She paused in the act of picking up the spoon. "I was going to feed you."

"I can manage."

"You shouldn't be using your arm. Tomorrow I'll fix a sling for it, but tonight—"

"I'm left-handed."

With unmistakable relief in her eyes, she stood and returned to the kitchen. Some small part of him regretted her retreat; there was something vaguely comforting about having her so near. The larger part of him was glad for the reprieve. He didn't need a reminder that—right now, at least—she was by far the stronger of them, and *she* didn't need a reminder that he was disgustingly weakened. He didn't need to be fed like a baby, taking food from a spoon that *she* held because he couldn't. He didn't need that helplessness, that embarrassment. That intimacy.

Like hell he didn't.

His face warm, he reached for the spoon and, keeping his gaze down, began eating. The stew was rich, heavy with tomatoes, carrots, potatoes and onions, but he would have eaten just as appreciatively if it had come in a can from some unimaginative company. By the time she returned with her own bowl to sit on the hearth near the fire's warmth, his bowl was empty. He laid the spoon inside carefully so it didn't clatter. "That was good."

Acknowledging his words with no more than a nod, she set her bowl aside on the stones, refilled his and brought it back, then seated herself again. They ate in silence, her gaze directed into the distance, his traveling around the room but all too often returning to her.

When he had literally stumbled out of the forest and into the clearing, he had first noticed the darkened cabin and had thought he'd found the perfect place—dry and empty. Even when he'd seen her van—probably thirty years old, its dominant color gray primer and missing body parts—his first thought was that the vehicle had been junked long ago. Then he had moved closer, and he had seen the lights on in the workshop. After only a moment he'd caught a glimpse of her—young, blond, vulnerable. For a while he had simply watched her, feeling sneaky and shameful. Even now, every time his glance strayed her way, he felt guilty for it.

But he could live with guilt. What he couldn't live with was prison. Being locked away for much of the rest of his life. Living up—or down—to the expectations of everyone who knew him. Taking the blame, as he so often had in his life, for something he hadn't done.

"Why do you live up here?" he asked, awkwardly peeling the golden crust away from a slice of bread with one hand, then taking a bite from it.

She looked startled, almost as if she had forgotten that he was there, then abruptly her expression turned blank and she shrugged. "I like my own company."

"You can be a loner in town, where it's safer."

"I lived in town. In Raleigh. You want to talk about how safe life is in the city?"

"You could live in Catlin."

"I've lived there, too. I prefer it here."

"Don't you get scared?"

She gave him a long, steady look that made him want to squirm. "Only when I have good reason."

"You should at least have a gun."

She shrugged again. "I would never shoot anyone."

"That's nice to hear," he said dryly.

She stood up, her skirt falling in swirls almost to her ankles, and came to the bed, adding her soup bowl to his dishes on the tray, picking all of it up. Before she walked away, though, she spoke again, her voice as soft as a whisper, sending a chill up his spine. "I don't need a gun. There are easier, simpler, subtler ways of stopping someone."

Facing her reflection in the uncurtained window, Ashley filled the sink with hot, sudsy water, then slid the dishes in. Across the room, Boone was still puzzling over her last remark, wondering if she had been teasing, no matter how unexpectedly or more ominously, giving him a warning. She would know what he'd decided when morning came and she served him breakfast. If he refused to eat, no doubt he would have decided that she wasn't to be trusted.

He would have decided wrong. He could trust her. She wasn't going to do anything foolish that might result in her getting hurt or worse. She wasn't going to race across the room, grab her keys and dash out the door, even though she could probably be halfway to the van before he even managed to get to his feet. She wasn't going out into the rain that was streaming down now, beating a steady rhythm on the roof, wasn't going out into the cold dark night.

However, that didn't mean she intended to do absolutely nothing. He would surely fall asleep soon. His body had been taxed to its limits; only sheer determination had brought him this far. He was warm and dry, his injuries had been treated, his stomach had been filled, he was as comfortable as he was going to get outside of a hospital, where pain-relieving drugs could give him peace. Exhaustion was going to take over any minute now, and he would sleep soundly enough that nothing she did would disturb him.

So what would she do?

She could find his gun wherever he'd hidden it . . . but after her comment—*I could never shoot anyone*—how much impact would it have?

Better still, she could tie him to the bed. She could make him her prisoner. She had some cord in one of these baskets, and if there was one thing hours of crafting had taught

her, it was how to tie a strong knot. The bed was sturdy and
had both a headboard and a footboard; there was no way
he would be able to pull free. She would have to be careful
of his shoulder, of course, but she could rig up something
that would cause him no harm and would do her a world of
good. Then she would drive down to the Parmenters' and
use their phone to notify Seth that he could pick up his es-
capee at his convenience. Within an hour, two at the most,
Dillon Boone would be out of her house and out of her life.
He would be in jail, where he belonged.

He *did* belong there... didn't he?

"How long have you been divorced?"

She rinsed the last bowl and placed it in the drainer before turning around. He was pale, almost as white as the
sheets, and he looked miserable enough to make her feel
more than a twinge of sympathy. He needed better care
than she could provide, but not even the best M.D.s in the
state could make things right for him. They couldn't keep
him out of prison. They couldn't fix a life that had long ago
gone wrong.

Drying her hands on a tattered towel, she answered his
question. "Four years."

"How long were you married?"

"Four years."

"And you're still friends."

She hung the towel over the front of the sink, then began turning off lights. "Best friends."

That was what she and Seth had always been—*all* they
had ever been. If they hadn't found themselves in Raleigh
at the same time, Seth finishing his degree at the state uni-
versity there when she had started, if they hadn't both felt
out of place, if they hadn't both been homesick and lonely,
they never would have married. They never *should* have
married. It had taken them no time at all to realize that
they'd made a mistake, that friendship was no basis for a
marriage—at least, not the sort that they both wanted—but
nearly four years had passed before they were able to admit that marriage was destroying their friendship, which
was far more important to them both. She was glad that

they had managed to save it. They were closer now than ever before.

Still, she couldn't help but wish briefly that they *were* still married. Then Seth would be coming home tonight. Then she would have told Boone yes, she had a husband, and he was due home any minute. Then she probably wouldn't be in the situation she was in.

But she would find a way out of it, and she would do it without Seth's or anyone else's help. She was strong. Independent. Capable. She could take care of herself. She could take care of Dillon Boone.

"Why does he come out every Saturday?"

"To check up on me." She sat down at the far end of the hearth where she could lean back against the warm fireplace stones and tucked her skirt around her legs. "To make sure I haven't fallen from the roof and broken my neck or had trouble with Bessie, my van."

"Or to make sure you haven't been taken hostage by an escaped prisoner."

Thinking about his words, she nodded. *Of course.* With an armed and dangerous fugitive loose in the mountains around her home, Seth wouldn't wait until Saturday to warn her. If he didn't take time this evening, he would surely come first thing in the morning. She might be rid of Boone sooner than she'd hoped.

"That van..." His voice sounded weaker, fading. "I wouldn't take that van even if I were desperate."

"I thought you *were* desperate."

"Something that ugly and beat-up would draw too much attention."

"Bessie suits my needs just fine. She gets me and my stuff where we need to go, and all she asks in return is a tank of gas, plenty of oil and a kind word now and then."

That last made him smile just a bit. He wasn't a man smiles came easily to, she thought, and that was a shame, because they made a handsome face more so. That one little beginning of a smile softened the hardness, warmed the chill and lessened the sense of danger swirling around him. "All of us do better with a kind word now and then," he murmured. "But sometimes they're damned hard to come by."

And that was a shame, too, she silently acknowledged.

He shifted in the bed, making the springs squeak, then, almost immediately, he grimaced. Even across the distance that separated them, Ashley could see the sweat bead across his forehead as he tried to find a position where the pain was tolerable. It wasn't fair that he should be suffering so, wasn't fair that after nearly a year on the run—nearly a year that he had passed presumably unscathed—he should suffer so many injuries as soon as he was taken into custody. Police custody was one place where a person should be safe, one place where he should be able to count on being treated fairly, on being protected.

Obviously it wasn't.

"Put some more logs on the fire, then come over here, will you?"

Although the room was warm and certainly didn't need more heat, she did as he asked, placing another four logs at angles to those already burning, then crossing to the bed. She sat down next to him and raised her right hand to wipe the perspiration from his forehead. That was how he caught her off guard when he snapped one half of a pair of handcuffs around her left wrist.

For a moment Ashley stared uncomprehendingly at the bracelet that now circled her wrist and connected her, via pathetically few steel links, to the other bracelet that he'd fastened around his own wrist. Then, with a surge of anger, she tried to yank free. "Let me go!" she demanded, twisting her wrist, trying in vain to force the wider part of her hand through the small opening. "Get this off of me *now!*"

Her struggle made him groan with renewed pain, but she didn't care. Her sympathy was gone, disappeared inside an ever-growing panic. He couldn't do this! He couldn't chain her to him, couldn't make her, in every terrifying aspect of the word, truly his prisoner. Damn him, he couldn't take away her options and leave her totally at his mercy!

She tried to rise from the bed, but he caught her with his free hand, tugging her down again so that she sprawled half across the mattress and half across him. "Ashley, damn it—" His face contorted with every shallow breath he drew, with every move she made. "Jeez, don't do that," he whispered. "You're killing me."

Very carefully she pushed away from him and sat on the bed, utterly still, glowering at him. "Take this off right now," she demanded, her voice low and threatening and trembling.

"I can't. I'm sorry."

"What do you mean you can't? Where's the key?" If he didn't have a key, if they were stuck together until *someone* managed to separate them . . . Oh, God.

"It's over there." He gestured vaguely toward the rest of the room.

She twisted around to look behind her. The most likely place was the pocket of his jeans, still lying on the rug where he'd undressed earlier, but she knew from living with Seth that a handcuff key was small; Boone could have hidden it anywhere. He'd stood at the door, where baskets were stacked on a small half-round table. From there he'd moved to the dining table, with more baskets, a dried flower centerpiece and a tatted lace runner. He had walked past the sofa, had sat in the armchair and passed close to the fireplace, where the mantel was filled with pottery and wooden boxes. He could have dropped the key behind the logs stacked on the hearth, could have slipped it into the drawer of the table next to the chair or the one next to the bed. He could even have the darned thing in bed with him. She hadn't watched him closely enough, had been all too willing to turn her back on him.

She faced him again. "You can't do this," she pleaded, the words broken by a hiccup that sounded suspiciously like a sob. "You just can't—"

It was the look in his eyes that stopped her. Just a short while ago, when they had stood face-to-face in front of the fireplace and he had commanded her to undress right there, the complete emptiness in his eyes had frightened her into compliance. Now there was emotion in that deep brown. There was guilt. Shame. "I have to," he whispered. "I can't let you go. I can't let you turn me in."

"I won't—" Once more she broke off.

He waited a moment, but seemed to know that she wasn't going to continue. "Go ahead, Ashley. Tell me that you won't try to escape. Tell me that you'll sit there while I'm asleep, and you won't do anything to get away." He paused. "Go ahead. Make me believe you. I would *love* to believe you."

She sat silent, her mouth clamped shut.

"As soon as I'm able to travel, I'll be out of here. I won't make you go with me, and, I swear to God, you won't be hurt. I know you don't believe me, but it's the truth. But because you don't believe me, and because I can't afford to trust you, I have to do this."

He raised his right hand, and the cool steel tugged uncomfortably at her hand, sending a shudder of revulsion through her. "I *can't* spend the night like this."

"*I* can't spend it any other way." He sighed grimly. "Get comfortable. It's a long time till morning."

Scowling, she turned away and slid off the mattress to sit on the floor. Her back was supported by the bed, her bottom cushioned by the handwoven rag rug beneath her. Her right arm dangled awkwardly in midair, suspended by the steel cuff. He was right: it *was* going to be a very long night, and she didn't intend to sleep through one bit of it. How could she, when she was chained to the side of a wanted felon? How could she possibly relax enough to sleep when every move brought discomfort, when every brush of the metal on her skin brought a new sense of helplessness?

"Ashley?"

She stared hard into the fireplace, concentrating all her energies on the flames that would surely go out and leave them cold before morning, trying desperately to ignore the drained voice above and behind her.

"Ashley." He jangled the chain that connected them, making her arm twitch. "You don't have to spend the night on the floor."

"Oh, yeah?" she responded belligerently. "Are you going to sleep down here instead?"

"The bed is big enough for two."

His voice was as gentle as hers was caustic, and it fed the anger she needed to remain in control of the fear seeping through her. "Not even in my worst nightmare."

"I *am* your worst nightmare, aren't I?" There was a moment of silence before he spoke again—or, at least, she thought he did. The words were so soft, so hesitant, so insubstantial that they might have been nothing more than the whisper of the wind. "I'm sorry."

Dillon awakened Wednesday morning, feeling cold, stiff and worse than half-dead. The pink blanket was heavy, but not heavy enough to combat the early-morning chill by itself, and he'd given up its accompanying quilt right after the fire had gone out sometime during the night.

Rubbing his hand over his face, then over his hair, he felt the stubble of beard and hair standing on end. Ignoring that, he closed his eyes and did a rather uncomfortable assessment of his condition. Breathing still hurt like hell, but he thought he detected a slight improvement—or was that merely wishful thinking? His legs were stiff, his muscles taut, his joints sore. His shoulder was hot and so tender to the touch that he didn't bother trying to move it. He wondered if it was infected, or if some of that herbal stuff Ashley had used on it had caused further damage. Last night it had been sore; after her ministrations, this morning it was sore *and* his right arm felt unusually heavy, his hand unusually numb.

Then he looked down and saw the reason for the discomfort: sometime in the past few hours, Ashley had fallen asleep deeply enough to seek whatever comfort she could find. What she had found—*all* she had found—was the slight pillow of his hand. Her cheek was pressed against his palm, her chin tucked into the curve of his fingers. His arm felt as if he'd held a bowling ball all night, deadening the nerves, stiffening the joints. But he had never touched a bowling ball so soft, so smooth. Even with his hand half-numbed, he could feel every place her skin touched his, could feel the differences between his own callus-roughened skin and hers, as delicate and fine as anything he'd ever touched.

Moving cautiously so he wouldn't disturb her, he flexed his fingers, touching the tips to her jaw. Squared off, it gave her a stubborn look and kept her just barely from crossing over from mere attractiveness into prettiness. Better than pretty, though, her face was interesting. It showed character. Personality. She was strong. Generous. Kind—and he had known so little kindness in his life that he recognized it instinctively when he saw it. Her eyes were bright, clear, probably filled with trust for everyone in the world but him, and her mouth seemed to want to curve into a smile as naturally as *his* didn't. Altogether it was a good face, one that would age with great grace. When she was eighty years old and her blonde hair had turned white, when fine wrinkles had replaced the smoothness of youth, she would surpass prettiness with uncommon beauty.

With a heavy, suddenly almost forlorn sigh, he fixed his gaze on the kitchen window and wished he had the keys that were in his jeans pocket halfway across the room. She was sleeping so soundly that he was sure he could unfasten the cuff from his wrist and secure it for safety to the bed frame. Then he could get up, build a fire, see about breakfast. He could make rather urgent use of her bathroom, could wash his face, brush his teeth, maybe even shave. All that would go a long way toward making him feel human again.

Setting her free would go even further.

Who was he kidding? He was still weak, still feeling some serious pain. He would be lucky if he could even get to his feet without help. Building a fire, fixing breakfast, finding a steady hand for a razor? Not likely. And setting her free? Letting her go, when he knew the first thing she would do was turn him in, when she hadn't even bothered last night to deny that she would? Letting the only thing that stood between him and a jail cell walk out of his reach? Not a chance in hell.

Not even if refusing did make him feel like the lowest of bastards.

Outside, the sky was dreary and dark, although it looked as if the rain had stopped, at least for a while. Had the weather slowed the search party yesterday as much as it had hindered him? Had they continued through the night, or had they taken a break so they would be well rested this morning? How long would it take them to follow his trail here? He didn't kid himself that they wouldn't. There were men up in these mountains who could track a sparrow flying too close to the ground. There was no way they could possibly miss the tracks he'd left for them—the footprints in the mossy ground, the scarred places where he'd slid down hills, the broken foliage, the overturned stones, the unmistakable signs of passage. He might as well have painted signs pointing to Ashley's cabin and proclaiming Here I Am.

He had to get out of here today, even if he did feel like death warmed over. Even if another day or two in this bed would go a long way toward physical healing. Even if another day or two in this place—with this woman?—might go a long way toward spiritual healing.

He could use some spiritual healing.

No doubt the North Carolina prison system would be happy to provide him with many long months where he could concentrate on just that.

So what were his options? There was no way he could leave here on foot. Hadn't he just admitted that he probably couldn't even make it twenty feet to the bathroom without help? He could steal her van, but the piece of junk was a stick shift, and he was pretty sure that, with this shoulder, shifting gears was out of the question. He was also pretty sure that there was no way he could drive that van through the town of Catlin without being noticed, and that was a risk he couldn't take. Besides, taking the junk heap— What had she called it? Bessie? Taking Bessie would leave her stranded up here all alone. If something happened to her... That was another risk he couldn't take.

That left only one choice. He would ask her to take him outside the county, maybe even outside the state. They weren't far from the state line; maybe the Tennessee cops weren't looking for him yet. He would have her let him off somewhere outside the immediate area, and he would do something to temporarily disable the van—let the air out of the tires, maybe—so that she couldn't notify the authorities right away. He would get a head start, and she would be rid of him. They would both be happy.

He could actually remember the last time he would have described himself as happy. It had been nearly a year ago, and his good friend Russell had sent him to Catlin to install an alarm system in the local bank. He had liked the town, had liked the people. He had thought it must be a nice little place to live, and he had enjoyed the few weeks he had lived there.

Then everything had gone more wrong than it had ever been in his entire life, and it wasn't ever going to be right again.

On the floor beside the bed, Ashley stirred, drawing his attention back to her. A shiver rippled through her, and she huddled deeper into the quilt he'd wrapped around her during the night. Its warmth wasn't enough to reverse the waking process, though; gradually her sleep lightened. Her eyes moved restlessly behind closed lids. Her breathing changed, becoming more measured, and her jaw tightened against his hand.

At last she opened her eyes. Dillon looked down at her, and she gazed up at him. Already there was wariness in her expression. There was no moment of confusion, no drowsy bewilderment, no lack of awareness. One moment she was asleep, and the next she was looking at him with such distrust and resentment that for a second he thought it actually hurt. But it was just his ribs, he told himself, and a breath taken the wrong way.

She raised her head from his hand and used her free hand to rub her face. Her hair stood high on top, was crushed flat on the side that had rested in his palm and curled in wayward wisps all over. She looked about ten years old, innocent and defenseless.

But she was closer to thirty. She was no child, but a woman. Very much a woman.

It had been a long time since he'd felt like much of a man.

"I need the key."

He knew exactly what she needed; it had been a long night. "You'll have to help me get it."

Shrugging off the quilt, she awkwardly got to her feet. She rolled her head to ease the kinks in her neck, then started to stretch her arms over her head. The handcuffs stopped her. "Can you stand up?"

He pushed the covers back, then swung his feet to the floor. The rug where she had spent the night was warm beneath his toes, but that was the only warmth he found. The room was cold, and Ashley's gaze was even colder. Holding his arm to his ribs and taking the deepest breath he could manage, he pushed himself to his feet. His vision dimming, his knees threatening to buckle, he muttered a savage curse that ended in a sound too close for comfort to tears.

Cool hands closed around his upper arms, lending support. "Try to relax and breathe evenly. It'll pass."

Not before it killed him. How was he ever going to get out of here today if he couldn't even manage standing on his own feet without assistance?

With more will than he'd known he possessed, he forced the pain to the back of his mind, forced it under control. When he thought he just might survive, he carefully moved her out of his way and, one awkward, agonizing step at a time, he made his way, Ashley trailing at his side, to where his jeans lay on the rug. She bent and picked them up, patted the pockets and found the keys, then offered them to him.

For the second time in less than twenty-four hours, he unlocked the handcuffs, removing them from his own wrist, then hers. "You can go first."

She started toward the bathroom.

"But you have to take your clothes off."

That stopped her in her tracks. For a long moment she stood motionless, then, very slowly, she turned to face him. Her voice was as unforgiving as the wintry mountains outside. "Excuse me?"

He shifted uncomfortably. "You have to take your clothes off out here first. I can't let you climb out the window, and I'll be damned if I'm going to keep you company in there, so taking your clothes seems to be the only choice."

"But I'm not wearing anything under—" She broke off, and he briefly squeezed his eyes shut. He knew. As if by magic, the image from last night popped into his mind: Ashley, standing in front of the fireplace, all soft, bare skin backed by rugged stone, arms raised to reveal a tantalizing glimpse of breast. Sweet damnation, he *knew*.

As she realized that he was serious in his demand, expressionless ice turned to mutiny. "I won't."

"It's the only way you're getting out of my sight," he said, hearing the regret in his voice. "If you're worried about your modesty, don't be. I'll look the other way. If you're worried about your virtue... Hell, even if I could get hard, which I seriously doubt, it's for damned sure I couldn't do anything about it."

In an instant her face flushed from pale shock to the fiery heat of... What was it? he wondered. Embarrassment over his crudity? Anger that he wasn't going to give in? Revulsion at even the mere idea of being intimate with him? Probably a combination of all three, he admitted, the acknowledgment accompanied by a stinging bitterness.

"Take your clothes off," he ordered, his words sharp, his tone defensive, "or sit down so I can cuff you to the leg of the sofa so *I* can go in there."

She stared at him for a moment, pure hatred contaminating the blue of her eyes, then she walked to the bathroom door, where she stopped and faced him once again. With slow, deliberate, precise movements, she reached beneath her sweater to the waistband of her skirt. She unfastened the top three or four buttons, opening the skirt enough that she could slide it down her hips and step out of it. Next she grasped the ribbed bottom of the sweater in both hands and peeled it up and over her head, and the whole time, except when the fabric covered her face, she never took her eyes off him.

Wearing nothing but lacy little panties—he wasn't looking; he swore he wasn't—she bent to pick up the skirt, bundled it together with the sweater and flung both pieces at him. An instant later the bathroom door slammed shut, followed by the unmistakable click of a lock.

Wondering how he could suddenly feel so feverishly warm when only minutes ago he'd been close to freezing, Dillon clutched the clothing he'd caught. The sweater was warm with her body heat and fragrant with her scent. Simply holding it made his fingers itch to hold *her*. Simply smelling it made him wonder how much sweeter, how much more enticing those scents were on *her*.

Muttering a curse, this one no less desperate but far more vicious than the earlier one, he threw the garments away from him, sending them sailing across the room, bouncing off the closed, locked door. He was a fool. He should have taken one look at her yesterday through the workshop window and known that this was no place for him. He should have listened to the first sound of her voice—*Can I help you?*—and kept right on going. He never should have come inside here. Never should have made her undress in front of him. Never should have made her touch him. Never should have looked at her just now.

He was such a liar. He wouldn't look, he'd said. He wouldn't threaten her virtue, he'd promised. He couldn't even get hard, he'd assured her. But he *had* looked, and if he thought there was any chance he could sweet-talk anything at all out of her, he would damn well try. And, as if he didn't have enough problems, as if he weren't already suffering enough, he *was* hard. As a rock.

He'd made it a habit over the years to avoid exercises in futility. Trying to change people's opinion of him, trying to prove that he wasn't a total failure, trying to convince anyone at all that he wasn't guilty of the crime he'd been ac-

cused of—those were all lost causes. They weren't worth the
breath he would expend arguing.

Wanting this woman...

That was the biggest lost cause of all.

Chapter 3

Ashley was so damned cold that her teeth were chattering and goose bumps had popped out all over very private parts of her body. Mouthing silent curses, she tried wrapping up in the only bath towel that hung on the bar, but it was too small to provide decent coverage, and the robe that usually hung on the back of the door was gone—tossed into the washing machine three days before. She had never bothered, she remembered, to transfer the load to the dryer, which meant it was still wet and quite possibly growing all sorts of nasty mildew.

For the first few minutes after she'd taken care of business, she had been smug. Maybe she was practically naked and cold, but at least she'd gotten to use the facilities. *He* was half-naked and cold, too—although he did have the option of wrapping up in one of her quilts—and he had the added misery of being unable to heed Mother Nature's call. But about five minutes ago, she had smelled woodsmoke, and her smugness had disappeared. He'd built a fire, and she wanted to be in front of it, absorbing its heat until she sizzled. She *needed* that warmth, almost as much as she needed her clothing and the false sense of security it gave her.

She had to admit that he'd made the best choice. If she were in his position, she would have made the same decision. She certainly couldn't escape this way, and being naked was a sight better than having his company in here.

But she was still angry. And *cold*. She didn't tolerate cold well. Hot, muggy summers didn't faze her, and the mountains' frigid winters were fine, too, as long as she was prepared. Coats, scarves, gloves, fires, blankets, quilts. She believed in staying warm.

Reaching out, she laid one hand flat against the door. Was the wood warm? Could there be such a tremendous difference between the room temperature out there and the chill inside, or was she simply so cold that even the slightest warmth felt like a heat wave to her blue fingers?

This was ridiculous. She couldn't stay in an unheated bathroom all day. So she was naked and there was a man on the other side of the door. It wasn't the first time, and—she fervently hoped—it wouldn't be the last.

But it *was* the first time with a man like Dillon Boone. The other men in her past—Seth and one other—had been lovers; they had been a part of her life, invited in, cared for. Boone had simply barged in, pointed a gun at her and made threats. He had chained her like an animal, had forced her to sleep on the floor at his side, had demanded not once but twice that she strip in front of him.

But once he'd gained her cooperation, she felt compelled to admit, he had put the gun away and she hadn't seen it since. He had offered to share the bed with her, and when it had gotten cold during the night, although he'd needed all the warm covers for himself, he had given up the warmest of them all to tuck around her. And although he *had* made her undress, he had been as uncomfortable with her nudity as *she* was.

She simply had to gather whatever dignity she could find, open the door, walk out and find her clothes and put them on. Then she would huddle on the hearth until the fire's heat had seeped into every bone in her body.

Discarding the skimpy towel, she walked to the door, drew a deep breath, then stepped into the outer room. Before she'd taken more than a few steps, she reached her clothes. Hastily, gratefully she pulled them on, burying her hands in the sweater's long sleeves, padding barefoot to the fireplace, where Boone was standing. He gave her another of those oddly regretful looks, this one not quite reaching her face, and gestured toward the couch. Biting her tongue on the protest that bubbled up, she sat down where he indicated, on a rug in front of the old sofa. One end of the handcuffs was already attached to the left sofa foot; bending cautiously, he fastened the other around her wrist.

Instead of going straight to the bathroom, though, he picked up a quilt from the chair. It was the Shoo Fly off her bed, the first quilt she'd ever made. He held it close to the fire, warming the layers of cotton, batting and muslin, and then he brought it to her, stooping, gathering it around her.

Then *he* went into the bathroom and closed the door.

Barely moving, barely breathing, Ashley stared into the flames. Damn these little gestures of his! He wasn't supposed to be this way. He was a crook—a bank robber, an escaped fugitive, a hardened criminal. He had forced his way in here with a gun, scaring her senseless, and had made her his prisoner. He cared about nothing but himself—*his* escape, *his* needs, *his* freedom. He didn't give a damn about anyone else, didn't give a damn whom he scared or whom he hurt.

But he didn't want her to be cold. He hadn't wanted her to sleep on the floor, hadn't wanted her to wear wet clothes. He had offered her every assurance possible, had promised that he wouldn't hurt her, had *sworn* that he wouldn't hurt her. He wasn't supposed to be that way, not if he was everything people said he was.

So maybe he wasn't.

Maybe he wasn't such a loser. Maybe he wasn't a hardened criminal. Maybe he wasn't a sociopath, unburdened by conscience or guilt, as Bill Armstrong would have everyone believe.

But he *was* a bank robber, and he *was* holding her hostage. He *was* a wanted man, and she had seen in his eyes last night that he *was* a dangerous man.

But maybe he wasn't dangerous for her. Maybe he saved his ruthlessness for people who threatened him, and she certainly didn't fall into that category. She couldn't hurt him, couldn't do anything that might bring harm to him. She couldn't get to a phone to notify Seth of his location. She couldn't—so far—outsmart him. She couldn't get him recaptured. She was no threat at all, and maybe, because of that, he presented no danger at all.

Her stomach growled, distracting her from her thoughts. On a normal day she would already be eating breakfast by now. Of course, it was too much to hope that Boone might have bothered to fix her a bowl of cereal or a cup of tea while he'd waited for her to give up her refuge in the bathroom. She was lucky he had built a fire. Knowing the toll his injuries had taken on him, she was surprised that he had managed even that task.

On a normal day... This undoubtedly was *not* going to be one of those. On a normal day she got up between six and six-fifteen, built a fire and got dressed. She fixed her tea first and if it was even remotely comfortable outside, she drank it on the porch, sitting in an old hickory rocker, listening to the birds, looking for deer, squirrels and other wildlife that often wandered out of the woods, watching the sunrise and gathering wool as the fog slowly drifted across the valley. Breakfast came next—whole-wheat pancakes with butter and syrup, a frittata heavy with vegetables from her own garden, biscuits floating in a platter of cream gravy or, if she was short on time or just plain lazy, a bowlful of granola with nothing but fresh yogurt for a garnish.

On a normal day she was in the workshop by eight. She followed no set routine there, unless she had an order to fill or an upcoming craft show to attend. She might spend the morning cutting reed for baskets, make eight dozen rose-scented, heart-shaped bars of soap after lunch and blend potpourri, work on her latest quilt, sketch a design for a new shawl to weave, tie together a twig tray or dip candles until quitting time. Lunch was always leftovers from last night's dinner, and dinner was usually something easy—a pot of stew that would yield several days' worth of meals, a meat loaf that could be sliced for sandwiches or frozen and reheated next week or a roast that would be wonderful tonight in thick slices, even better tomorrow in cold sandwiches with spicy mustard and best of all the next day chopped and cooked in gravy with potatoes and carrots.

In the evening on a normal day she would work on her counted cross-stitch samplers, or she would make herself comfortable on the rug while she fashioned the miniature sweet-grass baskets that commanded amazing prices from people familiar with such baskets in the Lowcountry of South Carolina. If her fingers grew tired, she might read or put a tape in the little deck on the night table, and she would fall asleep to music.

Normal days might be gone forever. Even if Boone kept his word, even if he left her physically unhurt, there were other harms that he would be responsible for. She might never again feel safe in her own home. She might need weeks or even months to forget the fear he'd caused. She would probably never again look without suspicion at a stranger who wandered her way.

She would have lost some of her innocence, and after a lifetime in *this* world, she didn't have much of it left to lose.

The bathroom door opened with a creak, and he came out, looking cold, pale and miserable, as if all he wanted was to crawl back into bed and sleep for a week. That was probably the best thing he could do. Sometimes the body needed to simply shut down all nonessential functions in order to handle the injuries dealt it. Twenty-four, thirty-six, forty-eight hours of sleep would do wonders for him, but she wasn't going to suggest it. Whenever he slept, no doubt, she would be handcuffed nearby. She didn't care to spend any more time than absolutely necessary wearing these bracelets.

He knelt beside her, leaning forward to unfasten the cuffs. There was a faint lavender smell about him, from the soap he'd used to wash up. His hair was wet and slicked back, and he had no doubt made use of one of the extra toothbrushes in the medicine chest—she could smell the minty toothpaste when he made a pained exhalation—but he hadn't tried to shave. The heavy stubble that had covered his jaw yesterday was going to soon become a full-fledged beard that gave him a slightly sinister look.

As soon as her hand was free, Ashley slid away from him and got to her feet. "I'm going to fix breakfast," she announced, giving him a chance to stop her before she turned away to the kitchen. She was putting water on the stove to boil when he finally spoke.

"Do you have any aspirin?"

"No, but I have some white willow bark." Without glancing his way, she knew the look he was giving her. Seth gave her those same looks, as did most of her friends, but she'd learned to ignore them. She had come by her faith in alternative treatments legitimately. Her mother, her grandmother and all the women before them had believed in natural remedies. She'd grown up using licorice for sore throats, ginger for upset stomachs and evening primrose oil for PMS, along with a host of other herbal concoctions taken daily as a preventive measure. She couldn't remember the last time in her adult life that she'd been bothered by even anything so minor as a stuffy nose.

After filling a glass with cold water, she took a bottle from the cabinet and carried both to him at the table, where he'd taken a seat. For a moment he didn't move, but finally he extended his hand, palm flat, and accepted the two capsules she shook from the bottle. He didn't take them right away, though. Instead, he looked at them as if he might rather suffer the headache instead of the cure.

She gave an exasperated sigh. "I'm not going to poison you, Mr. Boone. It wouldn't do much for my reputation if I did."

He glanced up at her. "What reputation?"

"Some people on the mountain don't have much faith in doctors or much money to pay them. They prefer the old ways, the natural ways. I put remedies together for them."

"You're an herbalist."

"Or a quack, depending on who you ask."

"You 'put' this together." He held up the capsules.

"You buy the capsules, and you can fill them with anything you need. For myself, I generally prefer to take herbs in tea form, whenever possible, but sometimes a capsule is better," she said with a shrug. Before returning to the stove, where the water was starting to steam, she hesitated long enough to speak again. "Besides, if I were going to poison you, I would have done it last night, *before* you got too comfortable in my bed."

Back in the kitchen, she added tea bags to two cups and poured hot water over them, then took a bag of baking mix from the cabinet. She wanted biscuits this morning, she decided, hot and flaky, with apricot preserves and honey and the butter that old Granny Tompkins had churned herself and traded for one of Ashley's egg baskets. Humming to herself, she prepared the mix, rolled it out on the floured counter and was in the process of hunting for her biscuit cutter when, unexpectedly, Boone appeared behind her, grasping her arm tightly.

"What—" Breaking off, she followed his gaze outside. A truck was slipping and sliding its way up her muddy driveway. She didn't need to see the blue light bar on top or the Catlin County Sheriff's Department seal on the door or to hear Boone's savage, almost frantic curse to know who was driving it: Seth.

"Son of a bitch!" Boone dragged her back a few feet from the window. When she looked back to tell him that he was hurting her, to insist that he let go, she saw the reason his grip was hurting so: he held the pistol in the same hand he had wrapped around her, and her tender skin was pinched against it. The sight of it, and the absolutely palpable panic emanating from him, made her heart skip a beat.

"You don't need the gun," she said quickly. "Please, just put it away. I swear, I'll get rid of him, but you have to promise not to do anything, *please!*"

"What is he doing here?" he hissed.

She swallowed hard and glanced out the window. The Blazer was coming over the last small rise. In another moment it would be parked behind the van, and another moment after that, Seth would be at the front door—unless she stopped him first. "It's my ex-husband," she admitted. "I told you he comes by to check on me."

"Your ex—" Dismay and disbelief made his eyes even darker. "Sheriff Benedict? Sheriff Benedict is your *ex-husband?*"

She gave a small nod. "Please... He just wants to let me know that a prisoner has escaped. He'll want me to move into town until you're caught. He'll tell me to be extracareful. That's all, I swear it is. Please just let me talk to him, and I'll send him away. I won't tell him anything. I won't make him suspicious. *Please,* Dillon, please let me talk to him."

He looked out the window, then back at her. "If you try to warn him—"

"I swear to God, I won't."

He glanced out again, then released her. "Go on. But don't forget—if you can't get rid of him...*I* will."

She took a quick look. Seth was still inside the truck, pulling on a jacket. It was raining again, she realized numbly, a heavy mist that seemed to fall in slow motion. Twice she'd looked outside and hadn't noticed. Then, giving herself a mental shake, she went to the counter. She carried the mugs to the table, setting them down, removing the tea bag from one as she slid her feet into a pair of stretched-out loafers kicked underneath the table. She was about to turn toward the door when a set of keys, half-hidden in the folds of a lace runner, caught her attention—*her* keys, dropped there last night when he'd closed the door and pulled that gun on her.

Seeing that his attention was still on Seth, she slid the keys into the deep pocket of her skirt, then took her tea to the door, pausing only long enough to take down a heavy woolen shawl from its peg and wrap it around her shoulders. With one last look back at Boone, she opened the door and stepped outside, leaving the door open a few inches behind her. "Morning."

Seth came to the top of the steps and stopped, the width of the porch between them. He was wearing his uniform, khaki trousers with a green shirt and a shiny green jacket. His boots were muddy, the uniform was wrinkled, as if it had been slept in, and his face was lined, as if he hadn't slept at all. "Good morning."

"What brings you out on a day like this?"

He drew a pair of black gloves from his pocket and tugged them on, reminding her of just how chilly it was and how poorly dressed—cotton skirt, sweater, shawl, bare legs—she was. "We lost a prisoner yesterday morning. The deputy who was transporting him, Tommy Coughlin, apparently lost control of the car and went into a ravine over near Sadler's Pass. The prisoner then somehow got his gun, shot him and escaped."

Ashley's throat went dry, but her expression didn't change. Had Boone lied to her? Had it happened the way he claimed—an ambush, an accident that was no accident, three attackers who'd shot both men—or was Seth's version correct? She didn't know, and she desperately needed to. "Jeez, I'm sorry, Seth. Is Tom okay?"

"He's in a coma. Besides being shot, he got pretty banged up in the accident. Apparently he suffered some head injuries. I talked to his mother this morning, and she said the doctors are guardedly optimistic—whatever that's worth." He removed his green baseball cap, bearing the county name over an embroidered sheriff's star, and shook the rain out of it, then hung it over the hand-carved wooden pineapple that decorated the railing there. "Anyway, I came to help you pack."

She kept her gaze even and cool. "I'm not going anywhere."

"You've got to get out of here, Ashley. You can't stay up here alone with that criminal on the loose. I won't be home much until Boone's in jail again, so you're welcome to stay there. Just get your stuff, and I'll follow you back into town."

She ignored the part about leaving—as she knew he would expect her to—and focused instead on what he would expect her to find interesting. "So you've caught—or almost caught—Dillon Boone. Bill Armstrong must be delirious with joy. What about the money?"

"It wasn't on him when they arrested him over in Mossville," he said dryly.

"Mossville. That's Sylvan County." She pretended she hadn't already known that that was where Boone had been captured. "Dillon Boone is an extraordinarily unlucky man."

"He's a *desperate* man. That's why you're going to do what I say. Pack whatever you need for the next four or five days and get the hell off this mountain."

She wrapped both hands around the mug to keep them from trembling and lifted it for a hot sip. Feeling only slightly fortified, she lowered it again and gave him a reproving look. "You expect me to drop everything and leave my home on the remote chance that some convict might come by here? You know me better than that, Seth. There's nothing here that Boone could possibly want—no telephone, no weapons, no money. Only poor Bessie. Besides, Sadler's Pass is miles from here. What are the chances that he could make it this far without getting caught?"

"It's only five miles over the mountain."

"*Only* five miles over the mountain?" she repeated, exaggerating the words and rolling her eyes. "What are the chances that he could even find his way here? You and I grew up in these mountains, and we still get lost from time to time. Boone's an outsider. A flatlander. He's from Georgia, for God's sake. He's a city boy." After another sip of tea, she grew serious. "What are the chances he could even survive the weather last night? He must have been hurt, bouncing around in Tom's car when it went into the ravine. Hell, coming from the Sylvan County Jail, he was probably hurt *before* the car went into the ravine. I don't know if you had it any better in town, but up here it was pretty darned cold last night, and the rain didn't stop till morning. You know how quickly exposure can kill a man."

Seth's expression turned grim. "We're considering that possibility, but until we find him—or his body—we have to assume that he's still out there. The first thing he'll want is shelter, then transportation." He gave the van a derisive look. "I'm not sure even Boone is desperate enough or crazy enough to believe Bessie qualifies. Not that transportation will do him any good. The county is pretty much sealed off. The highway patrol has roadblocks on the only roads in and out."

"Seems like a lot of effort for a bank robber."

"A bank robber who shot a cop," he corrected her. "A bank robber who nearly *killed* a cop."

She leaned her shoulder against the doorframe, feeling the rough wood prick at her shawl. If Boone *had* lied, if he had shot and almost killed a good man like Tom Coughlin, then she was a fool to protect him—even if protecting him also meant protecting Seth. But he'd told a different story—*We were ambushed.... There was a van and three men.... They opened fire....*—and he'd told it convincingly. Last night she had believed him. This morning—this morning she thought she still believed him.

What was Seth's explanation for Tom losing control of his car? she wondered without asking. Tom was a good driver, never reckless, certainly not with Catlin County's Most Wanted in his back seat. Yes, it had been raining, but not hard; it hadn't started to come down hard until after lunch. Yes, the road might have been a little slick, but like her and Seth, Tom had grown up in Catlin. He'd logged tens of thousands of miles on the county roads. He would have been prepared for that.

Also Seth apparently thought Boone had taken the gun and shot Tom after the accident. *Why?* If the deputy had suffered serious head injuries in the wreck, there was no reason for his prisoner to shoot him. He could have simply walked away. And Seth's assumptions left no room for one other small detail that she knew and he didn't: Boone's own gunshot wound. If he'd stolen the gun from Tom and shot him, then *who* had shot Boone?

There was a van and three men....

"I really am sorry about Tom," she said. "I hope he's all right. But I can't run away every time something happens in the county, Seth. This is my home. This is where I belong. I can't be afraid of everything, or I won't be able to live here anymore. We've had this discussion often enough, Seth. You understand."

He looked anything but understanding. "This is different, Ashley. We're talking about an escaped fugitive who shot an injured cop! God only knows what he might do to you if you get in his way."

She remembered waking up this morning to a cold cabin and the warm quilt Boone had covered her with. She thought about him taking the time just a short while ago to heat that same quilt and tuck it around her before he went into the bathroom. Those didn't seem like the actions of a man who could cold-bloodedly shoot an already injured man and leave him to die.

She gave Seth an apologetic smile. "Sorry, sweetheart, but I can't go. The gift shop over near the parkway has an order in for more trays, and I've got to get six dozen candles in the mail to South Carolina this week, and there's that market basket I'm making for a certain person's grouchy mother's birthday. I've got too much going on to waste even a minute of time packing or moving into your house or moving back out here."

"Ashley—"

"Seth." She mimicked his strained-patience voice, then smiled.

He stared at her for a long moment, his eyes dark, his entire face dark and handsome and dear. She kept her smile in place by sheer force of will, wishing all the while that he would simply leave, praying that he would leave before Boone's patience ran out or his fear grew unmanageable. Finally, running his fingers through his hair, Seth grudgingly asked, "You'll be careful, won't you?"

"I'll keep the doors locked and the windows barred and my hickory stick at my side."

"I'd prefer that you keep my shotgun at your side." He added hopefully, "It's in the truck, loaded and ready to go."

"I've never handled a gun in my life, Seth, and I don't intend to start today. I'll be careful. I'll stay inside. I'll keep the doors locked. If any escaped prisoners happen along, I'll cower and hide until they've gone on their way."

"Don't joke about it, Ashley," he said sharply. "If anything happened to you—"

"Nothing will. I'm safe here. Dillon Boone, if he makes it this far, will take one look at this place and at Bessie, and he'll keep on going." Reaching out, she gave his hand a squeeze. "*You* be careful, Seth. You're the one who's going off into the mountains in the rain and the cold to track down a desperate fugitive. You're the one who will be out there with a bunch of nervous, trigger-happy cops. Take care of yourself, and don't worry about me. I'll be fine." She was counting on that.

He held her hand and her gaze for a moment, then, releasing her, he turned to look out across the valley. With the low clouds, the mist and the fog, visibility was at a minimum. Tramping around in the forest looking for signs of Boone was going to make for a miserable day, and Ashley felt guilty that she couldn't spare Seth the discomfort. But how could she try to give him any sort of message when the man he was looking for was on the other side of the door at her back and holding a gun? When he was prepared to use that gun?

After a moment Seth faced her again and, changing the subject, tried to lighten up. "That wouldn't be hot coffee you're drinking while I stand here and freeze, would it?"

"When have you ever known me to drink coffee?" she asked chidingly. "This is green tea. I have more inside. Would you like a cup?"

His answer came quickly and was delivered with conviction. "No, thanks."

"Are you sure? It's good for you."

He didn't look convinced.

"I can fix you some ginger tea—it'll warm you up from the inside out. Or chamomile to ease your stress. Or how about some cayenne—"

"How about I wait until I stop by the Parmenters' on the way back down? Nell will have a pot of strong coffee on the stove."

"Strong enough to melt iron," she said with a touch of scorn. "It'll destroy your stomach lining, but suit yourself." She swallowed the last of the tea, then dangled the mug from one finger by its handle. "I appreciate your coming by, Seth."

"But you're not going to reconsider my request."

"Your *request?*" she echoed. "I must have missed that. All I heard was orders."

He put his cap on, pulling it low over his eyes. "Go in and lock up."

"I will."

"Stay inside."

"Absolutely."

"Don't do anything foolish."

Too late, she wanted to reply, but she smiled brightly and gave him the answer he wanted. "I promise I won't."

Coming forward a few steps, he bent to kiss her forehead. "Be careful."

"You, too." Tugging the shawl tighter, she watched him move down the steps and sprint across the saturated ground to the truck. She watched him climb inside, start the engine and back away, and all too soon she watched him drive out of sight. As his taillights disappeared down the hill, she gave a sigh. Seth was safe, for the time being.

But *she* still had to deal with Dillon.

Inside the cabin, Dillon was watching, too, his fingers tightly gripping the pistol, as the sheriff drove away. He didn't breathe a sigh of relief as the Blazer disappeared from sight. Benedict could change his mind and come back, could get to the bottom of the driveway and decide that he would *make* Ashley leave. She might be stubborn, but act-ing in his official capacity as sheriff, her ex-husband was probably just as stubborn.

Her ex-husband. Jeez, how bad could his luck get? Of all the women in Catlin County, the one he took as hostage was the sheriff's ex-wife—an ex-wife whom, judging from that exchange on the porch, the man was still quite attached to. He'd just given Benedict reason to make this whole thing personal, and when cases got personal for cops, they could also get deadly.

But this case was already deadly. Russell's men had tried to kill him once; they wouldn't miss on their second chance. Every cop in this part of the state believed he had shot an injured deputy; if they found him, they weren't going to be inclined to exercise much restraint in dealing with him. The fact that Ashley's ex-husband and best friend was the county sheriff was just the icing on a very bad cake. If anything happened to her, Benedict would surely see that the person responsible was punished for it.

And so much for his plans to have Ashley take him outside the area today. They would never get through the roadblocks, and he would prefer not to involve her in his capture. It could get nasty.

He wished he had never met Russell Bradley, wished he'd never heard of Catlin, North Carolina, and had never set foot in the First American Bank. He wished that son of a bitch on the highway had been a better shot, wished that the ravine had been deeper, that his miseries had ended at Sadler's Pass.

He wished like hell that he'd never met Ashley Benedict.

Wondering why she was dawdling so long in the chill weather, he pulled the door open just in time to see her reach the bottom of the steps. Her head was bent against the rain, and her hands were clutching the edges of the shawl together. Her right hand was also clutching something else: keys. He had forgotten about the keys she'd dropped on the table last night. He had seen them this morning, had noticed that there were only two—one to the cabin, presumably, and one to the van—and then he had promptly forgotten them. *Fool.*

Switching the gun to his right hand, he stepped outside, the cold hitting him with a vengeance. The porch, at least, was dry, but only a few strides took him to the steps, icy wet, and into the rain. Looking ahead, he saw that Ashley had reached the van, had climbed inside and was probably trying to still her shaking long enough to get the key into the ignition. He reached the bottom of the steps, and mud, squishy and frigid, closed over his bare feet. He ignored the discomfort, though, the pain and the chill, and made his way, limping and awkward, to the driver's side of the van.

She was trying to start the engine and having no luck. Jerking the door open, he leaned inside, grabbed the keys and threw them as hard as he could into the weeds that separated the house from what had once been tilled fields. Catching hold of her upper arm, he hauled her out and to the ground, fighting to maintain control when she resisted, when she struggled against him. He lost that control when she shoved him hard, both hands banging on his chest, over his ribs, sending bolts of pure agony shooting through him.

Doubling over, he released her and turned away, his knees buckling. Sinking to his knees in the mud, he tried to breathe, but his lungs refused to expand, refused to accept even one particle of oxygen that might increase the pain radiating through him. Oh, God, he'd never known what it was like to hurt so bad, to feel such torture. For a moment he couldn't breathe, couldn't see, couldn't hear anything but a loud rush in his ears; then there was a voice, soft, feminine, frightened.

"Are you all right?"

Rain was dampening his hair, running down his back, and the mud where he knelt had quickly stolen the last of the warmth that had taken him all night to find. The pain was gradually receding, though, the edges dulling, the sick churning in his stomach calming. He was going to survive.

She touched him, her hands cold but infinitely warmer than he was, but he pushed her a few feet back and held her there with the pistol, pointed level at her throat, as he staggered to his feet. She swallowed hard. The fear was in her eyes once again, exactly where he wanted it. "I—I'm sorry," she whispered. "I didn't mean—"

"Move." He gestured toward the cabin, and she started hesitantly in that direction. Together they climbed the steps, then went inside after she'd paused to remove her shoes. He paid no attention to his muddy feet, made no effort to wipe them on the mat outside the door or the rag rug just inside.

When she came to a stop near the table, he nudged her with the barrel of the gun. "Go over to the bed."

There she stopped again and waited silently, not turning to look at him. She couldn't see the handcuffs he'd picked up as they'd passed the table, but he had no doubt she knew what was coming. That was why, when he moved around her, she was so pale, why, when he shoved the nightstand aside and reached for her hand, she was trembling. She opened her mouth, but no words came out on the first try, and by the time she tried again, he already had one half of the cuffs fastened around her wrist.

"Please don't," she whispered. "I had to try. You would have done the same thing. Please . . ."

The headboard of the bed was wood, solid, and there was no place where the remaining cuff could be secured. Pushing the covers back, though, he found that the metal side rail supporting the mattress and springs on wooden slats was more than adequate. He closed the cuff around it, locked it down tight, then moved to the warmth of the fire and drew a calming breath.

Laying the gun on the mantel, he faced the fire and braced his hands on the rough-hewn wood. Bearing only a small portion of his weight made his arms tremble, and his legs were also unsteady. He hadn't been in great shape before the sheriff's arrival, and that little exertion—down, then up, one short flight of steps, across thirty feet of rain-saturated ground, pulling her out of the van—left him almost too weak to stand. And he'd had hopes of being able to move on today, he thought scornfully.

Behind him there came the scrape of wood on wood, and he turned his head to see that Ashley had pushed the

nightstand farther from the bed and was now sitting on the
floor between the two pieces of furniture, her back against
the wall, her face dark with anger as she scowled at him.
She'd discarded the woolen shawl, tossing it onto the rug.
Her skirt was stained with rain, her legs splashed with mud,
but he didn't offer her a chance to change clothes. The
shawl should have kept her sweater dry, and it was only the
bottom few inches of her skirt that had gotten damp. She
wasn't going to suffer for wearing it until it dried.

He, on the other hand, felt wet from head to toe, and it
was definitely adding to his misery. "Do you have any more
of Seth's clothes here?"

The gruffness of his voice made her mouth thin into a
narrow white line as she shook her head.

Great. The sweats were wet and caked with mud from the
knees down, and his jeans, left in a heap all night, were also
still wet. Modesty be damned, he was going to find comfort somehow.

Turning away from the fire, he spread his jeans out to
dry, then grabbed the quilt from the sofa, carrying it along
with the gun into the bathroom. He didn't bother closing
the door; he had learned quickly this morning that the
fireplace was the only source of heat for the entire cabin,
and he wasn't going to freeze in the name of privacy.
Bending over the tub, he turned the water on, waited until
it got warm, secured the rubber plug, then stripped off the
sweats and carefully lowered himself into the tub.

The first rush of liquid heat sent a muscle-relaxing
shudder through him. The water was hot enough to steam,
rising up to warm his still-exposed skin, carrying with it a
familiar fragrance. Honeysuckle. A bottle on the window
ledge was labeled Honeysuckle. There were others alongside it, fanciful glass shapes filled with jewel-toned gels and
labeled in flowing script. Tea Rose. Chamomile. Lavender. Vanilla. He reached for the honeysuckle, removed the
glass stopper and started to pour a thick stream under the
faucet, but stopped before the first drop escaped. Returning it to the ledge, he took down the vanilla and added it to

the water instead. It was better, he thought with a scowl, that he smell like a vanilla bean than like Ashley.

Leaning back in the tub, he closed his eyes and was about to settle down so that as much of his body as possible was underwater when a grudging warning came from the outer room. "Don't get your dressing wet."

With a grimace, he resettled so that his shoulder with its white gauze bandage was well above the surface of the water.

"I don't suppose I'm going to be allowed to take a bath this morning."

He didn't suppose so. In fact, he didn't plan on leaving the tub until every last drop of hot water had been sacrificed for his comfort.

"What about fixing breakfast? Or changing your dressing?"

He didn't answer. Eventually, of course, he would have to let her go, but until that moment came, he would find relief in knowing that, for *this* moment, he was safe. He didn't have to worry about her, and he didn't have to be close to her. He didn't have to fear that she might try another escape. He didn't have to breathe in her scent. He didn't have to spend hours only inches away from her. He didn't have to worry about what she might do.

He didn't have to fear what *he* might do.

As the water neared the top of the tub, he leaned forward and shut it off, suppressing a groan of discomfort. He didn't think his ribs were broken, after all. Cracked, maybe, or perhaps he'd just torn some ligaments in the accident. As painful as their little struggle had been outside, he assumed that getting hit the way she'd hit him, directly above a broken bone, would have been even worse.

If her escape attempt had taken him by surprise, that blow she'd dealt him had left him shocked. He had begun to believe that he could trust her, he realized. It didn't take much to sucker him—a few tender touches, a little genuine concern and a pair of innocent blue eyes. She could never shoot anyone, she'd insisted, and she had passed up more than a few opportunities to do him harm. She'd had a number of weapons in her hands last night—the scissors with which she had cut away his shirt, the logs she'd added to the fire, the knife she'd used to slice the bread for their dinner. She could have cracked open his skull with that heavy crock she'd used when she had cleaned him up, scalded him with hot tea or poisoned him with one of her herbal concoctions. He had believed that he was safe with her, that she wouldn't deliberately hurt him.

Once again he'd been wrong.

How many times did he have to get knocked to his knees before he learned to quit trusting? How many times did he have to get let down hard? He was a reasonably smart man; he should be capable of learning from his mistakes. But he just kept repeating them, and he kept falling harder.

Ashley Benedict could be the hardest fall of all.

Sliding a little lower in the water, he yawned. She had mentioned breakfast a few minutes ago, and it had sounded like a good idea, but right now all he wanted—all he really needed—was sleep. As long as he was asleep, he couldn't worry, couldn't be bothered by the mess he'd gotten himself into. He couldn't wonder how in God's name things had gone so bad. He couldn't brood over whether they could ever be set right. His body could continue the healing processes, and he could escape to some dreamland where Russell Bradley, Catlin, prison and Ashley Benedict didn't exist.

Finally he pulled the plug, then stood up, stretching slightly less sore muscles, drying much warmer skin. When he was done, he wrapped the quilt around him, returned to the fireplace and added several logs to the fire, then, in a carefully controlled move, dropped down on the sofa.

"You need to eat."

He glanced across the room at her. She was probably hungry herself. Maybe it would do her good to miss a meal. Maybe she would think twice next time about trying to run off before she'd eaten.

"You can take these off now." She rattled the cuffs against the metal rail. "Obviously I'm not going anywhere. I don't have an extra set of keys to Bessie, and, as you heard, she wasn't about to start. Sometimes she gets cranky when it's wet. Seth says it's the distributor cap and I should get it replaced, but I just tend not to drive her when it's raining.''

The sofa was old and well-worn. The fabric, an ugly green weave, was threadbare in places, and the cushions were lumpy underneath him. Still, he could easily see why she didn't throw it out. With one of her quilted throw pillows under his head, he was almost as comfortable there as he'd been last night in her bed.

On the floor, she lost her patience with his silence. "Damn it, Boone!"

"Dillon." The fire was burning brightly, filling the cabin with heat and soft yellow-red light, and he was sinking into the drowsy, otherworldly land of sleep, his eyes closing, his breathing evening out, his voice husky and distant. "When you were pleading for Seth's safety, you called me that." He finished in a yawn. "You called me Dillon."

So she had, Ashley silently acknowledged. *Please, Dillon, please let me talk to him.* She hadn't meant to. He was a bank robber, for heaven's sake, who might have shot a wounded deputy, who definitely had barged in here and taken her hostage. His name had slipped out only because she'd been afraid for Seth, not because she'd wanted to be on a first-name basis with him.

She had never heard anyone call him by his first name, she realized. In all the talk she'd heard about him in town right after the robbery, people had called him Boone or Dillon Boone. They had called him thief, liar, lowlife and bastard, but not once had anyone called him simply Dillon. Not Seth, who had liked him, or Bill Armstrong, who had—through the security company—employed him. Not Daphne Meadows at the boarding house, who'd rented a room to him, or Harry Lightfoot at the diner, who had served him dinner every day for weeks, or any of the people at the bank who had worked with and—presumably—liked him. No one had wanted to claim that little intimacy.

She wasn't thrilled with her first name; given a choice, she would have been Rachel or Sarah, Katherine or Anna. Still, she *liked* being called Ashley, not simply Benedict or, worse, Ms. Benedict. She liked the friendliness of first names, the acceptance. She wondered if *he* missed it. If Dillon missed it.

He was asleep now, his face turned away from her, his breathing even and just a little ragged. She hoped that raspy sound was just a variation on a snore and not the first symptom of an oncoming cold or flu. The last thing he needed in the condition he was in—especially with the rib pain—was a coughing-and-sneezing cold.

No, the *last* thing he needed, she admitted with a scarlet face, was getting hit in exactly the spot where he'd displayed such tenderness last night. She hadn't meant to hit him there, hadn't meant to hit him at all. She had only wanted to push him away, to gain a moment's freedom and possibly make her escape. She hadn't wanted to hurt him.

When he had fallen to the ground, the color in his face had disappeared, leaving him a sickly, ghastly gray. For a time, she was sure, he had stopped breathing, and his voice, half curses, half agonized groans, had been raw. She'd had terrible images of serious injuries made worse, of cracked bones fracturing, of broken bones puncturing lungs. She honestly hadn't meant to hurt him.

With a sigh, she pulled a pillow from the bed, slid it behind her back and settled more comfortably. She couldn't blame him for cuffing her here. If she had to be restrained while he slept, she preferred it like this, across the room from him. In some crazy way, she didn't feel as vulnerable, sitting on the floor and handcuffed to the bed, as she did when she was handcuffed to *him*. Over here she felt safer, more comfortable. A little damp, maybe, and definitely hungry, but less at risk.

Less at risk for what? she wondered. He'd had plenty of chances to hurt her or even kill her, and outside she had definitely given him reason, but he hadn't touched her. She honestly believed that she wasn't in physical danger from him. Maybe from the people looking for him, but not from him.

So why was she afraid?

Maybe because, next to Seth, he was one of the handsomest men around. Because he was a dangerous man, in ways that had everything—and nothing—to do with his alleged crimes. Because his story of being arrested and probably mistreated in Sylvan County, ambushed at Sadler's Pass, shot in the back while unarmed and most likely handcuffed, roused her sympathies. Because he had little reason to smile and found kind words from others difficult to come by. Because he hadn't asked for a fire when he was cold, food when he was hungry or dry clothes when his were soaked. Because he had been ashamed of his actions last night when he'd fastened the handcuffs around her wrist. Because he wasn't the lawless, unprincipled, psychopathic criminal he was supposed to be, but an apparently decent man who'd gotten himself into the sort of trouble that just might get him killed.

She wished he would wake up, wished she could ask him why he had robbed the bank in the first place. He'd had a job that he was apparently pretty good at. Maybe he hadn't made a lot of money, but a person could live on very little and be happy; she was proof of that. With his aversion to prison, why had he stolen so much money that a jury would be more likely to put him under the jail rather than in it? Had the temptation just been too great—seeing all that cash, knowing that, with his inside knowledge, he could simply waltz in, pack it up in a bag and walk out again?

And what had he done with the money? That was the big question, the one that would interest everyone in town. Where had their four hundred and fifty thousand dollars gone? He didn't look as if he'd spent much of it living the good life. If the lines on his face and the expression in his eyes were anything to judge by, the last year had been a tough one. He'd had little comfort and no peace.

He didn't seem to have spent the money on material goods. His jeans had probably cost less than twenty bucks new and were long past new; his shirt was a simple white

T-shirt, three to a pack for six dollars anywhere; and the tennis shoes drying over near the fireplace were inexpensive, an off brand, and had seen many better days.

Pulling another pillow from the bed, she rested it against the nightstand and laid her head on it. Sometimes life just wasn't fair. Many mornings she had awakened from a restless night's sleep and wished for the opportunity to stay in bed and snooze the morning away, but she'd never allowed herself to do it. When she had made the decision to move out here to the cabin and try to become self-supporting, she had also determined that discipline was the key. If she didn't work, she didn't eat, get paid or pay her creditors. She had to keep fairly regular hours, had to treat her crafting as a regular job and not the hobby it had been for so many years.

Now she had the chance to sleep in and be lazy, and she was wide-awake and handcuffed to the bed frame while an escaped prisoner lay snoring on her couch. Lay *naked* on her couch.

A blush warmed her face as she recalled the instant she had realized that he was going to strip down for his bath without closing the door. The thought had popped into her mind that a proper young woman would close her eyes or look away, followed immediately by the acknowledgment that she just must not be as proper as she'd believed, because she had looked enough to see that he was lean, muscular and the same smooth golden brown shade all over. But then he had stepped into the bathtub and out of sight before she'd seen anything else.

Outside, a gust of wind rattled through the house and drew her attention to the windows. The rain was coming down hard again, the sky dusk dark. Poor Seth and his men, out beating the brush in this weather for someone who was safe and warm by a fire. She wished she could have talked to Seth privately, wished she could have told him to call off his search and his roadblocks. All he needed to do was post a few deputies at the bottom of her driveway and wait a few days, and she would send their quarry to them. It wouldn't have been hard, if Dillon hadn't heard about the roadblocks, to persuade him to take Bessie and leave the county. After all, he desperately wanted out of North Carolina as quickly as possible, and in this terrain, on foot *wasn't* the way to go. She would have offered him Bessie, and knowing that it was his best choice, he would have accepted. He would have left her behind—he had promised he would—and he would have driven down her narrow driveway, and when he cleared the grove of oaks and hickories growing so close that their branches blocked out the sun and scraped Bessie's roof, he would have been in perfect position for another ambush, only this time without the shooting. Angry as Seth was about Tom Coughlin's injuries, he would see to it that no harm came to Dillon.

But she hadn't had a moment's private conversation with Seth, and Dillon had heard about the roadblocks. So what would he do now? Stay for the days, weeks or even months it would take for the urgency of the search to calm? Stay only long enough to regain his strength, then set out once again through the mountains? Either plan was impossible. If Tom Coughlin died from his injuries, the Catlin County Sheriff's Department would *never* let up on their search. Seth would be back, probably in a day or two, just to check on her, and sooner or later the trackers would make their way to her cabin. As for Dillon trying to get out on foot, if the cops didn't get him, exposure and the mountains, combined with his injuries, would.

Maybe she could provide him with a third option. Thanks to Seth and the better part of a lifetime spent in this county, she knew virtually every law-enforcement officer in the area, including those troopers with the highway patrol. If she loaded up her van with baskets, blankets, quilts and boxes that could provide a hiding place to anyone who didn't mind the cramped quarters, she could probably talk her way right through any roadblock using friendship and Seth's name, no questions asked. She could drive Dillon Boone out of Catlin County, out of North Carolina and out of her life.

But she would be helping a fugitive—a dangerous man—escape. Could she live with that?

Better than she could live with *him*, she thought grimly.

Far better than she could live with watching him walk into the mountains to almost certain death.

Chapter 4

The rain was coming down with a vengeance, blowing against the windows, beating a steady cadence on the roof. Dillon lay on his back, propped up by pillows, and gazed out the window. If he hadn't found this cabin yesterday, if he had managed to survive last night, today definitely would have killed him. This rain would have made him so miserable that he would have simply stopped. He would have waited to die or get caught, with little preference for which came first. In his situation, getting caught was as good as dying.

He wondered what time it was and how long he'd been asleep. Through the workshop windows yesterday, he'd seen the big clock on the wall, round, white with sharp black numerals. If Ashley kept one inside, he hadn't seen it anywhere; there wasn't even an alarm on the bedside table. He liked the idea of being able to live without timekeepers, of setting his own pace and answering to no one, of not worrying over hours and minutes, about being late or having enough time. Unfortunately he couldn't imagine many places where such a life was possible. Everything was regimented, with hours to keep and schedules to maintain.

Everything except Ashley's life up here.

From over by the bed came a restless sigh, soft and barely audible but registering instantly. When he'd first awakened, he had sneaked a look at her. She had been sitting exactly where he'd left her, between the bed and the night table, her head tilted to one side, her eyes closed. It had been impossible to tell if she was sleeping or simply resting. He certainly hadn't given her many possibilities for getting comfortable. He could have at least put her on the bed . . . and then he could have crawled in beside her.

Then neither of them would have gotten any rest.

Now he slowly turned his head until his gaze connected with hers. Her hair was mussed again, her skirt dry once more, her expression telling him nothing about her mood. She simply looked at him as he sat up, gathering the quilt close. "You said something about food," he said after it became apparent that *she* wasn't going to break the silence.

For a time he thought she would continue the mute act, then she gave a sardonic reply. "About six hours ago."

No wonder his stomach felt so empty. But in general he felt better. A few more days of rest like that, and he would be up to taking off again. There was just one little problem: he had nowhere to go and no way to get there.

Sliding to the edge of the sofa, he stood up and retrieved his jeans from the hearth. The denim was stiff, but as dry and warm as if he'd taken them from a dryer. He made a trip to the bathroom, got dressed, then came out and got the handcuff key before approaching her. He was a half-dozen feet away when she straightened, pushing the pillows away, drawing her feet together, anticipating being free again. He stopped and studied her distrustfully. "You aren't going to try something stupid again, are you?"

A blush coloring her cheeks, she glowered at him. "I'm sorry I hit you."

"Uh-huh. I got an apology more sincere than that from one of the deputies over in Mossville after his fist connected with my eye."

"If you were in my place, you would have done the same thing." She sniffed haughtily. "You *did* do the same thing."

Balancing with one hand on the mattress, he crouched in front of her. "There were people trying to kill your deputy and me. If I wanted to stay alive, I had no choice but to escape."

Her gaze didn't waver. "Seth says *you* shot the deputy."

"Do you believe him? Is that why you ran?"

Clearly she didn't want to answer. She caught her bottom lip between her teeth, looked away, then sighed heavily. Was she afraid her answer would anger him? She needn't worry. He was used to being distrusted. He was accustomed to people thinking the worst of him, expecting the worst from him. Under the circumstances, she was entitled to it.

But her answer, when it finally came, surprised him. "No," she said quietly, looking at him once more. "I don't believe you shot Tom."

For just a moment he sat motionless, hearing her words echo in his head, feeling the warm rush of pleasure they brought him. It was an amazing thing, being believed by someone who had no reason to believe him and every reason in the world not to. If there was one little bit of trust inside her, then maybe he could find more; if he could, maybe he could get her help in leaving North Carolina.

The rattle of the handcuff chain against metal brought him out of his thoughts. Moving forward, he leaned close to her and opened the cuff, freeing her. At first she didn't move, didn't even seem to breathe, then she raised her right hand and began an even, steady massage of her left wrist. He watched as her fingertips made slow circles over her skin, pushing with enough pressure to reach deep into the muscles. His stiff joints and strained muscles could use a little of that kind of attention. Hell, *he* could use any kind of attention she had to spare.

"You need a new dressing, and we both could use some food." Her voice was cool. The moment of trust was gone, the wariness back. "If you'll move . . ."

He stood up and backed away. She stood, too, stiff, stretching before she started toward the kitchen. "Sit at the table," she ordered over her shoulder as she began washing her hands.

He obeyed, pulling out the same chair where he'd sat that morning, settling in. Scents that he recognized but couldn't identify—vanilla, he thought, and spices, maybe cinnamon—came from a basket of potpourri that shared the center of the old table with another basket of dried flowers. Underneath them was a piece of lace, diamond shaped, one point dangling over the center edge of each side. "Is this your work?"

She glanced his way. "Yes."

"The baskets, the flowers or the lace?"

"All of it, including the table. I made it from an old shed that Seth and I tore down."

He fingered the lace, pretty, delicate, the color of old, old ivory. "There was a lot of lace in the house where I grew up—curtains, tablecloths, doilies, sachets."

Bringing the basket of first-aid supplies, she sat down in the chair on his right. "Your mother liked lace?"

He shook his head. "My grandmother did, or so I was told. She died before I was born."

"You lived with your grandfather?"

"Until I was eleven. Until my mother didn't have much choice but to move us to Atlanta." He felt rather than saw the curious look she gave him, but he didn't explain. Telling her what his childhood had been like—the looks, the whispers, the gossip, the hostility, the fights—would earn him nothing but her pity, and he'd had enough pity back there in Waterston, Georgia, to last a lifetime. "You grew up around here?"

She paused in removing items from the basket to glance around the cabin. "In town. This was *my* grandparents' place. My grandfather farmed those fields out front, and my grandmother cooked, cleaned, quilted and sewed, raised five kids and buried three babies and worked alongside him when he needed the help. He died just before I got married, and she died eight months later. She had always said she couldn't get along without him. I'd never guessed how much she meant it." Scooting her chair closer, she leaned forward and loosened the tape that held the bandage to his shoulder. It pulled on the tender skin, making him wince. "Is your grandfather still alive?"

He realized he was holding his breath and blew it out. "No. He's dead, too." After a moment he grimly admitted, "If he had still been living, this last year would have killed him."

"I imagine he had higher hopes for you."

"He was a farmer, too. He worked hard all his life and never had much of anything. He wanted better for my mother. When she let him down, he was hoping for better from me." And he'd let the old man down, too, in ways far worse than his mother had ever managed. As much as he missed his grandfather, sometimes he was glad he was dead. It truly would have broken Jacob Boone's heart to see all that Dillon had accomplished, to see what his only grandson had become.

"It looks good."

He glanced at her, then followed her gaze to his shoulder. She had the dressing off now and was using some cool, tinted liquid to clean the wound. It didn't look good to him; it was raw, red, hot and tender. About the best he could say was that it was no longer oozing blood. But he was no expert. What he knew about medicine began and ended with Band-Aids and iodine. *She* was the herbalist. The healer.

And he sorely needed healing.

"So you grew up in Catlin and moved to Raleigh," he said, seeking—needing—a change of subject. "Why?"

His question was followed by a moment of silence. He suspected that she didn't want to answer, that she didn't want him to know anything about her, that she certainly didn't want to know anything more about him. Then the moment passed and, with a hint of resignation, she replied. "I wanted to do something with my life, to live someplace else and meet interesting people and do exciting things."

"What went wrong?" At the questioning look she gave him, he shrugged. "You're living in your grandmother's cabin on top of a mountain only miles from the town you'd wanted to leave, without a telephone or neighbors, and supporting yourself weaving baskets and making lace. That's about as far from interesting people and exciting things as you can get."

Opening a jar of salve, she used a narrow wooden spoon to scoop some onto a pad of gauze. She laid it over his shoulder, then used two long strips of tape to secure it. "I make the lace only for myself. It's not cost efficient to sell."

She was entitled to avoid answering his question. Nothing in her past was any of his business. Nothing in her *life* except for these few days together was any of his business. But he wanted to know all the same, and so he pressed on. "Was it the divorce? Is that why you hid away up here?"

She picked up yet another jar and twisted the lid off. "I'm not hiding," she corrected. "I live up here because this life-style suits me. I was young and foolish when I thought I wanted something else." After a moment she set the jar aside and leaned back. "The Catlin County sheriff's job came open about the same time Seth and I divorced. He was with the Raleigh Police Department at the time, but he wanted to come back home, so he applied for and got the job. I stayed in Raleigh, kept my job as a teacher and tried not to feel so out of place. I had plenty of friends there, but I was lonely. My grandparents were dead, my parents and sisters had moved to California after I got married, my marriage had ended and my best friend had moved back to Catlin."

Best friend. He could buy that description of her ex-husband. He hadn't seen Benedict while he and Ashley talked, but he'd heard all the words and the intimate little silences. He'd heard the concern in the sheriff's voice. He'd seen the fear in Ashley's eyes when she had pleaded with him to let her send Seth on his way. There was no shortage of love and caring between the two.

So why had their marriage failed?

"It wasn't the happiest time of my life," she went on, "but I was making it. Then one day I went to school, and a fourth-grader in the class across the hall got angry with the teacher and pulled a gun on her. A *fourth-grader*. He wasn't even ten years old, and he was threatening his teacher with a gun. I decided that same day that I was giving notice and coming home to live in Granny's cabin."

Where she could be threatened by a man with a gun, Dillon acknowledged guiltily. Given a choice, she would probably prefer the fourth-grader...but she was safer with the man. *He* wouldn't hurt her. "How long ago was that?"

"Three years."

"Any regrets?"

She shook her head.

"Not even about the divorce?"

With a sweet smile that he wished was meant for him, she picked up the jar again. "I love Seth. I always have. But we weren't meant to be married—at least, not to each other."

It seemed that *he* wasn't meant to be married, period. He had never been against the idea. Most people he knew—his mother excepted—were married, or had been, and he'd always thought it would be nice to have that sort of relationship, that sort of commitment to someone else. But he'd never met the right woman, and then his life had gone sour, and any possibility of settling down had gone right out the window. If he got caught by the sheriff, he would spend the next twenty-five years in prison. If he got away, he would spend the rest of his life on the run, and if he got caught by Russell's men...he would be dead. What woman in her right mind would settle for a future like that?

"Where do your ribs hurt?"

He looked at the jar and the hands that held it. Small hands, fine boned, with long, slender fingers. For all their delicate look, they were strong; they had to be to manage all the work she did to support herself. Although marked with calluses, small cuts and faint scars, a legacy of all that work, they were soft. Gentle. Soothing. Arousing.

He didn't want them touching him any more than was necessary.

But after a lifetime of living alone, if he gave it a moment's effort, he could convince himself that even the slightest touch was necessary.

When he didn't answer, she brought one of those small, delicate hands to his chest, probing until her lightest touch made him wince. Marking the place, with the other hand she scooped up a dollop of cream and began rubbing it into his skin with the same easy, sure movements she'd used a short while ago to massage her own wrist. He wanted to believe that it was the coolness of the cream that made him shiver, that it was the discomfort her fingers were causing that made his breath catch, but he knew neither was the case. It was Ashley, touching him in a way he hadn't been touched in months. In years. In his lifetime.

"This is comfrey," she said, her voice soft, her tone conversational. "It's been used for centuries to treat wounds and skin irritations, to reduce inflammation, to heal damaged ligaments and tendons and to help heal the tissue damage caused by bone injuries."

"Where did you learn about all this stuff?" he asked, pretending he didn't notice that she was so close, that he couldn't smell the honeysuckle that lingered on her skin, pretending that there was nothing intimate about her touch, that his muscles weren't tensing, that his hands weren't shaky.

"From my mother and some of the other women in the area." She dipped into the jar again, bringing out more salve. "Mostly from my granny. She knew every plant that grew in the mountains and all its uses. She knew as much as any doctor."

He cleared his throat; his voice had gotten a little husky. "Did she teach your sisters, too?"

She shook her head, and a strand of soft blond hair fell to brush his arm. "Deborah and Gail weren't interested. Just me." She continued to massage the salve in, her fingers moving in slow circles, starting small, then widening. Did she notice, he wondered, that her attempt to provide comfort was making him *un*comfortable? Did she feel the change in his skin temperature, from cool to warm and well on the way to hot? Did she hear the change in his breathing, shallow as before but unsteady now? Did she see that his muscles had gone taut or feel the trembling that rippled through him?

Closing his eyes tightly, he tried to concentrate on the slight jarring pain every time her fingers passed over a particular point above his ribs, but that little bit of pain was nothing compared to the pleasure. The need. The hunger. It had been so long since anyone had touched him without causing pain, so long since a woman had touched him....

Abruptly he opened his eyes and clumsily brushed her hand away. His body hard, his face hot, his voice shaky, he said, "I'm kind of hungry. What about lunch?"

If she noticed anything brusque about his manner, she didn't show it. She simply drew back, screwed the lid on the jar, wiped her hands on a gauze pad and got to her feet. "I'll get it now," she said, gathering her supplies together in the basket again, then walking away. She was calm, collected and completely unaware—or uncaring?—of the effect she'd had on him. Worse, she was completely unaffected herself. *He* might be dealing with an incredible desire for *her,* but *she* didn't feel a thing for *him.*

Damn her.

Damn them both.

Making bread was one of Ashley's favorite tasks. It supplied her with food and—in the spring, when she sold fresh-baked loaves at the Hatfields' vegetable stand on the edge of town—money. It filled the cabin with its warm, rich, homey scent and reminded her of childhood days whose innocence and goodness she would like to recapture, when she had stood on a three-legged stool right at this counter and learned to measure, stir and knead from her granny.

It also provided her with a few minutes of hard work, kneading and manipulating the stiff dough, that were guaranteed to ease any tension affecting her. She needed that release now.

She hadn't meant to become so absorbed in tending to Dillon's injuries. She hadn't meant to lose her perspective, to forget the situation they were in, to forget that theirs was no normal association—that at best they were patient and practitioner, at worst captor and hostage. She hadn't meant to let the professional task of providing medical treatment somehow slide into pure personal pleasure.

She certainly hadn't meant to arouse him . . . or herself.

It didn't mean anything, she silently insisted as she began gathering ingredients on the counter. It was just that she'd been alone too long. Since the divorce, she'd made only one effort to revive her all-but-absent social life, and that relationship had died a natural death a few short months later. She was too young to live so all alone, her mother kept warning her. When she found herself attracted to a man like Dillon Boone—a man who had taken her prisoner, a man with a disreputable past, a man with no future—no doubt, her mother was right. She needed people in her life, needed friends and a lover.

She *didn't* need Dillon.

Even if he was the only person available.

With a deep, cleansing sigh, she forced her attention to the ritual of bread making. She measured each ingredient precisely, then ran the water in the sink until it was exactly the right temperature. She oiled the loaf pans, only two this time, and the big pottery bowl the dough would rise in. Next she returned the flour and sugar canisters to their place in the corner, put the milk back in the refrigerator and the shortening, yeast and salt back in the cabinet. While the yeast softened in warm water and the milk heated on the stove, she put a pot of water on for tea—also part of the ritual—then sorted through the various herbal varieties stored in Mason jars in the cabinet. Already feeling the slightest bit more relaxed, she took two bags from one jar and placed one in each of the two mugs on the counter.

"Isn't it easier to buy bread from the store?"

At the sound of his voice, the muscles in her neck tightened again. They hadn't spoken through lunch. He'd eaten two bowls of stew and thick slices of bread spread with the strawberry preserves she'd put up last summer, and he hadn't looked at her or talked to her or even seemed to notice that she was there. But now he was talking to her. Now he was looking at her. She felt his gaze.

"The nearest store is fifteen miles away," she commented, her tone chiding. "It's raining, so Bessie doesn't want to run, and even if she wanted to, someone threw my one and only key into the weeds, where it will probably get buried so deep in the mud that I'll never find it again."

From the corner of her eye, she caught the beginnings of a flush as it crossed his cheeks. Was that a little regret for his actions this morning? Had he realized too late that if *she* couldn't drive away in the van without the keys, then neither could *he?* Would he be out there in the weeds when the rain stopped, searching for the keys? Maybe he would simply hot-wire Bessie. He was a criminal; surely he knew how to do that.

If he didn't, once the rain stopped and Bessie's distributor cap dried out, maybe she would show him how.

Turning back to the stove, she checked the milk, found it ready and stirred it together with the sugar, salt and shortening. The recipe she used was her great-grandmother's, passed down through the generations. Like the herbs—and the quilting, the weaving, the needlework—her sisters had displayed little interest in baking. They shared Dillon's opinion that it was easier to simply buy. Someday she hoped to have a daughter to share all her knowledge with. Otherwise, when she was gone, her grandmother would be finally gone, too.

While the milk mixture cooled, she removed the kettle from the burner and filled the mugs with steaming water. She thought about leaving his there on the counter, where he could get it or not, and taking hers over to curl up on the sofa and enjoy the fire. But when she moved from the counter, it wasn't toward the fireplace with only one cup. She carried them both to the table, sat down in the chair opposite him and returned to the conversation. "'Easier' isn't always better, you know. Some things are worth the extra effort, and bread is definitely one of them." She drew a deep breath, savoring the aromas of the steeping tea: roasted grains, carob, chicory and spices. "Wouldn't it have been easier for you if you'd learned to live within your income instead of breaking into the bank?''

For a long time he simply looked at her, his eyes unreadable. Then he shrugged. ''Breaking into the bank had nothing to do with money.''

''Then what *did* it have to do with?''

''Proving a point. Learning a lesson.''

''Proving to whom? Learning from whom?''

Again he looked at her without speaking; again he shrugged. ''It doesn't matter.''

Oh, but it did. It mattered to Seth and to Bill Armstrong. It mattered to the company Dillon had worked for in Asheville and to every single person who'd had money in the First American Bank. It mattered to the district attorney, and it especially mattered to the government, which had made good on every depositor's funds.

It mattered to her, too. She wanted to hear that he wasn't guilty, that he hadn't done anything wrong, that it all had been a terrible mistake. She wanted to think that he was running and hiding to avoid a miscarriage of justice and not simply to avoid paying for his crimes. She would like to think that he was a better man than that. She wanted to believe that she was attracted to a better man than that.

Even though the evidence indicated that he wasn't.

Picking up one cup, she used a spoon to remove the tea bag. After sliding the cup to Dillon, she removed the bag from the second, stirred in a squirt of honey, then took a sip. ''Did you learn the lesson?''

His smile was humorless. ''I certainly did.''

''What was it?''

''Never trust anyone.''

She studied his face for a moment and saw that, yes, he had indeed learned the lesson well. There was nothing even remotely resembling trust in his expression, nothing that came close in his eyes. Looking away to hide the sadness that knowledge brought, she quietly commented, ''That's no way to live.''

''No,'' he quietly disagreed. ''In prison is no way to live. Dead in a ravine is no way to live.''

"Neither is on the run," she argued. "Why don't you turn yourself in?"

"I can't do that."

"They're going to catch you. You heard Seth say that the roads out of the county are all blocked. There are people out there searching for you now. Sooner or later they'll pick up your trail, and they'll follow you here."

"Maybe not. Maybe the rain will wash away enough to throw them off."

That wasn't likely to happen. She knew it, and she suspected that he did, too. Even if the signs were all washed away, rather than give up, the search parties would simply forget about picking up and following his trail and would instead focus on canvassing the entire area. They would make their way to every house in the mountains, would ask questions and look around. They would make their way *here.* "If you turn yourself in and get a good lawyer—"

He interrupted her. "And how would I pay for a good lawyer?"

She met his gaze evenly. "With the money you stole."

"When I got arrested, I still had most of the money from my last job—about two hundred and eighty bucks. I don't know where it is now. I assume the Sylvan County sheriff turned it over to your deputy and your sheriff has it, but it's all I have in the world."

"What about the four hundred and fifty thousand dollars you took?"

His grin was cynical. "I've never even seen four hundred and fifty thousand dollars, and I never will."

She toyed with her cup. Not once had he actually admitted that he'd robbed the bank—but not once had she actually asked. Nobody that she knew of had asked. He had been so easy to blame. He'd been a stranger in town, and he had helped install the very alarm system that had been bypassed in the break-in. He knew the system, the bank, the operations. He had known that the money would be there, had known how to get in and out. His fingerprints had been found inside the bank, in places where he'd worked and they were expected, and in places where they shouldn't have been. Blueprints and notes detailing how to circumvent the security system had been found in his room over at Daphne Meadows's boarding house. He'd been in trouble with the law before—although a long time ago, his boss had offered in his defense. He had even talked to his co-workers at the security company about how easy such a robbery would be.

No, there had been no reason to ask him if he was guilty. But she asked anyway. "Did you break into the bank?"

He didn't look away, didn't avoid her gaze, didn't back down from his guilt. "Yes," he said grimly, "I did."

"And you stole the money."

"I took *some* money. Not four hundred and fifty thousand dollars."

"Then what happened to it?" The money had been there in the vault when the bank closed for business that afternoon, and it was gone late that night when, after the robbery had been reported, Armstrong opened up the bank for Seth's investigation. It hadn't magically disappeared. *Someone* had taken it, and since Dillon had admitted to the break-in, to stealing *some* money, it seemed most likely that he had taken it all.

His expression made it clear that he knew the conclusion she had reached. Skeptical, mocking, sardonic, he shook his head. "Honey, you wouldn't believe me if I told you."

"Try me."

With a gesture toward the counter, he said, "Your milk's getting cold. You're supposed to add the flour while it's still warm." At her look, he raised one eyebrow. "My mother used to bake bread."

Because he was right, Ashley returned to the kitchen. She stirred the flour into the milk, adding extra to make up for the day's humidity. "So what are your plans?"

"Beyond staying alive, I don't have any. I don't know how I'm going to get out of here, don't know where I'll go or how I'll get there or how I'll live when I get there."

"Didn't you plan ahead? Didn't you think to put some of the money aside? Didn't you realize you would need a way to survive?"

There was the scrape of wood on wood, then he came into the kitchen, moving with care, his right arm bent and immobile against his chest. He rinsed his empty cup, set it in the sink, then leaned back against the counter to watch her. "There wasn't any money to put aside." His voice was strained. "I only took five thousand dollars, and I left that—"

She turned the dough out on the floured counter as she waited for him to continue. When he didn't, she began the job of kneading and considered the possibilities. He hadn't left any money at the bank; Seth would have found it there. He hadn't left any in his room, either. In fact, Seth didn't believe he'd even gone back to his room; if he had, surely he would have taken the blueprints and the notes detailing how he'd intended to accomplish the robbery—the strongest evidence, along with his fingerprints, against him. The authorities in Asheville didn't believe that he'd gone back to his apartment there. The manager hadn't seen him, and the girlfriend upstairs claimed—quite believably, Seth had thought—that she hadn't, either. Everything there had appeared untouched. His belongings had still been scattered about when they'd searched it; his clothes were still in the closet, and a few personal items—photographs, she recalled—had been left behind.

So where might he have left the money? Perhaps with an accomplice? There had been no evidence that anyone else was involved, but that didn't make it true. Maybe he'd had a partner, and he'd given the money to this person whom the police didn't know existed to hold until the heat was off. Maybe they'd had plans to meet up somewhere and split the take, but this person had never shown. After all, why should he—or she? He or she had nearly half a million dollars that Dillon was receiving all the blame for stealing. No one would ever connect him or her to the robbery.

Or maybe it hadn't been an accomplice but simply a woman whom he'd trusted. Maybe he'd thought her affection for him would outweigh the temptation of a half-million dollars.

Then she looked at him and reconsidered that last theory. She couldn't imagine him trusting *anyone*. But hadn't he said that to never trust anyone was the lesson he'd learned?

"Where did you go when you left here?"

"Back to Georgia. I stayed in Atlanta awhile, then did some traveling—Georgia, Mississippi, Tennessee."

"How did you support yourself without the bank's money?"

"The old-fashioned way. I worked."

She felt the skepticism cross her face. "You just applied for a job and got hired and worked like anyone else, and the police never caught you? Why didn't they check with Social Security, find out where you were employed and arrest you?"

His sigh started out heavy and impatient, but with a wince at the movement, it ended hushed. "No, I didn't just walk into a place and apply for a job. I worked the kind of jobs where you get paid in cash and no one worries about taxes, withholding forms or things like that."

He was talking about day-labor sort of work, drudge jobs where a man worked very hard for very little pay. It was a tough way to earn a living. She couldn't imagine anyone who had any other choices at all choosing to live that way. But surely it beat going to prison, which was all he'd been facing.

Giving the dough one last turn, she formed it into a ball, placed it in the oiled bowl and coated it, then washed her hands. She dried them, then carried the bowl to the hearth, set it a fair distance from the fire and covered it with a towel. Next she took a piece of fabric from the tall lidded basket that sat in one corner, got pinking shears and a safety pin from her sewing kit and laid everything out on the clean counter next to the stove.

"What is that for?"

"A sling. You shouldn't be using your right arm."

"I'm not using it."

"You're moving it a little, even if you don't mean to. A sling will more or less immobilize it and your shoulder, and it'll help your shoulder to heal more quickly." She measured out a piece of cotton, about forty-five inches square, cut it, folded it on the diagonal, then approached him. He watched her warily—no more so, she suspected, than she was looking at him. She wished he could fashion the sling for himself. It was possible, of course, with a lot of trial and error, tying, trying on, adjusting, retying. It was also silly to even suggest.

She slid one short side underneath his bent arm, then brought the ends up around his neck. It wasn't possible to reach high enough to tie them, though, without asking him to sit down ... or getting very close.

For reasons she couldn't begin to understand, she chose to get close.

She took one step, then one more, until the only way she was going to get any closer to him was in his embrace. Her feet were between his, her thighs only a millimeter from his. She swore she could feel the heat radiating from his body... or was that her own warmth? She certainly had gotten hot in the past few seconds.

Rising onto her toes brought her a fraction nearer. She could smell the vanilla bath gel he'd used this morning, could feel his breath on her forehead, could hear each measured intake and each slow breath out. She could feel his skin—warm, smooth, her fingers lingering over each small touch.

This was ridiculous, she scolded herself as she fumbled with the cloth. She had nursed other men and had done far more intimate things with two of them. Heavens, she'd been nursing *this* man for nearly twenty-four hours now. Touching him now was no different than touching him all those other times had been.

Oh, but it was. This time he was standing up, looking strong, vital, virile. He wasn't lying in bed, so miserable that he might rather be dead, or sitting in a chair, pale with pain. He wasn't so weak that he couldn't remove his own shoes, so cold that he couldn't stop shivering, so tired that

he could barely hold his head up. This time she wasn't seeing him as just a patient, an unwanted visitor, a criminal to
be feared. This time she wasn't afraid—although she had
no doubt that, if he wanted her fear, he could easily pro-
voke it.

This time was definitely different.

She tied the two corners into a neat, square knot, ad-
justed it on the side that wasn't injured, then began gathering the excess fabric over his elbow, folding, tucking,
securing it with the safety pin. When she finished, she took
a step back, smoothed a wrinkle from the cotton and
cleared her throat. "Is that comfortable?"

Still looking uneasy, he nodded.

For his peace of mind, as well as her own, she moved
farther away, busying herself with cleaning the counter. She
imagined she heard a sigh of relief as the distance between
them increased, but she couldn't say whether it came from
him . . . or her.

She'd had plenty to worry about in the past twenty-two
hours—whether he might mistreat her, force her to flee with
him or maybe even kill her. Those concerns, it appeared,
had been groundless. He'd promised he wouldn't hurt her,
had promised he would leave her behind when he left, and
she believed him. But now she had another worry, one that
could potentially be as big a threat to her well-being as any
of those others.

God help her, what if she was falling for Dillon Boone?

Moving each log with care, Dillon stoked the fire, then
rested his good arm on the mantel, leaned his head on it and
closed his eyes. He was tired and expecting a better night's
rest than he'd gotten last night. He didn't know if it was the
comfrey that Ashley had used or the natural healing process—or if he was gullible enough that simply being told
that the herb would help had made him believe it as fact—
but his ribs weren't quite so tender this evening. He could
even manage an occasional deeper breath without feeling
as if he might pass out from the pain.

"Are you ready for bed?"

Ashley's voice came from the chair behind him. She'd been curled up there since dinner, a wooden frame holding a piece of needlework in her lap. He had lain on the couch most of the evening and watched her work, lit by the harsh yellow light of the lamp on one side and the softer golden glow of the fire on the other. That was all he'd done for the better part of two hours, just watched her, and he had enjoyed it in ways he'd never imagined.

It had been such a homey scene, one that would have appeared so normal to someone looking in: the well-lit room, the blazing fire, the freshly baked bread on the counter, the man stretched out on the couch, the woman bent over a cross-stitch sampler a few feet away. The only things missing were the kids at play and the dog curled up on the rug. And the conversation. The connection. The caring. The intimacy.

He'd never had many normal, homey scenes in his life. The closest he'd come had been in his grandfather's house, where they'd had the woman, the kid, the dog, but the man—the father—had been missing. As much as Dillon had loved his grandfather, Jacob hadn't quite taken the place of the father he'd never had.

Even though that father was one hateful son of a bitch.

"Yeah," he said at last in response to her question. "Do you want to change into a nightgown or something?" A flannel nightgown, he hoped, something with a high neck and a hem that dragged on the floor when she walked, something that not even his long-unsatisfied lust could find attractive.

He seriously doubted that such a garment existed.

She was quiet for a moment, then she softly, hesitantly replied, "Yes, I do."

He turned around and watched as she went to the dresser and took a cotton gown from the top drawer, shaking it out. So much for hopes. The gown wasn't flannel, the hem wouldn't come within six inches of the floor once it was on and as for the neck... He couldn't see its line, but he could tell it wasn't anything high and substantial. Damnation.

He'd be better off if she slept once again in that skirt and shapeless sweater.

Clearing her throat, she asked, "Do I have to change out here... with you...?"

Sweet damnation, that was all he needed. Not trusting his voice enough to answer, he simply shook his head instead. With a quavery smile brought on by gratitude, she hurried across the room to the bathroom.

Muttering soft curses, Dillon went to the bed. She'd made it that afternoon, folding the covers down invitingly. He sat down on the edge, then leaned forward to reach the handcuff that was still fastened to the frame. He wished like hell he could leave it there, wished he could trust her not to try anything during the night, but he had trusted her this morning and look what it had gotten him. She had almost escaped, and he had suffered for her attempt. He couldn't risk it again.

So what would they do? Pass another night as they had last night, with him in the bed and Ashley handcuffed to him and on the floor? Maybe tonight she would be brave and would choose to share the bed with him. Yeah, right, and then *he* would be the one sacked out on the floor. Last night he could have slept beside her. He had been so cold, so weak, so exhausted from the pain. Tonight... What a difference a day had made.

She came out of the bathroom, wearing the gown. It had no sleeves, a V-neck that dipped too low and was made from a fabric almost sheer enough to see through. God, why hadn't he kept his mouth shut? Why hadn't he left her in wrinkled chambray and heavy knit?

At the couch she scooped up the afghan there and wrapped it around her shoulders. "My robe's in the washer out in the workshop," she said apologetically, uncomfortably. "It has been for days." Her gaze focused on the handcuffs he held, and her mouth thinned as revulsion tempered by resignation slid across her face and flattened her voice. "Where do you want me?"

He almost groaned aloud. *Right here in bed,* he wanted to say. *Underneath me, on top of me, however I can man-*

age it. Instead, he forced some steadiness into his voice and asked, "Where do you want to sleep?"

She glanced at the bed where he sat, then at the sofa, then dug her bare toes into the rug she was standing on. "Here."

"You won't be very comfortable." He swallowed hard and made the offer that just might kill him. "You're welcome to half the bed. I won't bother you. I won't touch you."

Without even a second's consideration, she shook her head. She didn't want to be that close to him, he realized bitterly. "Do you have some extra blankets?"

She went to the far end of the room, where a large wooden quilt rack stood in one corner. A moment later she returned with an armload of quilts and started to dump them on the bed. "Not for me," he said, laying his hand on the top one to steady it. "Make a bed for yourself."

After a moment's hesitation, she set the covers on the chair, then began spreading them out, each one folded in half lengthwise, on the braided rug. She laid two aside to cover up with, then brought the last one to the bed. "I won't be able to keep the fire going," she said, her voice subdued. "It may get cold."

She laid the quilt, neat geometric shapes with sharp corners and rounded sides, across the foot of the bed, then returned to the pallet in front of the fireplace. He followed her, standing back as she laid the afghan aside and stretched out. Once she was settled in, the covers snug around her neck, only her left arm remaining uncovered, he knelt beside her and secured the handcuffs, one around her wrist, one around the ball-shaped foot of the sofa. He moved the afghan so she could use it to cover her arm once the room cooled down, then stood up, switched off the lamp on the chair-side table and returned to the bed.

The entire time she never stopped looking at him, her gaze disappointed, faintly accusing.

He removed the sling, sliding his arm free and lifting the cloth over his head, then unfastened his jeans. Getting them off was easier this time, but it was still painful, still slow going. By the time he'd finished and swung his legs underneath the bed covers, he'd broken into a sweat and raised his heart rate substantially. He had made himself weak again...though not so weak that he could sleep right away. He lay back against the pillows, weary but not yet sleepy, and stared up at the ceiling, at the strange swaying shadows there created by the fire's dancing flames.

"Can I have a pillow?"

There were five or six on the bed, most of which he was using, but he took one of the others and started to push the covers back.

"Just throw it, if you can." Her voice was soft in the dimly lit cabin, too feminine to be comfortable, too sweet to be uncomfortable.

Sitting up, he swung the pillow into the air. She caught it, stuck it under her head, then settled in again. She was so quiet that he thought she'd fallen asleep, but when he looked, he saw that she was staring into the fire. Only this morning he'd thought that she wasn't quite pretty, that there was strength, character and generosity clearly defined in her face, but not beauty. But he'd been wrong. In this light—warm, yellow gold—and this pose—thoughtful, subdued, serene—she was very definitely pretty. There was such softness in her face and yet strength, too. Such fragility. Goodness. Hopefulness.

Such faith.

"When the weather has cleared and Bessie will run—" she shifted her glance his way for only a moment "—I can get you out of here."

"How?"

"My crafts are sold at a number of shops in western Carolina and eastern Tennessee. I make deliveries, pick up supplies and go to craft shows on a fairly regular basis. No one in Catlin gives a second look to Bessie loaded to the max with stuff."

Stuff that could provide him with a place to hide. "What about the roadblocks?"

"I know all of the deputies around here and most of the state troopers. They would never dream that I might voluntarily help you escape."

"You think you can talk them out of searching the van?"

"If I make it difficult enough. If I make it appear that there's no room to hide anything. If I fill it with boxes and baskets." She smiled faintly. "If I mention Seth's name often enough."

And what if they did search the van? he wondered, watching a bunch of dried sunflowers sway in the hotter air above. What if she happened to approach a roadblock manned by cops she didn't know, strangers who couldn't care less that she was Sheriff Benedict's ex-wife? What if they wanted him so badly that they refused to overlook the slightest possibility? Not only would *he* get caught, but the circumstances would certainly make them look closely at *her*. The fact that he was armed might be enough to protect her, but there was a chance that it wouldn't, a chance that they might suspect her of collaboration and not forced cooperation.

There was a chance that they might arrest her. Seeing her in handcuffs here was bad enough. Seeing her arrested, chained and taken away and knowing that he was solely responsible... That was too much.

But what choice did he have?

"Where would you go?"

"I don't know."

"Isn't there someone who could help you?"

Once before he had accepted help—from Russell Bradley. He and Russell had lived in the same poor neighborhood in Atlanta, had come from the same background and had faced the same future. They had played together, raised hell together, fought together and grown up together, only somewhere along the way Russell had straightened himself out. He had left Georgia for a hitch in the navy, where he'd learned a few things about electronics. Once he got out, he'd begun working in that field, moving up every few years to a better job while Dillon had simply kept moving on to a different one. By the time they'd met again two years ago, Russell had settled in Asheville and was running his own company and he'd offered Dillon a job.

It had seemed to Dillon at the time that his life had been on one long downhill slide, and he'd seen Russell's job as a chance to stop it, to turn things around, to quit being the failure everyone had always expected him to be and maybe make something of himself. Even though he'd known nothing about alarm systems, he had accepted the offer, moved to Asheville and gone to work installing the alarms and learning the business. Eleven months ago he had discovered the hard way—for him, wasn't it *always* the hard way?—that he'd learned entirely too much about the systems . . . and not nearly enough about his old friend.

So was there anyone who could help? "No," he said, disliking the flatness in his voice, hearing the disappointment and the utter *aloneness* that formed it, hoping she missed it.

"What about your mother?"

"What about her?"

"Is she still living?"

"I suppose."

"Where?"

"I don't know. Marietta, Smyrna, Conyers—somewhere around Atlanta, I guess."

"When was the last time you saw her?"

He had to give the answer a moment of serious thought. He knew in an instant the last time he had talked to Carole—he had called to tell her that her father had died—but the last time he had actually seen her . . . "I guess it's been about ten years. I don't really remember."

It took some awkward maneuvering, but she managed to roll onto her side and face him. With the covers pulled high, most of her face was in shadow, but that was all right. He didn't need to see her dismay and censure; he could clearly read them in her voice. "How can you not remember the last time you saw your *mother?*"

"When's the last time you saw *your* mother?" he asked defensively.

"Christmas, three years ago. But it's a matter of logistics that keeps us apart. She lives on the other side of the country, and neither of us has the money to be traveling back and forth. But she and Daddy are coming to visit this summer, and we write at least two or three times a month, and I call her from Seth's house on all the holidays.''

"Well, my mother and I are different." Hostility edged into his voice. Carole had never been an average mother. If she hadn't honestly believed that a baby on the way would force his father to make good on all the promises he'd given her, she wouldn't have chosen to ever *be* a mother. But instead of divorcing his wife, leaving his family and thumbing his nose at everyone in Waterston, Alexander had left Carole. He had denied paternity, had refused support and later had even denied their affair. He had led the entire town in scorning her and her illegitimate brat.

The first job Dillon had ever been given to do—bring his father together permanently with his mother—and he had failed. He smiled bitterly. Jeez, he'd been a failure from the moment of his conception.

"Do you have any brothers or sisters?"

"No."

"Will your father help you?" Her voice was softer, more subdued, as if she thought that she'd hit a nerve in talking about his mother. He considered telling her that it didn't matter, that he'd never had a mother in the real sense of the word, that he couldn't miss what he'd never had, but it wasn't true. He'd never had a woman like Ashley, either, but when he left here, he would miss her. He would regret that he had nothing to offer her but trouble, fear, inconvenience and discomfort. He would regret that there was no future for them, and he would especially regret that he wasn't the kind of man a woman like her got involved with.

"My father has never claimed me as his son. He has, however, made a fool of my mother, shamed my grandfather and made my life hell. He always said I would wind up in prison someday. If he knew the trouble I'm in now, he would no doubt subsidize the search and offer a generous reward for my capture, preferably of the dead-or-alive variety and preferably dead.''

Out of the long silence came her voice, softer than ever, sweeter and with enough pity in two little words to make his jaw clench in revulsion. "I'm sorry."

"I'm not." He said it forcefully, so she would understand that, while he wanted many things from her, pity sure wasn't one of them. Then, wanting to bring the conversation to an end, he added in a brusque, strained tone, "It's late. Go to sleep."

There was a soft rustle as she rolled over, her back to him now, a long slender form under a pile of covers. Intending to follow his own advice, he slid down in the bed, seeking a position he could bear for the rest of the night. He'd just found it when she spoke again, little more than a whisper in the still night.

"Good night, Dillon."

He sighed grimly. She had just ensured, with no more than the voicing of his name, that sleep wouldn't come easily tonight.

So much for a good night's rest.

Chapter 5

Ashley had heard of cabin fever, but she had never experienced it. She always had plenty to do and had never, in her three years on the mountaintop, seen weather so bad that she couldn't make the journey between the cabin and the workshop. But this dreary, rainy Thursday morning, she was restless, edgy and fairly certain she would go crazy if she didn't get a breath of fresh air and find *something* to do with her time.

The only problem was the work that needed doing was out in the workshop. Somehow she didn't think Dillon was going to let her go out there alone, not even just to get a few projects and bring them back. She could ask that they both spend the morning over there, but it wasn't the most comfortable place for someone recuperating from the injuries he'd suffered. She didn't have even one decent chair in the place—just the tall stool she used when she was working at the table and Granny's old ladder-back chair that was just the right height for the quilt frame and the loom.

She sighed heavily. If she were home alone, on this third day of rain and fog, she would forget about work, put on her heaviest sweater, add her yellow slicker, gloves and rubber boots and go for a hike. Seth hated when she did that. What if she fell? he argued. What if she got hurt and couldn't make it back home? How slim were the chances that anyone would find her—or even miss her—before exposure took its toll?

Still, she'd been tramping around the hills in all kinds of weather ever since she was a little girl, and she loved them best in the rain. She had seen the peaks wreathed in frothy, cottony fog, had seen the trees and hillsides drenched and washed clean, had smelled the rich, refreshing scent of rain and lush earth. She had watched the thin rays of gold pierce the clouds as the sun broke through and had seen, heard, even *felt,* thunderclouds rumbling in. Not even for Seth would she give up those vistas, those smells and feelings, for the dry, warm safety of her cabin.

But if Dillon wouldn't trust her alone in the workshop, he certainly wouldn't trust her to come back from a hike into the woods.

"What is it you're so anxious to do?"

She turned from the window to find his attention on her. He had been quiet most of the morning. Moody. She disliked moodiness in herself and had learned in the last months of their marriage to dread it in Seth. His moods had usually led to arguments that had left her feeling abandoned and utterly alone.

As Dillon was.

She knew he'd misinterpreted her apology last night. She hadn't meant anything by it. She had simply meant to say that she was genuinely sorry that he wasn't close to his mother and had never gotten along with his father. She certainly hadn't meant to make him feel pitied.

She couldn't imagine not being close to her parents. Even though they lived on the California coast, they were—and always had been—the anchors in her life. They, along with her grandparents, had taught her everything important she needed to know. They had shaped her into the woman she was today.

Dillon's parents, she supposed, had shaped him into the man he was: a bank robber, an escaped criminal, facing a lifetime in prison if he was caught, a lifetime of fear and uncertainty if he managed to flee. Surely some of the blame for that lay on a mother who lost touch with her only child, on a father who always told that child that one day he would end up in prison. What great expectations the man had had for his son.

"Ashley?"

She shrugged. "I'm just bored. I'm not used to sitting around doing nothing all day."

"What would you like to do?"

"Go for a walk."

The look he gave her was scornfully dry. "Right."

"Or I could go to the workshop and work for a while."

"Uh-huh." More derision.

"You think I would make a beeline for the nearest neighbor, don't you?"

"Or the nearest search party."

"I wouldn't. If I were going to turn you in, it would be to Seth, no one else."

"Why? So he would get the credit for my apprehension?"

"No. Because he would keep you safe."

He put down the book he'd been reading the better part of the morning and leveled his gaze on her. "Safe from what?" he asked evenly.

"From angry cops who believe you shot an injured deputy." Her gaze was just as level, her voice just as even. "From whoever shot you. From whoever believes that robbing the bank is worth killing for." Those last were his own words, the only explanation he'd offered Tuesday evening for his own gunshot wound. She hadn't pressed him for more that night; he'd been too weakened from exposure and pain, and she had been afraid for her safety. She wasn't afraid now, though, and he was getting stronger, it seemed, with each passing minute. "Who would that be?"

He studied her for a long time before shaking his head slowly from side to side. "You don't need to know that. *Nobody* needs to know. Keeping my mouth shut just might keep me alive."

"Or it might mean that if they succeed in killing you, they get away scot-free. But if you tell me..."

"Then they'll kill you right along with me. I don't want to die with your death on my conscience. And, yes," he added sarcastically, "I *do* have a conscience."

She tried to ignore the ominous little shiver the mention of death sent dancing up her spine. "I know. I've seen evidence of it."

"You have, have you?" He almost smiled then. It was a pretty dismal attempt, but the corners of his mouth did lift and his eyes lightened about a dozen shades. Then he seemed to remember that he wasn't supposed to be relaxed or amused or friendly, and his eyes went dark again and his mouth compressed once more into a thin line.

"Well, since you won't let me go to the workshop, I suppose I could spend the rest of the morning shaving you," she said, her voice determinedly lighter.

Giving her an owlish look, he blinked once, then scratched his chin, a habit she'd noticed for the first time this morning, one that seemed to have developed as his beard grew heavier. "Shaving me," he repeated blankly.

"You don't ordinarily wear a beard, do you?"

He shook his head.

"I didn't think so. It makes you look rather sinister, and when you're wanted by the police, the last way you want to look is sinister. I could shave it off for you."

"You and a razor and my throat? I don't think so."

"You don't trust me, do you?" She wondered what it would take to earn his trust. How many promises would she have to make and keep? How many times in how many different ways would she have to prove that she was reliable? How many months and years—if he had months and years to spare—would she have to pass how many tests before he would judge her worthy of his trust?

The answers were too depressing to even guess at.

"It's nothing personal. I told you, I don't trust anyone."

"Because of what happened with the robbery."

He looked at her for a moment, then pointedly opened the book to the page he had marked.

"What did happen, Dillon?" she persisted. "You said you didn't do it for the money but to prove a point. What point, and to whom? The people who tried to kill you?"

"The people who will kill *you* if they think it's to their advantage," he said heatedly. "Drop it, Ashley. You don't need to know more than you already do."

He was wrong. She needed to know a whole lot more. She needed to know *everything*.

And she wasn't even sure why.

What kind of point could a person prove by breaking into a bank? That he could do it. That he was smart enough. That he was capable enough. That he could outwit the security experts and the electronic systems and make it in and out without getting caught. Obviously Dillon *was* smart and capable, and according to Seth, in his time with Bradley Electronics, he had become something of a whiz with the systems. The owner of the company had given him a job as a favor—they were old friends—but all he had expected, again according to Seth, was a day's work for a day's pay. He had never imagined that Dillon would have such a knack for electronics, alarms and codes. In no time at all, he had taught himself everything there was to know about the high-tech security systems Bradley Electronics installed. Including how to disarm them.

To prove a point.

To his boss and old friend?

Watching him closely, wanting—needing—to see every bit of expression that crossed his face, she asked, "Was it Russell Bradley?"

The look he gave her should have killed the last bit of curiosity she could muster. The tautly controlled anger made his eyes darken to almost black, and narrow white lines formed around his mouth. He closed the book, very carefully, very quietly, and leaned forward to lay it on the table, then he looked at her, simply looked. It was like that look two nights ago that had convinced her more thor-

oughly than anything else could have that he was a dangerous man . . . but worse.

From somewhere she found the courage to go on, but her
voice shook just a bit and her hands, shoved into the hip
pockets of her jeans, were curling tightly. "It *was* him,
wasn't it? He was the one you were trying to prove a point
to. The one who taught you not to trust anyone."

His voice was low, intense, a warning for all its softness.
"This is none of your business."

She swallowed. "You said you didn't take the four hundred and fifty thousand dollars. Did he?"

"*I* was the one who was there. *I* was the one whose fingerprints were all over the place."

"And were *you* the one who stole nearly half a million
dollars? Did you lie yesterday when you said you didn't?"

His smile was cool, unpleasant. "Funny you should ask,
since you didn't believe me when I said I didn't."

Ashley shifted her weight from one foot to the other. He
was right. She had reached the conclusion just yesterday
that he probably *had* stolen the money, even though he'd
denied it. Had she changed her mind so quickly? Had she
really come to believe that, while he might be guilty of
many things including the break-in at the bank, he was
truthful when he said he didn't take the cash?

Or did she simply *want* to believe that because she
thought he was handsome, because she was attracted to
him, because she felt sorry for his lack of family, because
she felt his loneliness?

"If you were set up—"

"I wasn't."

Ignoring his interruption, she went on. "Maybe Seth
could help prove it."

"There's nothing to prove."

"Then what happened to the money?"

He looked away. He didn't have a lie prepared for her last
question. That was what his previous two responses were:
lies, short, simple but none too convincing. He *had* been set
up, she believed, by Russell Bradley. There was nothing to

make you lose faith in people like being betrayed by an old, good friend.

But if that was the case, who had taken the money? Dillon had made a valid point: *his* fingerprints had been all over the place. Not Russell Bradley's or anyone else's. In fact, there was nothing she was aware of that might point to anyone else. All the evidence led back to Dillon, and only to him.

"You don't know, do you? Or if you do know, you don't want to say."

"It's none of your business," he repeated stiffly.

"If you'd tell the truth, maybe I could help you."

He rose from the couch and approached her, stopping a few feet away. "You? Help?" he repeated, a touch of scorn in his voice. "How? You live in a log cabin at the top of a mountain with nothing but deer for neighbors. Your only form of transportation is a piece-of-junk van that won't even start when it's raining. You don't have any money. You peddle little baskets and candles and stupid twig trays to support yourself. You play with your roots and fruits, you make god-awful tea and you pretend that this is a reasonable, rational way for a woman to live. You don't even have the good sense to protect yourself. How could you help me?"

Biting the inside of her lower lip, Ashley dropped her gaze to the floor. She was used to being considered a little odd. Weird, others said; eccentric, she preferred, or unconventional. Her mother called her a free spirit; Seth's mother called her a hippie. Her friends back in Raleigh thought she was crazy, and even Seth insisted that this was no way to live. But she had never minded the judgments and the names. She had never cared much what others thought, except her family, and as long as they loved her, what did it matter if her father described her to their California friends as his little Bohemian?

But she cared what Dillon thought. She cared that he obviously thought she was foolish. She cared that he found her life-style—and therefore *her*—deserving of mockery and scorn.

Drawing a deep breath, she looked up, though her gaze went no farther than his jaw. "You're right. The only help I can give you is to get you out of here, and I promise, as soon as the rain stops, that's exactly what I'll do."

She turned to walk away, but suddenly his left arm snaked around her from behind, crossing her shoulders, stopping her short. "Ashley—"

Stiffness shot through her, making her voice cold and flat. "Don't touch me." After one still moment he let go, and she headed for the door. "I'm going over to the workshop. You can come, you can stay here or you can go straight to hell. Either way, it doesn't matter to me."

Expecting him to stop her at any moment, she took her woolen shawl from its peg, wrapped it around her shoulders and opened the door. Her mud-caked loafers were on the porch where she'd left them yesterday morning, cold and damp but comfortable enough for now. She slid her feet into them, walked down the steps, then, when the rain hit her, lifted the shawl over her head and dashed for the workshop stoop. A glance back from beneath its shelter showed the front door still open but no sign of Dillon. She couldn't believe he had let her walk out, couldn't believe she wasn't now sitting on the hard floor beside the bed wearing those handcuffs.

Lifting the latch, she went inside and flipped the lights on. The first order of business was to get a fire going in the potbellied stove. The second was finding some interest in working. Yes, just a short while ago, she had been craving something to do, had thought that working sounded like a fine idea, but now all she wanted to do was curl up in front of the fire in one of her ready-for-market quilts. Now all she wanted to do was brood.

Over Dillon.

Sinister.

Dillon studied his image in the bathroom mirror and saw that Ashley had been right. The beard did make him look sinister. Shifty. Unworthy of trust. Maybe it wasn't his usual look, but this morning it seemed an accurate reflection.

Her razor rested on the windowsill between bottles of chamomile and lavender bath gel, and a can of shaving cream—Specially Formulated For A Woman's Skin—was on a triangular shelf in the corner above the tub. He squirted a bit of the cream into his hand and sniffed it. Specially *scented* for a woman's skin, too, but it would have to do. Besides, what could it possibly matter how he smelled? He didn't have a snowball's chance in hell of getting close to anyone around here.

Turning the hot water on, he leaned against the sink and stared out the window at the workshop across the clearing. Through the big windows the lights gleamed yellow, two lone bright spots—three, if he counted Ashley—in yet another bleak day. He'd stood at the kitchen window for nearly an hour, watching her work. She'd been perched on an unpadded stool before the tall worktable, assembling the materials for a tray, putting them together, weaving the thin cord over and underneath the twigs. The work seemed to go quickly, not because she hurried but because her movements were so sure, so exact.

Stupid twig trays. For the hundredth time in an hour, he cursed himself. All he'd wanted to do was make her back off and quit pushing for answers he couldn't give her. He hadn't meant to be so snide, hadn't meant to insult her work or mock her choices. And he sure hadn't meant to hurt her.

Or maybe he had. Maybe his subconscious had figured that the best way to be with her was at a distance. Maybe he'd thought that if he angered her, he would be safe from her. Maybe he'd believed that if he hurt her, she would quit caring what had happened that April night a year ago; Russell would have no reason to suspect anything, and maybe she would stay safe.

Feeling the faint warmth of the steam rising from the sink, he turned, bent and splashed warm water over his face. Lathering up with only one good hand was awkward, but he managed. It would have been easier if the scent of the shaving cream was minty or medicinal instead of sweet, light and very feminine. It would have been much easier if he hadn't taken a deep breath that made him wonder if this same fragrance clung to Ashley's skin after she used it.

It would have been easier by far if he'd had sex sometime in recent memory so that everything he did, saw, smelled and touched didn't make him think about sex—and not just sex, but sex with *her*. That was what he wanted. Just her.

He finished and rinsed his face, patted it dry on her towel, then stared into the mirror again. It wasn't much of an improvement, he conceded. Maybe *sinister* was gone, but *shifty* and *untrustworthy* remained.

He had never cared much for his own looks. From the time he was old enough to notice, he'd known that the opposite sex found him appealing, but he'd seen too strong a resemblance to Alexander Waters to find much appeal in himself. After a lifetime of being denied by his father, he'd been tempted a few years back to visit Waterston, just to show everyone that neither blood tests nor an admission from Alexander was necessary to prove his paternity. Genetics had put the proof right there on Dillon's face for all the world—all the town, at least—to see.

But he'd gotten a job offer, and there was really nothing to gain by showing up in Waterston after all these years. There was nothing he wanted from the Waters family, nothing he wanted from the town. And so, instead, he had come to North Carolina. If he'd had any idea of the trouble he was walking into, he never would have set foot across the state line.

And he never would have met Ashley Benedict.

One last glance out the window showed that she was still seated on the stool, still bent over her work. He turned off the light and, knowing he shouldn't bother, knowing it would be better for both of them if he stayed over here and she stayed over there, he made his way around the furniture to the armoire near the bed.

From a rod across the top on the right side hung a few summery dresses and a number of skirts similar to the chambray one—long, full, casual. Shelves on the left side held lingerie, socks and a variety of T-shirts, sweatshirts and sweaters. The first one he picked up—a sweatshirt, black and bearing the teal-and-purple logo of the Charlotte Hornets—looked adequate. Removing his sling, he carefully tugged it over his head and *very* carefully slid his right arm into the sleeve. The movement tugged at this morning's dressing and made his wound throb, but by the time the shirt was on and his arm was back in the sling, the pain had subsided.

The shirt was a snug fit, washed until the colors had faded, until the cotton had gotten soft, and it smelled of her. For months after he left here, he was going to live with her scent. It was going to infuse every waking breath and haunt him every night. *She* was going to haunt him.

Scowling, he sat down on the hearth to put his tennis shoes on. They were mostly dry and stiff. Rather than trying to tie the laces with his one good hand, he yanked them out, then left the cabin. He walked as quickly as he dared across the muddy ground, breathing a sigh of comfort as he stepped onto the small porch, out of the rain, then another as he opened the door and felt the first rush of heat.

Ashley didn't even look at him, but she was obviously aware of him; her scowl matched his own. She had finished with the trays in the past few minutes and was now measuring lengths of cotton wicking. Boxes of candles sat in front of her, hand dipped, rich colors—red, green and deep translucent blue. The reds and greens, when he picked up their boxes, smelled simply of wax, but the blues... They had a fresh, clean, wintry scent that he couldn't begin to identify.

"You told the sheriff that you have to send six dozen of these to South Carolina. To sell?"

For a long time she ignored him, concentrating harder than necessary on the easy task of measuring and cutting. Hell, this was the woman who could effortlessly lace together a rustic tray, weave a basket, dress a wound or whip

up a few loaves of bread. This little job didn't need even a
fraction of her attention. She just didn't want to give *him*
any of it.

And suddenly, foolishly, perversely he wanted it. *All* of
it.

As he moved slowly around the table, she finally answered. "They're used in some of the historic house mu-
seums down around Charleston and Beaufort."

"The blue ones smell nice. What is that?"

"A combination of roots and fruits."

Inwardly wincing at the cold disdain in her voice, he
reached the end of the table, where basketry supplies were
gathered, turned the corner and started up the other side.
Toward her. "My grandmother quilted," he remarked,
studying the quilt in the frame on the opposite side of the
room. "I have—I *had* some of her quilts in Asheville. I
guess they're gone now."

He had asked the deputy only one question before they'd
reached Sadler's Pass: what had happened to the personal
belongings left behind in his apartment when he'd fled the
state? He'd broken the lease, Coughlin had explained, and
under the law, the landlord was entitled to box up everything left behind and dispose of it however he wanted. Dillon hadn't had much and had cared about little of it, but he
would have liked to have his grandmother's quilts, the
family Bible that had passed to him on his grandfather's
death and the family photographs. He wondered what the
landlord had done with it all—kept or sold the quilts,
probably, and tossed the rest. Who wanted a Bible docu-
menting a family of strangers or snapshots of people they'd
never known?

He stopped right beside Ashley. She pretended not to
notice, but he saw the faint tremble in her hands. Was she
uncomfortable because he was invading her space? A little
nervous because she sensed that something was going to
happen? Or uneasy because she meant what she'd said in
the cabin? *Don't touch me.* It wasn't the words that had
made an impression on him so much as the emotion behind them. Anger. Insistence. Revulsion?

She continued to work, continued to ignore him until he reached out and laid his hand over hers. Instantly she went still, as motionless and lifeless as the slab of wood in the middle of the table. She didn't move, didn't blink, didn't even breathe. For a moment he forgot to breathe, too. When the tightness in his chest reminded him, he drew a breath that was fragrant with her varied scents—honeysuckle from this morning's bath, almond from the shampoo they had both used, roses from the lotion on her hands. They were simple scents, homemade every one of them, and they were sweeter, more intoxicating, more enticing than the most expensive designer fragrance in the world.

He moved a step closer, so close that when he spoke, his breath stirred a strand of pale blond hair above her ear. "Ashley." He flexed his fingers, pressed them against hers, drew his fingertips across her hand. He felt the little shiver that rustled through her, starting in exactly the spot where his finger stroked the web of skin between her thumb and index finger and intensifying as he slid his finger between hers, over that skin, into the hollow formed by her loosely clenched fist.

This was crazy. Didn't he have enough fantasies to torment himself with without touching her? Didn't he already want her more than he could remember ever wanting anything? Did he have to add sensation to fantasy, to lust, to need? Did he have to torture himself further?

Why not? He'd learned as a kid that life was hard. Just once he wanted it hard in a way he could enjoy.

Finally she breathed, a quavery little sound as erotic as any he'd ever heard, and her eyes fluttered shut. Watching her, he moved his caress from her palm to her arm, feeling her pulse, rapid and erratic, when he brushed across her wrist. Her arms were slender, tanned, strong, the muscles swelling and rounding to soften the straight lines. The few women he'd shared serious relationships with had all been petite and very feminine, and he had assumed that fragile, delicate and helpless was his type. In the past few days, he had discovered that strong, muscled and independent had an appeal all its own.

His fingers curved over her shoulder, glided across soft fabric to softer skin, followed the line of her throat to her jaw. It took just a slight pressure—and ignoring the voice in his brain suggesting that he stop—to turn her head toward him. Just the slightest bending to bring his mouth into contact with hers.

He half expected her to flinch, expected her eyes to fly open, her feet to hit the wood floor with a thud and her demand—*Don't touch me*—to echo through the room with more loathing than he'd ever been treated to. But she didn't flinch, didn't stare at him, didn't jump to her feet and flee. She didn't do anything at all but open her mouth to him and raise one hand to his chest, bringing it gently to rest on his ribs, then letting it slide down until her fingers hooked in the waistband of his jeans.

So long. It had been so long since he'd kissed a woman, so long since he'd touched a woman, so long since he'd been intimate with a woman. So long that the sweet taste of her mouth was something new, never experienced, as intoxicating as the best aged whiskey, as full of promise as a spring morning. So long that her fingers, snug against his stomach, stirred an ache that spread until it threatened to engulf him. So long that he felt every bit as weak as she was strong. So long—and so good—that he had to stop.

For one brief moment she clung to him, seeking more of his mouth, tightening her fingers around his waistband. When he pulled, though, she let go. She let him go.

He wished to God that she hadn't.

She was looking at him now, her blue eyes curious, a little surprised, a little disappointed. He knew that if he kissed her again, that disappointment would go away, and sweet damnation, he wanted to make it go away. But if he kissed her again, he might not stop, not until it was too late. Not until they'd traveled to hell and gone beyond what was safe. Not until he'd learned all sorts of new meanings for the word *torment*.

As he forced himself to take the first step back, then the next and the next, her gaze never left him. It followed him the length of the table and back up the other side, where he'd started out, where he leaned against the solid table and finally returned the look.

After a time she spoke. She had to clear her throat first. "Well . . . that was interesting."

The droll evenness of her comment forced a choked laugh from him. "Interesting?" he echoed. "That's all?"

"How would *you* describe it?"

There were a hundred ways to put that moment into words, but he settled on the easiest and simplest of them. "Nice. Very nice."

"I'd rather be interesting than nice."

"You're both," he said, suddenly serious. "You're a better hostage than I deserve."

"So that's your way of saying thanks?"

"No. My way of saying thanks will be to walk away from here and never look back. To leave you the way I found you—unharmed. Safe. Too trusting, but out of danger." Damned if he wasn't sure he could do it. Two days ago he'd *known* that he could. All he'd wanted was shelter from the rain, heat to ward off the cold and a little precious rest to deal with his injuries. Today. . . Today he wanted Ashley.

And he couldn't have her. She wasn't the sort of woman a man could seduce, then forget, wasn't the sort a man walked away from. She and the sheriff had been divorced as long as they'd been married, but Benedict hadn't yet walked away from her. He still loved her, was still part of her life.

The only way Dillon could begin an affair with her was if he stayed long enough to let it run its course, to come to a natural end or go on forever, and he couldn't do that. He couldn't put her in any more danger than he already had. He couldn't risk getting caught for her. He couldn't risk getting both of them killed simply because he harbored this incredible lust for her.

She gathered the wicks and laid them off to one side, then rested her arms on the table and laced her fingers together. "You know, you could stay awhile," she said quietly.

"Don't say that." *Don't tempt me.*

"You could. You talk about running and hiding. Once they move their search out of this area, what better place to hide than right here?"

"Anyplace where they've never heard of Catlin, North Carolina." Someplace where all the women had dark hair and dark eyes, where the only tea they drank was iced, where the bread came in plastic wrappers from the store, where herbs were for cooking and never for nursing. Someplace where he wouldn't be enticed, where he wouldn't find hope, where he wouldn't have a future. Someplace where he would never fit in, where he could never belong. Someplace where he wouldn't even want to try.

He could belong here. He could live on this mountaintop, could till those fields, chop firewood and keep the van running. He could spend his days doing the kind of hard work his grandfather had always done, and he could spend his nights . . .

Heat flushed his face as he turned away from the words that would naturally complete that sentence. He would spend his nights in hell if he even contemplated making a future here. Making a future with her.

"Right now you can't get to someplace where they've never heard of Catlin, North Carolina," she observed, sounding cautious and a little off balance. "But you're safe here."

"And what about when the search parties come? You know they will. It's just a matter of time."

"You're right. They may come today, maybe tomorrow, maybe even the day after. When they come, chances are good that you'll still be here. Once they're gone, they won't come back, so there's no reason you should leave, too."

She was the best reason he had to leave. The way she had nursed him. The way she had lied to Benedict to hide him. The way she had touched him, looked at him, listened to him, kissed him. The way she was looking at him right now. If he stayed, he might forget the lesson Russell had gone to such pains to teach him, and he might start trusting someone again. He might start believing he could have a normal life, with a home, a family, a future. He might start thinking he could make things right, with the sheriff's help, with Ashley's help. He might tell the truth, and it very well might get him killed.

He very well might get Ashley killed.

"What's wrong, Ashley?" he asked softly, seeking to avoid temptation in the only way he could manage. "Been alone too long?"

Her eyes widened, and her breath caught. Then she breathed deeply and offered him a chilly smile. "Yes, I guess I have."

"Since the divorce?" Stupid question, he warned himself. Her sex life was none of his business. He didn't need to know that maybe she'd been celibate since the breakup of her marriage, didn't want to know that there might have been men other than Benedict in her life, men who had kissed her, men who had done with her the things that he'd spent much of the past day—and especially the past night—aching to do.

"Not quite."

In thirty-four years he'd never had occasion to discover that he was a jealous man. Now, in only an instant, he knew. He was. Feeling hot, frustrated and just a little mean, he asked—demanded, "Who was he?"

"A man in Raleigh. His sister was a teacher at my school. He was an accountant who certainly destroyed every preconceived notion *I'd* ever had about accountants." She stopped, then added, "He was much easier than you are."

Easier to seduce? Dillon wondered. Easier to be around? Easier to want? Damn her, easier how?

Sliding off the stool, she went to the deep cubbyholes that lined one wall and selected a few items: loose coils of reed, oval hoops, a gracefully curved handle. She laid them on the table, picked up a bucket and came around to his side to fill it with water in the small bathroom behind him. When she came back, she stopped close to him, lifting the bucket onto the table in front of him, then giving him a steady look. "But you know what, Dillon?"

He didn't speak but simply looked at her as she leaned closer, close enough that he could sort out all her scents, close enough that he could feel her heat, close enough that he could hear her words even though they were merely whispered.

" 'Easier' isn't always better."

Ashley looked up at him and waited for him to back off. She knew he would, just as she'd known he would end that sweet, unexpected kiss, just as she'd known he would shy away entirely from the possibility of an affair. She didn't have long to wait—just a minute, maybe two. After about ninety seconds by her estimate, he took a long step away, removing himself from what he surely perceived as imminent danger, then moving another dozen feet for good measure. As she returned to her stool, he pretended great interest in everything in the workshop except her.

Maybe his sarcastic little remark had been right on target, she thought with a suppressed sigh. Maybe she *had* been alone too long. First she'd gotten turned on doing nothing more than rubbing comfrey salve over his ribs; then she'd given her cardiovascular system quite a workout with the simple task of fitting a sling to support his arm. Now after one kiss—one simple little kiss, one nothing-special, shared-by-millions-every-day kiss—she was willing to make room for him in her life on a permanent basis. She was offering to live a life of deceit, to lie to Seth and everyone else in her world in addition to breaking who knew how many laws, just so Dillon could stay.

Oh, but that kiss *had* been something special. She wasn't the most experienced woman around, but she knew a good kiss from a so-so one; she knew a sizzle-and-burn kiss from the gee-that-was-nice variety. And it didn't matter, anyway, because Dillon didn't *want* to stay. He didn't *want* to be a permanent part of her life.

Resting her chin on her cupped hand, she considered the materials she'd gathered. She needed to mark the middle of each of the reeds before putting them in the bucket of water to make them more pliable, then she would lay out the bottom of the small market basket, weaving over and under the handle to secure it. Or she might sit here, watch the weather, listen to Dillon prowl and pray for the longest, heaviest rains since Noah built his ark.

What she needed was physical activity—*real* activity. Something like stacking firewood under the shelter of the porch roof...but the porch already held all the firewood it could hold. After running out of wood nearby in her first heavy snow up here three years ago, she'd become almost obsessive about keeping a good supply handy.

She could always go back in the house and bake more bread...but there was no room for it in the freezer, and she would hate to see it grow old and stale before they could eat it.

Maybe she could...

"You do nice work."

Slowly she shifted her gaze to Dillon, standing beside the quilt frame, tracing one fingertip over the stitching that secured the three layers together. He sounded grudging and looked annoyed, but she accepted his compliment anyway. "Thank you."

"How long does it take to do one of these?"

"For me, months, but I do them along with everything else. If I devoted my time exclusively to a quilt, I imagine it would take me three or four weeks."

"How much do you sell them for?"

"It depends on the size, the fabric, the intricacy of the pattern and where it's sold. Anywhere from a few hundred dollars to a thousand or more." She gestured to the partial quilt over on the sewing table. "That one will go to the most upscale of the shops I sell in, and it will probably bring fifteen hundred, maybe more."

He circled the frame to look at the unfinished one. "I don't like it as well as this one," he said, comparing it to the one in the frame. Then he gave her a quick, sheepish look. "I mean—"

"I don't, either, but it's not for me." The quilt in the frame was a Jacob's Ladder, a series of squares and triangles placed to create a crisp geometric pattern in sharply contrasting colors. It was bright, clean, pleasing to the eye. The other was a Cathedral Windows. Each window consisted of two squares of fabric, one soft ivory, the other varying. Once each piece of ivory was folded, pinned, stitched and reduced to half its original size, the second fabric was slipped underneath and the four outer edges were slip-stitched to create the effect of looking through a window. Each window was time-consuming, and the entire quilt required hundreds of windows. It was going to be a *long* time in the finishing. "Fifteen hundred dollars for a bed cover sounds like a lot, but when you consider the time invested, it's not much of a return."

"So why do you bother?"

"Quilts are never a bother," she chided. "They're folk art. Americana. A piece of history." Then she shrugged. "I started out making them for myself. I never intended to sell them, but one day the owner of an antique shop in Durham came to buy some baskets. He saw the quilts stacked on the rack in the cabin and said he could sell as many as I could make. I agreed to make a few for him, and I've been doing it ever since."

Finally he faced her again. "You should have been born a hundred years ago."

"So I've been told. My chosen life-style and I are throwbacks to an earlier time." She made no effort to temper the sarcasm that crept into her voice, even though, once again, his face turned a deep red.

"I shouldn't have said . . ."

She mimicked the shrug that followed his trailing words. "Why not? Everything you said was true." It wasn't *what* he'd said that hurt, but the *way* he'd said it. With derision. Scorn.

Dragging his hand over his face, he muttered a curse. "Hell, who am I to criticize the way anyone else lives? I've screwed up every thing I've ever done. I'm hiding from the cops because I can't face twenty-five years in prison. I don't have a place to live. I don't even know *how* to live except on the run. I should be—I *am* grateful that you've chosen to live up here, because without you, I don't think I would have made it through that first night.''

Before she could think of a response, a sound outside drew her attention. Slowly she rose from the stool and started toward the window.

Halfway there, though, she stopped and abruptly stepped back. ''Oh, no.''

Dillon moved away from the quilt frame toward the opposite window, but she quickly stopped him. ''It's one of the search parties. You've got to hide.''

''Where?''

''In the bathroom. Go on, hurry.'' She didn't wait to watch him, didn't wait to hear the click of the door as it closed behind him. Instead, she grabbed her shawl, went to the front door and stepped outside. ''Good morning.''

There were four men coming into the clearing. Two were civilians, the Briggs brothers. They had lived all their lives in these mountains; they were skilled hunters, trackers and expert shots. She recognized the state trooper following them and was fairly well acquainted with the Catlin County deputy bringing up the rear. Steven Vickers was a few years younger than her—Gail's age—and had been one of Gail's many boyfriends their last year of high school. After school her sister had moved to California with the rest of the family, finished college and started her own business. Steven hadn't done much of anything at all before he'd been hired a few years ago as a deputy, but he seemed to enjoy the job and Seth said he did it well.

All four men looked cold, tired and grim.

All four of them were armed.

''Mrs. Benedict.'' The trooper spoke first. Jess Briggs's greeting was less formal. ''Miss Ashley.''

She drew her shawl tighter. ''Any luck yet with the search?''

''A little bit,'' Steven replied. ''We tracked him as far as that bluff a couple hundred yards back of here, then lost his trail again. Have you seen anyone suspicious around here?''

Ashley forced a smile, hoping it appeared somewhere close to natural. ''Steven, I live five miles from my closest neighbor. *Anyone* around here would be suspicious." Then she let the seriousness she was feeling take over. "Seth came by yesterday morning to tell me about the escape, but he's the only visitor I've had in weeks. So... you think he came that close to my house."

"We *know* he came that close," the younger Briggs answered. "Those were his tracks, all right. He was walking with a bit of a limp, which makes a difference in the footprints, and there was a cut on the sole of his left shoe. Easy tracks to pick up. Easy to follow."

"Except when he goes across two hundred feet of rock," his brother added.

Ashley's breath was trapped in her chest. Just a short while ago, Dillon had walked from the cabin to the workshop, minus the limp but wearing the same shoes with the same cut on the sole. Surely his footprints were still there, clearly visible for all the men to see. What if they *did* see? They would insist on searching the workshop—how could she tell them no?—and they would find Dillon. There was no way they couldn't.

Then what would she do?

Quickly she did a mental scan of the cabin. The dishes from a breakfast for two had been washed, the bed was made, and the quilts she'd slept on were all folded over the back of the couch. Dillon's shirt was in the wastebasket under the kitchen sink, he was wearing his jeans and shoes, and Seth's sweatpants were in the bathroom hamper. There was nothing in there that might give him away...except the handcuffs. What had he done with the handcuffs this morning?

Unable to remember, she clenched her fists over the edges of the shawl and moved to the edge of the stoop, one step away from the rain. "I don't drink coffee, gentlemen, but I do have a wide assortment of herbal teas in the cabin. I'd be happy to fix you some—although I'll warn you that I *have* been told it's god-awful. How about it?"

There was a moment of collective hesitation, then Jess Briggs grinned. "After six hours out in this weather, *anything* hot sounds good, Miss Ashley."

Out of habit, she reached back and secured the door of the workshop; then she led the way to the porch steps. Every stride was longer than usual, every step landing squarely in the center of a bigger and—according to the Briggs brothers—distinctive step. When they reached the cabin, she stifled a sigh of relief and instead offered a silent prayer that Dillon's other footprints—when he'd arrived Tuesday evening and when he'd followed her to the van Wednesday morning—had apparently been obliterated by the rain.

Stopping in the cabin door, she paused to hang up her shawl, dawdling, subjecting the cabin to a quick look. There was nothing out of place, nothing to indicate that she hadn't been alone, as usual, the past two days. She needn't have worried, though; all four men refused to come inside. Their clothes were wet, their boots muddied, they explained. She didn't mind; they could get warm, and she could clean the floor later, she insisted, but they still refused. Just the tea on the porch, Steven requested.

Inside she put a pot of water on to boil, placed tea bags in four mugs and watched nervously out the window. The men were talking, their voices a low rumble through the glass, their words indistinguishable. There was no sign of life in the workshop. *Be patient,* she silently pleaded of Dillon. *Don't get nervous, don't wonder what's going on, don't come out to check.*

Trust me.

At the first sign of a bubble in the pot, she switched off the burner, poured the water into the cups, then nervously tapped her fingers on the counter. When the tea had steeped barely ninety seconds, she fished out the bags, gave each cup a squirt of honey, placed them on a tray and carried them outside, serving each man in turn. "Maybe I should have taken Seth's advice and moved into town."

"You probably don't need to worry, Mrs. Benedict," the trooper said. "The boys think he passed through here at least twenty-four hours ago. If he'd thought he could stay around awhile, he would have made his presence known by now. Still, it might not hurt to think again about staying in town. Boone's a dangerous and desperate man. While he's never used violence before this incident, there's no telling what he might resort to now. After all, he *did* almost kill Tom Coughlin.''

Poor Tom, she thought, feeling guilty that she'd let him slip completely out of her mind. "How is Tom?"

Steven answered, his expression grim, his eyes cold. "He's still in a coma. The doctors say the longer he stays that way, the less his chances are of coming out of it okay."

"If you talk to Mrs. Coughlin, tell her my prayers are with them."

In the silence that followed, each man finished his tea—and she saw more than one grimace. Maybe Dillon was right, she mused, leaning against the doorframe and watching them. Maybe it *was* awful, and she'd just been drinking it too long to notice.

"We'd best get going," the trooper said, handing his cup to her. "Would you like us to look around before we go?"

"I appreciate the offer, but the only place to check is the workshop, and I've been in there all morning. If anyone were hiding in there, believe me, I would know it." She collected the last cup. "Steven, if you see Seth, let him know that I'm okay—but don't tell him I was in the workshop when you came. He seems to think I should stay behind barred-and-locked doors in the cabin until Boone is caught."

The young deputy looked at her. "He might have the right idea. I'll tell him that you were, that you wouldn't open up even for us."

"Thanks."

They trooped down the steps, one behind the other, and headed south across the clearing, toward the forest there. Ashley stood exactly where they'd left her and watched until they were out of sight. When the last glimpse—the bright yellow cap Jess Briggs wore—disappeared from sight, she gave a heartfelt sigh of relief . . . and promptly developed a case of the shakes so bad that she dropped the tray and all four cups in a glass-breaking crash.

Chapter 6

If there were room to pace in the tiny, closed-in space of the bathroom, Dillon would be doing it, but he could hardly turn around without banging his head or his elbow or some other portion of his anatomy. He couldn't even see what made the room so cramped. The light was off, there was no window and the door was extraordinarily tight fitting. He was in pitch black—couldn't see anything, couldn't hear anything, couldn't *do* anything.

That was the worst part—being unable to take action—that, and not knowing. When the door opened, it could be Ashley coming to tell him that it was safe, or it could be a cop. An angry cop. One who believed that Dillon was far worse than just an escaped prisoner. One who would hold him responsible for the misfortune that had befallen Tom Coughlin. Just this morning Ashley had said that she would turn him over—if she were so inclined—to Seth and only Seth, that her ex-husband could be trusted to keep him safe from other officers. She *knew* those other officers. She believed they presented a threat not to be considered idly.

Maybe, though, she had lied. Maybe she was out there right now, telling her rescuers everything that had happened the past two days, telling them exactly where he could be found. Maybe when that door opened, it *would* be a cop, led straight to him by the woman he was trusting to...

The thought trailed off, and he sank down on the only seat in the room, replaying the last words in his mind. *The woman he was trusting...*

Trusting...

Oh, God, he was in trouble.

He had trusted Russell Bradley, and now his good buddy wanted him dead. How much more dangerous could Ashley be to him? She could get him arrested. She could get him killed. Worse, she could make him believe in things he'd never believed in. She could make him want things he'd thought he would never have. Love. Respect. Acceptance. A family. A future.

She could break his heart.

She could destroy him.

But only if he let her, he insisted uneasily. Only if he let himself trust her. Only if he let her get too close. He knew how to avoid it. He'd been running, in one way or another, all his life. He knew how to avoid involvement, how to keep people at a distance. He had learned by example from his mother, from his father and the entire town of Waterston. He could do it with Ashley.

Couldn't he?

From the outer room came the sound of a door opening, followed by soft footsteps. Quickly he stood, moving the two steps necessary to reach the door. If it was one of Catlin County's or North Carolina's finest on the other side come to arrest him... Hell, he'd rather end it here than bother with the farce of a trial that was sure to follow and prison. And if it was Ashley...

She opened the door, then stepped back so he could leave the small room. "Are they gone?" he asked before taking that step out.

"Of course they are."

"It took you long enough to get rid of them."

"I made them a cup of tea."

"You're just little Miss Hospitality, aren't you?" he asked sarcastically as he left the bathroom's close, dark shelter. "First you invite the sheriff in for a cup of tea, then the search party."

"It's what they expect of me. If I didn't offer, they would think it was strange." Her voice was strained but soft, controlled. "I think we'd better go back to the cabin and stay there."

"Why?"

"Jess and Toy Briggs are good trackers, but they're not the best. They lost your trail back in the woods at the bluff, so they had no reason to believe you might be here. If they don't find something soon, they'll bring in one of the best—Dub Collins, Zeke Henderson or Mac Haney. If even the slightest sign still exists out there, they'll find it."

"So what does that have to do with staying inside? If they catch me there, I'll be just as screwed as if they catch me out here."

She shot him an impatient look. "You've been outside three times already. Every time you go out, you leave new footprints. *That's* why I offered them tea—so I could blur the latest set. I guess it worked. They didn't seem to notice a thing."

"What was it you were telling me just a little while ago? That once the search party comes here and doesn't find me, they won't come back?" He muttered a curse. "Now you're saying they *will* be back."

"Possibly. Probably."

"To try to pick up a trail they lost?" He lowered his voice. "Or because you told them to come back?"

She stared at him for a long time, her blue gaze softened by disappointment, then abruptly she turned away. Taking a big handled basket from a shelf, she began neatly placing materials into it: basket-weaving supplies, bolts of cloth, a gallon jug of something clear, small plastic bottles, smaller glass vials. When she was done, she left it all on the table, checked the fire, then picked up the basket, switched off the lights and waited at the door.

He knew he should let it drop, knew in his heart that she hadn't betrayed him to those men. But it would have made perfect sense if she had. She could have confided in the searchers, could have told them to get reinforcements, to come back when they could take him by surprise. For all he knew, she could be leading him into a trap. The men could be outside, just waiting for him to step into the clearing. They could be in the cabin, ready to ambush him when he walked in the door. "Ashley." Her gaze met his, but he couldn't read anything in her eyes. "Did you tell them to come back?"

She studied him for a moment, then slowly, coolly smiled as she approached him. "Yes, I did," she replied. "I told them to get Seth, to get all his men and all the troopers and all the guns they can carry. I told them to come back late tonight, when you're asleep. I told them I would slip into the bathroom and light a candle in the window when you were snoring away, that I would leave the door unlocked for them so they could sneak in and capture you before you knew what was happening."

She was lying. Dillon knew it as surely as he knew he wanted her. She was telling tales to alarm and frighten him, and, damn it all, he deserved to be alarmed and frightened. "And how did you plan to get out of the handcuffs so you could light a candle in the bathroom window?"

"I wasn't planning on wearing the handcuffs tonight." Now she was standing right in front of him, only the big basket separating them. She leaned across it, close to him, too close, and murmured, "I wasn't planning on wearing anything at all tonight."

That was a thought too tantalizing to consider. Just the brief image that formed before he stopped it was enough to make him squeeze his eyes shut and bite down hard on a groan. "Just for that, you *will* be wearing the cuffs tonight," he warned her. "I had been considering leaving you free, seeing that you've been so good lately, but now..." He shook his head.

Her smile this time was also slow and cool, but it was a totally different proposition from the last one. In fact,

Dillon feared, that was *exactly* what it was: a proposition. She proved him right when she said, "You put me in handcuffs tonight, it'll be in bed, not on the floor."

With that, she turned and walked out. Forgetting about search parties, guns and possible ambushes, he followed her. She latched the door, then set the basket down once more and walked out into the rain, checking to the south first, then the west, north and east. Raindrops staining her red sweatshirt crimson, she motioned for him to move and, head ducked, he made the short trip to the cabin. She followed more slowly, squishing in the mud, leaving nothing in each place he'd stepped but tiny hills and valleys that quickly filled with water.

He stepped over one of her woven trays and a pile of broken glass near the door, then removed his tennis shoes at the door. He hesitated just a moment, though, until, with a knowing, chiding look, she came up behind him, reached around and opened the door, then slipped past and entered the cabin.

"Look, Dillon," she said, turning in a circle, spreading her arms wide. "No cops."

He went in, closing and locking the door. "What happened to the cups?"

"Nerves," she said carelessly. "It's not every day I lie to the good guys."

He leaned back against the door. If the cops were the good guys, then that left only one role for him: the bad guy. He always had been. The Boone bastard. The punk kid. The budding juvenile delinquent. The loser. The failure. The sucker. The fugitive. The target. The prey. They were roles he knew well, roles he played well. He was used to them.

So why did it hurt to be cast in them by Ashley?

She laid the basket on the table and began unloading it. "It wouldn't be a bad idea to figure out a hiding place in here," she remarked, not noticing his silence. "Seth will come back whenever he's got time, and the next time he might expect to come in."

"So you'll have to stop him."

His curt response made her look sharply at him. "If he asks to come inside, I can't very well refuse without arousing his suspicion, which is the last thing you want me to do."

No, the last thing—and the first—he wanted her to arouse was *him*. "Fine. If he wants to come in, invite him. He can keep us company for a while."

"You wouldn't take him hostage. You're not that stupid. He's the sheriff, for God's sake. He's trained to deal with this sort of thing. He's an expert shot, an expert at self-defense. You would be lucky if he didn't kill you."

"He wouldn't do a thing." Joining her at the table, he stroked his hand lightly over her hair. "Not if he believed *you* would be punished for it."

A shudder rippled through her and into his fingers. "You won't hurt me. You promised."

"He already believes I would hurt you," he explained. "That's why he was so anxious to get you out of here. He expects the worst from me. He thinks I'm a dangerous man, a desperate fugitive who almost killed a cop. God only knows what I might do to you if you get in my way." Those last were Benedict's words, merely rephrased.

She was supposed to feel at least a little threatened, to stand utterly still, unable to move, or to tremble with fear. Well, she was trembling, all right, little shivers that intensified each time he drew his hand down her hair to her shoulder, but instinct told him there was nothing the least bit fearful about it. Her soft blue eyes, hazy now and barely open, confirmed it.

"Let me get in your way," she murmured, "and let's find out what you'll do."

He jerked his hand back and took a half-dozen steps away from her. "Ash, I'm not going to seduce you."

She smiled. "Actually I thought *I* might seduce *you*."

His breath locked in his chest, depriving his brain of the oxygen desperately needed to argue that point with her. Reason failed him, but imagination didn't. Without closing his eyes, without making even the slightest effort, he could see her, naked, lean, beautiful. He could feel her, soft and hot. He could smell her fragrances, light and erotic on her skin, between her breasts, on her belly, scenting her hip. He could taste her mouth, could savor the exotic forbidden flavor of her. He could . . .

He could die an early death from wanting her.

He could die a slow and very painful death from having her.

"Not counting your precious Seth, how many men have you been with?" he asked harshly, already sure he knew the answer.

"One."

"Your friend's brother the accountant. Were you in love with him?"

"No."

"But you cared for him. You thought something might develop with him. You thought he might be the next great love of your life."

Her head tilted to one side, she looked curiously at him. "Why do you think that?"

"Because that's the kind of woman you are. You don't have sex with men. You have *relationships* with *suitable* men. You've never gone to bed with someone you picked up one night in a bar. You've never had sex with someone whose name you never bothered to find out. You've never had sex for its own sake, because you'd had too much to drink or you'd been alone too long." His smile was thin and bitter. "Well, *that's* the kind of man I am. I don't have relationships. I don't meet *suitable* women. I meet women in bars, women whose names I sometimes never knew to forget, women who are interchangeable, who are just there for the using. You're not that kind of woman, Ashley. You're not *my* kind of woman."

"So you're saying that you don't want me."

He gave a short laugh. "I've done without a long time, and I've been alone even longer. Of course I want you. But—no offense, sweetheart—I'd want just about any woman under these circumstances."

"So what's the problem?" she asked stubbornly. "We're both adults. We're both capable of weighing the consequences and making the right decision."

Swearing silently, Dillon crossed the room to tend the fire. There, with more than half the length of the cabin between them, he felt a little safer, but not much.

God help him, she was going to kill him. She was absolutely going to destroy his good intentions, his resolve and, ultimately, *him*. He never should have touched her this morning, never should have kissed her...but he would sell his soul to the devil to do it again.

He just might sell it to the sheriff for a chance to make love with her.

"The problem, Ashley," he said, his patience severely tested, "is common sense—your lack of it. Women like you don't have affairs with men like me. Women like you don't have affairs, period."

"What do we do?" she asked dryly. "Live alone and unsatisfied all our lives?"

"You have relationships with men like your precious Seth. You get married. You have children and grandchildren, and you devote yourself to your family. Like your mother. Like your grandmother."

She came closer, stopping at the sofa, sitting on its overstuffed arm. "Is that what your mother did?"

"No. My mother picked up men in bars, men whose names she didn't bother to learn, men she used to help her forget the pain of falling in love with a *suitable* man." He stared at her for a moment, then exhaled heavily. "You're not my kind of woman, Ashley."

After a pause to let that sink in, he felt the bitterness cross his face in a smile again. "And I'm damned sure not your kind of man."

Their *problem,* Ashley thought as she got ready for bed that evening, had nothing to do with her lack of common sense. Maybe it was bad timing. Maybe if they'd met a year ago, when he had first come to Catlin to work at the bank, he would have decided he had too much to lose to risk the bank job.

But a year ago he'd had a woman in his life, and not of the pick-her-up-in-a-bar-and-never-know-her-name variety. She had been his neighbor, a nice woman, in Seth's judgment, one who'd had no idea at all what kind of man she'd gotten mixed up with. She'd had a silly name—Calla? Cilla? No, Pris, short for Priscilla.

After pulling her nightgown over her head, Ashley made a face at herself in the mirror. Could she simply claim an extraordinary memory for details, or had she been fascinated by Dillon Boone eleven months before meeting him? Was that why unimportant little things—like the photographs left behind in his apartment, the name of his former lover and the fact that the woman had red hair—were so clear in her mind?

So what was the big difference between her and Pris, other than the fact that Ashley wouldn't be caught dead answering to a nickname that, in other usage, was less than complimentary?

Other than the fact that, while Ashley wasn't Dillon's kind of woman, Miss Pris obviously was?

As she picked up her brush from the rim of the sink, a flash outside caught her attention. Switching off the light, she peered out the window into the darkness. There were often hunters in these woods, both in season and out, along with the hikers. She stayed locked up tight and ordinarily paid them no attention. After all, it wasn't as if she owned the mountaintop; her acreage was on the small side. The rest was private property or public parkland.

But this wasn't an ordinary night, and the scene in the next room wasn't an ordinary sight, at least not in *her* house. That light could be a hunter or a hiker, or it could be a search party or a lone tracker hoping to bag a reward.

Leaving the bathroom, she took the extra sheets from the armoire near the door, grabbed a hammer and a box of nails from under the sink and, giving herself a boost, climbed onto the counter that ran under the kitchen window.

Dillon, lying on the couch and reading, looked up. "What's wrong?"

"Nothing." Kneeling on the counter, she tacked a corner from the first sheet to the window frame, scooted across and nailed it again in the opposite corner. "When I moved in here, I always intended to make curtains—yellow gingham, just like my granny had. But there was so much work to do that I never got around to it. In the first year I was terrified that I wouldn't be able to stay, that I couldn't earn enough money, that I couldn't barter enough services, and so I worked ten, twelve and fourteen hours a day, seven days a week. I figured nonessentials, like curtains, could wait. I mean, the place is so isolated. It isn't as if there are neighbors around to peek through the windows."

Taking the sheets and tools with her, she moved to the next window and repeated the process. "After a while I got used to not having curtains. I thought maybe someday I would buy some gingham, or maybe I would make enough yards of lace to cover them all, but it wasn't any big deal."

"But now it is."

"Well, it occurred to me tonight—" Just a random thought, she hoped he believed; there was no sense in worrying him about the light she'd seen. It had been way off in the distance and probably didn't mean a thing, but he would surely believe it was a posse of angry, gun-toting men out looking for him. He might even begin to believe her lie this morning about instructing Steven Vickers and the others to come back tonight with Seth. "With the lights on in here and all these uncurtained windows, to anybody outside looking in, we may as well be in a spotlight. And since there very well *might* be people outside, why take a chance?"

By the time she'd finished, she had covered all the windows in the main room and used her last sheet. Without giving it much thought, she took one of the quilts from the back of the sofa and headed for the bathroom.

"Hey, what are you doing?" There was a thump as Dillon dropped his book to the floor, then the shuffle of footsteps behind her. She was holding a nail to the upper right corner of the quilt, the hammer poised in her other hand, when he yanked it away. "Stop that. You can't put holes in this."

"I don't have any more sheets."

"So keep this door closed."

Still holding the corner of the coverlet above her head, she scowled at him in the dim light. "Maybe you haven't spent enough time in this room to notice, but icicles form in here when the door is closed. When porcelain that cold comes in contact with human flesh, it can do some painful damage."

"You can't put nails in this. It'll ruin it."

"It'll put a few holes in it," she said with exaggerated patience. "Look, *I* made it. If I want to hang it as a curtain, I can. Besides, I think it'll look kind of nice—brighten the room. Give it a homey effect." Pulling the hammer from his hand, she stretched onto her toes and hit the first nail squarely on the head, sinking it with three strikes. Smoothing the fabric as she went, she added more nails, one every six inches or so, until she reached the corner. There, she climbed into the bathtub and affixed the other half in the same manner over the front window.

Climbing out again, she turned on the light to study her handiwork, then smiled. It *did* look nice. The bright shades of the fabric added color that the plain wood walls badly needed, and the straight, rectangular lines of the Log Cabin pattern nicely echoed the lines of the wall boards.

Then she glanced at Dillon again. He was staring at the quilt, a dismayed look darkening his face. "Hey," she said softly. "It's just a quilt. I've made dozens of them. I'll make dozens more."

He shook his head. "You've ruined it."

"Of course I haven't. Don't you know quilts aren't supposed to be perfect? All of the good ones have some rips, tears, lumpy batting or whatever. It gives them character. I bet your grandmother's quilts weren't in pristine condition." The look he gave her at that last part made her wince. He didn't have any idea what kind of shape his grandmother's quilts were in now. Someone else had them now, probably someone to whom they meant nothing, someone with no emotional connection. Heavens, for all he knew, they could have been thrown in the garbage with the rest of his stuff when he failed to pay his rent the month following his disappearance.

Moving past him, she smoothed the fabric in the corner. "This quilt will become a family heirloom now," she said lightly. "When I'm old and gray, I'll still have it, and I'll tell my grandchildren and great-grandchildren how those holes came to be there. They'll be intrigued that *their* granny once helped an escaped bank robber hide from the police. It'll probably make me a minor legend in their eyes." She turned to grin at him, but her expression soon turned sober. He was staring at her, his gaze as intense as any she'd ever seen, as hard and troubled as any she might ever see. "Dillon—" She reached out, but he turned and walked away.

She stood there a moment, then, taking a deep breath, joined him in the outer room. He had turned off all the lights and was now adding fuel to the fire. She returned the hammer and nails to their proper place, reclaimed the brush she'd forgotten earlier and went to sit on the pallet in front of the fireplace.

Finished with the logs, he went to the bed, removed the sling, stripped and slid under the covers. She didn't exactly watch him . . . but she didn't turn away, either. Sitting cross-legged on the thick pad of covers, she began drawing the brush through her hair. "Do you ever miss Pris?" she asked conversationally.

"How do you know about her?"

She smiled into the fire. "You forget, my ex-husband and best friend is the sheriff. By the time his investigation into the bank robbery was completed, he probably knew everything about you, and he told me the interesting stuff. So . . . do you?"

He was quiet a long time, then the bedsprings squeaked. "In a way. She was a nice woman. You would probably like her if you knew her."

"No, I wouldn't "

"How can you be so sure?"

"We can't possibly have anything in common."

"Why do you say that?"

"Because you slept with her. You won't even let me touch you." She thought back to that moment in the bathroom, how close her fingers had come to his shoulder, how quickly he'd avoided her touch, how hurriedly he'd put distance between them.

He fell silent. What kind of response could a man make to a comment like that? She didn't blame him for not even trying.

"What would I like about her?"

An impatient sigh. He didn't want to continue this conversation. She didn't blame him for that, either. "She's nice. Funny. Generous. She's a lot like you."

"How is she different from me?" She had to be, since he'd found her perfectly *suitable* for an intimate relationship.

"Come on, Ash..."

All right, so *all* nicknames weren't bad, she acknowledged. She could warm right up to "Ash," especially when it was Dillon saying it. His name didn't lend itself to shortening—"Dill" was definitely out of the question—but she could easily see herself calling him darlin'. Sweetheart. Baby.

"Satisfy my curiosity." *Since you aren't willing to satisfy anything else.* "How is she different?" When he didn't answer, she supplied her own answer. "I know she has red hair and that she lived upstairs from you. I assume she's prettier than me."

"Why?" He sounded as if he were scowling again.

"Because men like pretty women. Pretty faces, big boobs, long legs..." She laughed, but it wasn't with good humor. "At least I've got the legs."

"Yes, Pris is pretty, but you..." He sighed wearily. "Jeez, Ash, do we have to do this?"

"No," she whispered. That was enough of an answer. *Pris is pretty, but you have character, Ashley. You have inner beauty. You have so many talents.* So it wasn't the answer she wanted. It was exactly what she deserved for asking.

She was an enlightened, independent woman of the nineties, and *she* thought she was pretty. She liked her face. She realized there was more strength than daintiness, more character than conventional beauty, but she liked her looks anyway. What did it matter if he found his old girlfriend more attractive? *She* didn't find *him* as handsome as her ex-husband...at least, she hadn't in the beginning. Funny—the more time she spent with him, the better she came to know him, the more handsome he was.

So maybe, if the reverse was also true, in another...oh, fifty or sixty years, he would find her prettier than Pris. She could wait. She didn't have any plans for the rest of her life...but *he* did. He had his own plans, and Seth and the D.A. had their plans for him. Bill Armstrong had lots of plans for him.

Gazing into the fire, she continued to draw the brush slowly through her hair. When she was little, she had spent countless nights sitting right there, brushing her hair while, beside her, her grandmother did the same. For as long as Ashley could remember, the old lady's hair had been snow white, fine and long, reaching almost to her waist. During the day she'd worn it up, wound around her head into a bun and secured with long rippled pins. She had covered it with a scarf when she went outside, a simple square of calico folded into a triangle, the ends tied under her chin, or with an old straw hat adorned with one floppy, yellow cloth daisy. But at night, every night, whatever the season, she had sat on the braided rug in front of the fireplace—not this rug, but very nearly the same—and let her hair down, and she had brushed it, long gentle strokes gliding all the way to the ends, over and over, slow and easy.

While she had brushed—and Ashley followed suit—she had talked. She had told stories about her parents, had repeated tales her mother had told her. She had talked about herbs and flowers and the phases of the moon, about moonshine stills and soap making and the seasons of her youth. Ashley had learned much in those regular talks about living and dying, about love and joy, heartache and great sorrow.

In spite of the failure of her marriage, Ashley knew she'd been unusually blessed. She had her family and their unswerving love. She had a strong sense of who she was and a sure knowledge of what she wanted. She was living a life that she loved, a life that she wouldn't change one thing about...except for the fact that she was living it alone. She had never gone hungry, had never been broke, had never been afraid. She didn't know what hard living was. Her only sorrow had been losing her grandparents, and she had never experienced heartache, not even with Seth. She had, indeed, been fortunate.

But her luck, she suspected, had changed Tuesday evening when Dillon Boone walked into her cabin. Unless he left now—walked out of her life *right* now, right this very instant—she feared that she was going to find herself on a first-name basis with heartache. She was going to drown in sorrow, and she didn't have a clue how to save herself.

She wasn't even sure she wanted to save herself.

Dillon lay in bed, his eyes gritty and sore, his hands clenched tightly at his side. The cabin was quiet except for the crackle of the fire. Except for the softer crackle—real or imagined?—of Ashley's hair as she slowly pulled the brush through it. Except for the urgent pleas he'd been making for several miserably long moments.

Put the brush down.

Move away from the fire.

Find some clothing more substantial.

Go to bed and, please, God, don't ask me to join you.

Did she know that that flimsy little gown of hers, when backed by the flames, was nearly transparent? Did she know that, every time she raised her arms, he could see the curve of her breast almost as clearly as if she were naked? Did she know that he could think of few things more erotic than watching a woman brush her hair in the firelight?

Did she have any idea that she was killing him?

He wished he could believe the answer was yes. Yes, she knew her gown revealed as much as it concealed. Yes, she knew what a tantalizing sight she presented. Yes, she knew that she was arousing him, tormenting him, teasing and taunting him. If he could believe that, if he could believe that everything she was doing was calculated to seduce, then maybe he could find the strength to resist.

But there was nothing calculating, nothing manipulative about her. Hell, she was a grown woman, married and divorced, and she didn't even realize how pretty she was. She had no idea why he hadn't wanted her to touch him earlier. She didn't even begin to understand why he couldn't have an affair with her.

In all honesty, he was having a few doubts himself. They *were* both adults, as she'd pointed out, both capable of weighing the consequences and making the right decision. Wouldn't that make it all right? If she came to him, fully understanding that it wouldn't be a relationship but an affair, that there wouldn't be anything between them but sex, that it might last a day, three or four at most, and then he would be gone... If she knew all that, wouldn't it save him from burning in hell?

No. She didn't have affairs, and he couldn't have a relationship. There was a lot more between them than just sex, and three or four days would be plenty of time to figure out what it was. It would be more than enough time to damn him.

But he was damned anyway, wasn't he? Since he was going to pay for these few days here with Ashley with every bit of longing he'd ever known, with his peace of mind and just a little of his sanity, would it be so wrong if he made love to her before he left? If he had to suffer the torment anyway, couldn't he experience the pleasure first?

She laid the brush on the hearth—*thank God*—folded back the top quilt, fluffed the pillow, then glanced around. "Where are the handcuffs?"

"I put them away." While she'd been in the bathroom changing for bed, he had unhooked them from the leg of the sofa and tucked them, along with the key, underneath

the cushion. He wasn't going to need them anymore...
unless he had to chain himself in the corner to keep himself away from her.

"Does this mean that you've decided I'm worthy of your trust?"

"I don't trust anyone," he answered automatically as he
watched her settle on the pallet. She didn't have a pretty
face or big boobs, she'd said earlier, but at least she had the
long legs. Damned right, he thought as he caught a glimpse
of her legs, long, strong, the thin gown sliding up to reveal
more, now at the knee, now the thigh, the hip.... Catching his tongue between his teeth, he squeezed his eyes shut
and swore.

"Maybe you don't, maybe you do. How do you know I
won't sneak away during the night?"

Dragging in a breath, he forced his jaw to relax enough
to answer. "Where would you go? It's cold out there, and
it's not going to stop raining until we drown. Bessie won't
run, and your nearest neighbor is five miles away. Getting
there in the dark, in the cold and the rain wouldn't be the
easiest hike you've ever taken, and, honey, I promise you,
most of the people out there looking for me are much more
dangerous than I am."

"You trust me not to leave," she said simply.

"I believe you have the good sense to weigh the consequences and make the right decision."

"Which is the same as trusting me."

"It's got nothing to do with trust," he insisted, exasperation shading his voice.

She sat up, the quilt falling to her waist. "You're afraid
to admit it, aren't you?"

"The last person I made the mistake of trusting set me up
for a major fall, then tried to have me killed. I'm not afraid
of anything except him." And getting caught. Going to
prison. Dying in prison. Wanting Ashley. Needing her.
Making love to her. Not making love to her.

Russell, it seemed, was the *least* of his fears.

She stared at him, her gaze compelling even though her
face was mostly in shadow. "It *was* Bradley, wasn't it?" she

asked softly, and Dillon cursed aloud. "*He* was involved in the robbery. *He* took the money."

He swore again.

"What happened? How did he convince you to break into the bank? Did you take the money and take it to him?"

Why couldn't he learn to keep his mouth shut? The less she knew about what had happened that night and who was involved, the safer she would be. And he *needed* her to be safe. That was the thing he feared most of all: Ashley getting hurt because of him. Ashley being punished because of him. God help him, Ashley dying because of him.

"Forget it, Ash," he said—pleaded—wearily.

"In your dreams." She scrambled to her feet and came to sit on the bed. He drew aside so quickly that a sharp pain shot through his ribs. "Did he pay you? Bribe you? Blackmail you?"

He tried to ignore how close she was—always too close, never close enough—and focus instead on her last question. "What could I possibly have done that Russ could use to blackmail me?"

She shrugged. "You robbed a bank. Surely there must be other secrets in your past."

"Not one."

She allowed herself to be distracted for a moment. "You've never done anything you're ashamed of?"

He also allowed a brief distraction as he reached out and drew his fingers over the curve of her knee, making her shiver before he lifted his hand and tugged the hem of her gown down to cover her legs. "There's a lot that I'm ashamed of," he answered quietly. "Things I did, things I didn't do. But most of it isn't a secret, and none of it's worthy of blackmail."

"What sort of things?"

There were so many to choose from that he couldn't, starting with the trouble he'd caused when he was a kid—the fights he'd picked, the mischief he'd created, the embarrassment and pain he'd caused his grandfather. There was the sorry state of his relationship with his mother; granted, Carole had never been prime parent material, but then he'd never given her any reason to try. He had been more trouble than he was worth since before he was born, she had often declared to whoever would listen, and he had been determined to prove her right. She had been a bad mother; he had deliberately been a bad son.

There were all the failures in his life: the jobs he'd lost, the women he'd known, the disappointments he'd caused. As much as he'd loved his grandfather, and as much as Jacob had loved him, Dillon hadn't even been able to keep that relationship healthy. Weeks, months or—on a few occasions—entire years had gone by when he had refused to return the old man's calls, had tossed his letters in a drawer unanswered, had found it too much a bother to drive the few hours necessary for a visit. Only a few days before Jacob's death, Dillon had turned down a request that he drive out to the old farm for an afternoon. He hadn't wanted to go to Waterston, hadn't wanted to risk running into any of Alexander's family—at least, that had been his official reason, and partly true. The real reason was that he'd lost another job and another woman in the same day. He hadn't been able to face his grandfather, hadn't been able to bear seeing the disappointment in the old man's eyes every time he looked at him. Selfishness and pride had cost him one last meeting with the only person who had always loved him.

"Dillon?" Ashley's voice was gently prodding and as soft as her hand settling over his.

He looked down in the dim light, comparing, contrasting. His skin was dark and brown; hers was painted gold by the fire. His hand was big and strong; hers was deceptively delicate. His palm was callused from years of hard work; hers bore the traces of hard work, too, but was softened by cream that felt like powdered silk and smelled of roses. His hands could cause great pain. Hers could bring great peace.

He needed peace.

"Why are you always touching me?" Immediately she started to draw her hand back, but he surprised both her and himself by turning his hand, catching hold of hers.

"People need to touch and be touched." Her voice was throaty, unintentionally provocative, and her fingers were stroking his palm. "It gives us a connection to each other, makes us feel less alone." She slipped her hand free of his and raised it to his jaw, drawing her fingers along it, then down his throat, making him shiver. "It allows us to get closer, to build intimacy. It can comfort, soothe, reassure and encourage." Her fingers teased and tickled their way across his chest, skirting around the tender place on his ribs, turning away when they reached the covers and returning once more to his hand. "It can heal..." Her voice was softer now. "And hurt..." Breathier, too. "And bring great pleasure..."

And it could arouse. *He* was aroused, his body throbbing, and if she *wasn't,* it surely wouldn't take much to remedy.

But she was. If he needed proof, he got it in the next instant, when she lifted his hand to her mouth. Cradling it in both of her hands, she kissed his palm, her tongue moistening his skin, then she pressed his hand to her throat, holding it there, molding it to fit before slowly sliding it down.

He couldn't breathe, couldn't speak, couldn't find the words to stop her or the strength to stop himself. He simply lay there and let her guide his hand across warm, satiny skin, over delicate lace and thin cotton. He let her slide his hand along until it was cupped over her breast, cradling it in his palm, feeling the hard peak of her nipple like a brand.

For a moment he remained still and compliant. Then, no longer needing her guidance, he began stroking her, simple little movements, not much but enough to make her eyes close, enough to make her breath catch and her lips part on a silent sigh. He rubbed her, bringing each stroke slowly, deliberately over her nipple, creating friction with the heat and pressure of his palm and the barely there fabric, and he tried to remember one reason, just *one* reason, why he shouldn't do this. His mind was thankfully blank.

"Is that pleasurable, Ash?" he whispered.

Eyes still closed, she gave him a smile of such satisfaction and raised her hands, not to push him away but to fumble with the tiny white buttons down the front of the gown. He watched as she unfastened the top one, then the second, the third and the fourth. Holding on to him, she used her free hand to push the fabric aside, then clasped his hand to her breast, naked now, so smooth, so soft and hot. So beautiful.

She was right. He needed this—needed to touch her, needed to be touched by her. He needed her hands on his body, anywhere, everywhere. He needed to be stroked and petted until he died from the pure pleasure of it. He needed to kiss her breasts, to hold her, to explore and taste and savor her. He needed her body against his, her breasts flattened against his chest, her belly rubbing his, her hips sheltering his, her legs twined with his. He needed it all.

And what did *she* need?

Anything in the world but him.

She needed Seth, or someone just like him. Someone respectable, someone she could be proud of, someone who wasn't likely to end up dead or in jail before his thirty-fifth birthday. Someone who knew what it meant to love, who knew how to give it and receive it, how to care for it and keep it growing. Someone who would be there for her not just right now but five weeks and five months and five years from now. Someone whom the children she needed to provide the grandchildren and great-grandchildren she wanted wouldn't be embarrassed to claim as their father. Someone who could protect her and keep her safe and never, ever cause her a moment's harm, a moment's pain or a moment's shame.

Someone *else*. *Anyone* else. Anyone else but Dillon.

Giving up that touch was the hardest thing he'd ever done. His fingers literally ached, curving toward her, reaching in silent plea. His entire body ached, too, with disappointment, with regret and desire.

It took her a moment to realize that he was stopping. Her eyes slowly fluttered open, and she drew a deep, noisy breath. She didn't plead. If she had, he probably would have given in, and she would have made the biggest mistake of her life. But she simply looked at him, her eyes dazed, her expression hazy, her body all soft and invitingly warm.

He copied her earlier act, lifting her hand to his mouth, pressing a kiss to the center of her palm. "I want to make love to you, Ashley," he whispered, his voice not quite steady. "I want to pull you over here and slide inside you and stay there forever. I want to see you naked, to kiss you and touch you. Oh, God, I want to touch you...but it would be wrong, Ash. Can't you understand that?"

She shook her head.

Silently swearing, he squeezed his eyes shut on the tempting picture she presented, sitting there with her hair mussed from the moment she'd spent in her bed and her face flushed from the moments she'd spent in *his* bed, with her gown unbuttoned and her breasts uncovered.

When he opened his eyes again, he pulled the top edges of her gown together and, making a concentrated effort not to actually touch her, he buttoned it up. It didn't help, though. He had already seen, and he wasn't likely to ever forget. "You don't even know me."

"Yes, I do."

He wanted to argue, wanted to insist that she was wrong. In spite of the close quarters they had shared these past few days, in spite of the intensity of the relationship—the alliance, the companionship, whatever the hell it was—they had built, they were still strangers. She couldn't possibly have learned enough about him to believe that she wanted to have an affair with him, because knowing him should convince her of exactly the opposite.

But he couldn't argue a lie. These past few days probably *were* enough for her to reach that decision, because they had sure been long enough for him to reach it.

"I *can't* make love with you."

She treated him to a long, slow, appraising look that didn't stop until it reached evidence—still very strong evidence—to the contrary. Feeling stripped bare and frustrated, he shifted positions and pulled the covers higher.

"I *won't* make love to you," he amended, his voice sharp. "I've got to leave here in a few days, Ash, one way or another. Whether I get away free or go to jail, one fact doesn't change. There's no room in my life for you."

After a long moment she smiled the cool sort of smile she chose when she was hurt. "You have a high opinion of yourself."

He scowled at her. "Why do you say that?"

"You think a few days as your lover is going to be so meaningful that it will change my life, that I won't be able to live without you, that I'll pine away the rest of my life because you aren't here."

She waited, but he couldn't respond. To agree that, yes, that was exactly what he was afraid of was too arrogant, and to admit that, no, *he* was the one whose life would change, *he* was the one who would have trouble getting along, *he* was the one who would die missing her, would be too painful.

With a sigh, she rose from the bed. "We could have been good together, Dillon. You'll never know what you've missed."

Oh, he would know. Every lonely minute of every lonely day would remind him. Every empty night would torment him. Every image of her would haunt him. But instead of admitting that to her, instead of giving her something more to use against him, he echoed her sigh. "And you'll never know what you've escaped."

Chapter 7

"**D**o you have a map?"

At Dillon's question, Ashley looked up from the dining table. He'd been restless all afternoon, pacing the cabin, stopping occasionally to lift the corner of a sheet and peer out the window. She'd wanted to tell him a dozen times to calm down, to take it easy, read, relax, try to sleep, but she'd known instinctively that he wouldn't listen. He was fidgety. Nervous. Eager to be on his way.

Eager to leave her behind.

She pushed away from the table. "There's one in the van. I'll get it."

He started to protest, then shrugged. After putting on her loafers, she hurried out to the van. The rain was still coming down, but it was gentler this morning, warmer, a typical spring shower. The sun was trying to break through the clouds, and try as she might, she couldn't make out any more rain clouds to the west. A day or so of dry weather, and Bessie would be ready to go.

Dillon was already ready.

Leaning across the passenger seat, she pulled out the tattered atlas, then returned to the cabin and silently handed it over to him. While he flipped through the pages to the North Carolina map, she reseated herself at the table and went back to work. For small-ticket items, shower gels were among her more profitable enterprises. She bought the clear soapy gel by the gallon, colored it in rich jewel tones or soft pastels and added scents with essential or fragrance oils. She had a large collection of the oils, each in a small vial, but her own personal favorites were tea rose and honeysuckle. She hoped that wherever he went, whatever he did, Dillon never smelled either of those scents again without thinking of her. Without missing her. Without regretting her.

Just as she would never again breathe in the fragrance of vanilla without being reminded of him. When he left, she would send her last two bottles of the ivory-hued, vanilla-scented gel with him . . . and maybe a bottle or two of the deep red honeysuckle, too.

"This atlas is over ten years old." He tossed it on the table, nearly knocking over the round plastic bottle she was filling with the last of the jasmine-scented gel. Dragging out the chair across from her, he turned it around and straddled it.

"So?"

"So things change. New roads get built. Old ones get closed down."

"Not around here. I doubt that Catlin County's gotten a new road in my lifetime."

"So how do we get out of here?"

"That depends on where you want to go." She used a narrow spatula to scrape the last of the gel into the jar, removed the funnel, then capped it with a small white lid. Later she would label the jars with the pretty gummy labels her sister Deborah had had designed and made up for her last Christmas, but for now she was simply setting them aside. She wouldn't forget what they were and, if she did, she needed only a whiff to remember. "If you want to head into South Carolina or Virginia, we should probably take this road." Reaching across the table, she tapped one finger on a thin north-south line on the upside-down map. "If you want to go to Tennessee, Georgia or points west, you need to take this road to the interstate.''

He studied the map a moment. "Those are the two major roads out of the county.''

"Those are the two *only* roads out of the county," she corrected him.

"Surely there are some secondary roads.''

"There are lots of secondary roads, but those two are the only ones that leave the county. Catlin's a small county, and a lot of it is too rough for travel. We have plenty of little meandering country roads like the one I live on, but—like the one I live on—they dead-end after a while or they circle around and run into one of those highways. That's how we have to go.''

He stared at the map a while longer. Wishing he'd escaped in Asheville, maybe, where he knew his way around and Miss Pris would have helped him? Or maybe in a city like Raleigh or Charlotte, where the possibilities for getting out of town were endless, where there were so many roads that trying to close off the city with roadblocks would be impossible. Maybe he was wishing he'd never heard of Catlin, that he'd never left Georgia, that he'd never trusted his buddy Russ.

Maybe he was wishing he'd never met *her*.

Finally he looked up at her. She was measuring drops of oil into a bowl filled with gel in a rich translucent red, and the scent of honeysuckle drifted up between them. Reaching out, he caught the next drop on his fingertip, rubbed it together with his thumb, then sniffed it. "This smells like you.''

Her smile was hard to find, but she managed a faint one.

He drew his hand back and rested his arms on the back of the chair. "Once the rain stops, how long will it take Bessie to dry out?''

"A day, maybe two. It depends on how humid it is.''

"Why don't you get the thing fixed?''

She gave him a dry look. "That van is nearly thirty years old. You don't just walk into an auto-parts store in a place like Catlin and pick up a new part off the shelf.''

"Why don't you get something safer?"

"Bessie's perfectly safe."

"Something more reliable."

"Who's got the money to spend on a car?"

He scowled and muttered, "This is no way to live."

"This is exactly how I *want* to live," she responded quietly. "If you find it so unappealing, well, in another day or two, you won't have to endure it any longer. Whatever happens, in jail or on the run, you'll be living in a way that's much, much worse." That turned his mood a few degrees darker, prompting her to go on quickly. "Which way do you plan to go?"

"West."

"I have family in California. If you make it that far, look them up."

He disregarded the flippancy in her voice. "Why did they move there when their roots are here? When their daughter is here?"

"It was Daddy's dream to live someplace else."

"To meet interesting people? Do exciting things?" He almost smiled. "I guess you came by the desire honestly. Do you miss them?"

"More than you can imagine." After all, he'd never been close to his mother, and his father had never acknowledged him. He'd never had the sort of normal upbringing that she'd taken for granted—the typical family, the working father and stay-at-home mother, the annoying siblings, the rivalry, the vacations, the big holiday get-togethers. She would like the chance to include him in a few of her family's affairs.

Fat chance. Slim chance. *No* chance.

"Where is your father?" she asked, giving the gel one final stir, then setting up the first bottle with the narrow-necked funnel in place.

His scowl returned. "He lives in Georgia."

"Atlanta?"

"No. A little town called Waterston. He's one of the Waterses for whom the town is named."

"There's nothing quite like small-town aristocracy, is there?" she asked lightly. "In Catlin, the Benedicts are the most aristocratic of them all. Seth's mother was tremendously disappointed by our marriage. I was one of the riff-raff, my father worked in the mill that used to operate over on Tompkins Ridge." Waiting for the thick gel to ooze into the bottle, she sobered again. "I take it your parents weren't married."

He shook his head.

"You want to talk about it?"

He stared at the atlas for a moment before finally shrugging. "My mother was eighteen when she began her affair with Alexander. He was twenty-six, married and already had one kid and another on the way. He told Carole—my mother—that he loved her, that as soon as the baby was born, he would divorce his wife and marry her, and she believed him. She honestly believed that the only son of the Waters family, the richest family in town, with the oldest money and the bluest blood, was going to divorce his wife—from the second-richest family with the next-to-the-bluest blood—to marry the high-school-dropout daughter of a poor dirt farmer and take her away to a better life. She was a fool."

"Being in love can make you crazy," Ashley said softly. "It can make you do foolish things."

She felt his glower even though she wisely wasn't looking. "How would you know?"

Because *he* was teaching her. But she didn't say that. "What happened?"

"After four or five years, she got pregnant. By then Alexander had three legitimate heirs to the throne. He wasn't pleased with the prospect of an illegitimate one. As her pregnancy became obvious, there were rumors, of course. There had always been speculation about their affair, and people were apparently pretty curious about the new development. Alexander didn't like the gossip, and his mother and his wife especially didn't like it, so he denied being the father. He denied ever having been with Carole, and he cut her off—socially, financially, emotionally. All the years we lived there, he treated her worse than anyone should ever be treated. He despised her and made certain that everyone, especially my mother, knew it. It didn't help any that, to get back at him, she named me after him—Dillon Alexander Waters Boone.'' He gingerly touched his eye, where little sign of the bruising courtesy of the Sylvan County Sheriff's Department remained. ''The name alone got me about a dozen bloody noses and twice that many black eyes from Alexander Waters, Jr. Alex didn't like sharing his name *or* his father with me.''

Either Carole Boone had had a cruel streak running through her, Ashley thought grimly, or she had been too much a fool to consider what she was doing to her son with that name. If Alexander Waters had despised his ex— What had Carole been to him? Lover? Mistress? Plaything? Amusement? Whatever role she had filled for him, if he had come to despise her for the gossip and the notoriety, he surely must have despised their son as much. Giving Dillon the man's name—particularly when Alexander's legitimate son already had a claim to it—must have been like rubbing salt into an open wound. It must have made Dillon's life in Waterston, Georgia, pure hell.

''How long did you live there?''

''Until I was twelve. Things had gotten kind of tough by then. Alexander's family was determined to run us out of town so they wouldn't have to face the product of Alexander's indiscretion every day, and I was determined to help them. I hated it there. I hated the talk. I hated the way they treated my mother and especially my grandfather, just because the almighty Waters family decreed that they should be treated that way. I hated Alex beating the hell out of me every time I left the house... although I have to give him credit.'' He grinned sardonically. ''He taught me how to fight dirty, and that surely did come in handy in Atlanta.''

She set aside the filled bottle, then reached for another empty. ''You've either been looking for trouble or running away from it most of your life, haven't you?''

Sometimes she thought his face should be permanently etched with a scowl. In less time than it took to blink, it chased away his grin and the faint softening that had accompanied it and left him looking hard and unforgiving. Ignoring her question, he returned his attention to the atlas, flipping open to a map of the United States. "If I want to head out west, we pick up the interstate and cross into Tennessee. How far can you take me?"

Swallowing a sigh, she glanced at the map. "You want to try for California?"

The scowl deepened. "Be serious."

"I *am* serious. I told you that I haven't seen my family in over three years. I wouldn't mind surprising them."

"You think Bessie could make it all the way across the country?"

The scorn in his voice turned her smile sad. "Stranger things have happened." In spite of her insistence, it *hadn't* been a serious offer, she told herself. She couldn't just lock up and leave. If she wasn't here, she wasn't making money, and without money, she couldn't hold on to this place. It wasn't much, but it was all she had. It was her life. The offer had been a joke, all in jest.

So why did it sting just a little that he hadn't jumped at it? That he hadn't found anything the least bit attractive about it? That he no more wanted to take her with him than he wanted to stay here?

"How about Nashville?" It was four, maybe five hours away. The city was large enough that he would have some options, close enough that she could make the trip there and back without too much cause for concern.

He located it on the map, stared at it for a moment, then silently nodded.

"It would be in your best interests to wait at least a few more days."

"Why?"

"The roadblocks will have to come down pretty soon. It costs a lot of money to have officers assigned exclusively to one location, doing only one job. Frankly I don't think you're important enough to justify the expense for too long."

"You said you could get through the roadblocks."

She acknowledged that with a shrug. ''There's also the risk of recognition. I imagine your face has been plastered all over the newspapers and TV stations for miles around. It's not an easy one to forget.''

''And what am I supposed to do while I wait for the roadblocks to come down and for something more important to bump me off the front page of the paper?''

She could tell from his expression that he expected her to repeat yesterday's invitation, to say, *You could stay here. I could hide you.* Of course, that was what she wanted to say. She wanted to ask, beg, plead. She wanted to argue with him, wanted to insist, wanted to somehow convince him that *here* was exactly where he belonged. Instead, though, she shrugged carelessly and repeated an earlier suggestion.

''You could turn yourself in.''

Turn himself in.

For the first time in more than eleven months, Dillon gave the matter serious consideration. Always before, he had dismissed it out of hand as utter foolishness, a mistake he would pay for with the rest of his life. After all, who would believe anything he had to say? When he was pointing fingers at people like Russell Bradley, when he had a history of unreliability and minor run-ins with the law, when he had fled town that night last April like the guiltiest of the guilty, who would even listen?

Ashley believed Seth would. Maybe she was right. Maybe he would not only listen but actually even believe...but could Dillon stake his life on it?

What life? a mocking voice asked. On the run was no way to live, she'd once told him, and she was right. It was the loneliest, most miserable life he'd ever known...and growing up as Alexander's bastard son and Alex's punching bag, he'd known some miserable times.

But surrendering wouldn't give him any other choices. Instead of being miserable and free to go where he chose, he would be miserable and behind bars.

Unless Ashley was right. Seth could help prove that he'd been set up, she'd said. If he told Seth everything, if he revealed the entire story that he'd never shared with anyone, if Seth believed him and agreed to reopen the investigation... Dillon could clear his name and be free to live wherever he wanted, however he wanted, with whomever he wanted.

He could stay here. With *her.*

If there was evidence to clear him. *If* Seth believed him.

"What happened that night, Dillon?"

Those were mighty big *if*s. Besides, he knew better than to want what he couldn't have. That was one lesson he'd learned when he was a kid. He was wrong to want Ashley. To want to stay here. To want to make this old farm into a viable proposition once more. To want to spend his days working in the fields, the way his grandfather had, and his nights making love with her. He was wrong to think about watching a lifetime's worth of sunrises from that front porch with her, about sharing just as many sunsets.

He was wrong to think about marrying her, having children with her, growing old with her.

"I can't tell you."

"Why not?"

"Because there are people out there who want me dead! Have you forgotten that?"

Her gaze shifted to his shoulder, to the dressing that was hidden underneath the sweatshirt he wore. Though still tender, the gunshot wound was healing. Sometimes, if not for the sling, he could forget it was there—and that was dangerous. As long as he was here, as long as he was around Ashley, he needed to always remember that there were a lot of people out there who would be better off if *he* were dead.

"So tell me again what happened *then*—when they tried to kill you. You said the first night that you and Tom Coughlin were on your way to Catlin when you got ambushed at Sadler's Pass, that three men opened fire on you."

He made no response.

"Did you see them very well? Did you know any of them?"

When he still said nothing, she left her chair and came around to crouch beside him. Her fingers, very delicate and feminine in spite of their short, unpainted nails, rested on his thigh. ''Dillon, you aren't protecting me by keeping silent. Someone tried to kill you because of the bank robbery. You believe they're out there looking for you along with the police. If they find you here, what will they do?''

''They'll probably take me into custody to turn over to the sheriff. Unfortunately, somewhere between here and town, I'll try to escape, and they'll have to shoot me. No one will even question their story because I *did* get away twice before.''

''*I'll* question it, and when I do, what will *they* do?''

Sliding back on the seat, he rested his head on his arms and stared down, seeing nothing. If Russell and his accomplices were willing to kill to keep *him* quiet, would they balk at using the same deadly force to silence Ashley? He would give his soul to believe that the answer was yes—that, while they had no qualms about murdering someone who had been part of their plans from the start, they would draw the line at killing an innocent woman who'd been dragged into this mess through no fault of her own.

But try as he might, he couldn't believe it. Russell and everyone else involved had a lot to lose, and who better to put them in jeopardy than the investigating sheriff's ex-wife and best friend? They weren't fools. If they found him here, they would kill them both. Whether Ashley knew the truth would be irrelevant.

Tilting his head to the side, he met her gaze. ''Two of them were strangers. The third one—the one who shot the deputy... I'd seen him before, but I don't remember where.''

''Could it have been someone who worked for Bradley Electronics?''

He shook his head. ''Not while I was there. I knew everyone.''

''A friend of Bradley's? Someone you saw with him in Asheville?''

"No." That meant it was probably someone he'd seen around Catlin the weeks he'd lived there. An employee of the bank, maybe, or a regular customer at the diner where he'd eaten.

Her muscles growing tired, Ashley drew back, pulled a chair over and sat facing him. He immediately missed the touch of her hand on his leg. "What did he look like?"

He thought back to that morning in the cruiser. When the Sylvan County deputies had turned him over to Tom Coughlin, they had cuffed his hands tightly behind his back. Without a word to them, Coughlin had removed the handcuffs, then refastened them just tight enough to keep Dillon from slipping free, and he'd done it with his hands in front. Having ridden in a Sylvan County car with his hands behind him and the cuffs tight enough to make his fingers turn blue, Dillon had appreciated the small consideration.

The drive, for the most part, had passed in silence. The deputy had been all business, no chitchat or small talk. Dillon had asked him about the belongings he'd left behind in Asheville, and the deputy had told him that the law allowed the landlord to dispose of them as he saw fit. That was the extent of the conversation until they'd reached Sadler's Pass. Coughlin had slowed down for a tight curve, then suddenly hit the brakes and muttered, "What the..." and all hell had broken loose. Dillon had had only seconds to take in the scene ahead—the black van, its windows tinted, the three men. They had been all business, too—so cool, so collected, so deadly. As if this sort of thing came naturally to them. As if violence came naturally to them.

With a deep breath, he tried to focus on the man he'd recognized. He'd stood apart from the other two, right out in the middle of the lane, as if he'd had no fear. It was his shot, Dillon was pretty sure, that had hit Coughlin. He had no idea who'd shot *him* because the car was already going off the side of the mountain; the shot had come from behind, and he was being tossed around like a rag doll.

He had believed at that moment that he was going to die.

It still might happen.

"He was young, probably in his mid-twenties," he said at last, his voice flat. "He was about six feet tall, maybe a little taller, with black hair, kind of shaggy, a mustache, kind of cocky. He was wearing jeans and a green-and-yellow jacket—you know, a high school letter jacket."

More than a little of the color drained from her face, but she tried to hide her shock with a smile. It didn't work. "You just described Steven Vickers."

"Who is that?"

"My kid sister's ex-boyfriend. The star quarterback for the Catlin High Wildcats eight or ten years ago." That sickly little smile reappeared. "A member of the search party that came through yesterday. And one of Seth's deputies."

For a moment Dillon felt nothing. He sat there, leaning on the back of the chair, hearing her words in his head but not understanding them. Then he realized that his fingers were gripping the chair tightly enough to hurt, that his stomach had gotten queasy and his lungs felt as if they just might burst. The man who had tried to kill him had been right outside the cabin yesterday morning, and he was a cop. He wasn't sure which frightened him more.

A cop. He hadn't expected that. He'd known that there was more than enough corruption in this mess to go around, but he hadn't thought that it might have reached the sheriff's department. He hadn't considered that Russell might buy himself a cop, but really, it made perfect sense. If Dillon had been arrested eleven months ago, a deputy on Russell's payroll could have kept his old friend informed. He could have passed on every bit of inside information on the case. He could have told Russell and the others things like what Dillon was telling the sheriff. Things like if and when he was being transported, and by what route.

A cop. Even worse, a cop who had shot another cop, who had been willing to kill a fellow officer, a friend. It seemed the stakes had gone even higher than Dillon had imagined.

"You can't be sure that the guy with the gun is your deputy," he said stiffly. "Vickers can't be the only man in the county with shaggy black hair and a mustache."

Ashley gave him a chastising look. "Haven't you heard about the death of small-town America? Young people want excitement, education, opportunity, so they move away to the city. There aren't more than two dozen men in Catlin between the ages of twenty and forty, and only one who fits that description *and* has a Wildcats letter jacket." She drummed her fingers agitatedly on the tabletop. "I have to tell Seth."

"Like hell you do." Reaching out, he grabbed her hand and held it tightly in his. "What are you going to tell him?"

"That he might have a dirty cop working for him!"

"And he'll want to know where in God's name you got that idea. *Then* what are you going to tell him?"

"The truth. Dillon, he can help you!"

"I don't *want* his help. All I want is to get out of here." But that wasn't true. In the best of all worlds, accepting help from the sheriff would rank right at the top of his priorities. Getting help, clearing his name, staying here, making a life, loving Ashley—those would be his goals.

But this was far from the best of all worlds. If the sheriff knew he was here, Benedict would arrest him. He wouldn't believe his story about Russell and the money. He wouldn't make an effort to clear Dillon's name. He would lock him up in a cell guarded by the very man who had tried to kill him. Dillon would be lucky to live long enough to go to trial.

"So you're just going to run away without even a look back." The accusation in her voice made him uncomfortable, made him feel weak and cowardly. He wasn't weak—the fact that he could walk away from her proved that—but he *was* a coward. He was afraid of going to prison. Afraid of failing in exactly the way that Alexander and so many others had expected of him. Afraid of losing his freedom, his dignity and whatever was left of his pride.

Running away without looking back. ''That's what I do best,'' he replied grimly.

But that was a lie, too. He would be looking back. Until the day he died, he would look back with great regret on this place, this time and especially this woman.

Chapter 8

The dinner dishes were done and night had fallen when Ashley took her shawl from the peg near the door. "I'm going outside," she announced, then, at Dillon's sharp look, she hastily added, "Just to the porch. Just for a few minutes."

He didn't offer her permission, didn't respond at all except to watch with a scowl as she stepped into her shoes, then wrapped the shawl tightly around her shoulders. She gave him a quick, reassuring smile before she went out and closed the door behind her.

It was chilly, the sort of crisp, sharp cold that made her think winter was coming, not leaving. It felt good, though. Refreshing. The icy air chased away the heat that seemed to have seeped into her very bones, cleared the cobwebs from her head and cleaned the pungent woodsmoke from her lungs. It made her feel stronger. More alert. More alive.

She also felt incredibly alone.

With a heavy sigh, she moved a few inches closer to the steps. If the moon weren't so bright, she would go to the top step to sit, to breathe and brood. Tonight, though, she stayed in the shadows, nothing more than a darker shadow to anyone who might be out there looking.

She wondered whether Seth was out there somewhere, hoped and prayed that he was nowhere near Steven Vickers. She hoped the man Dillon had described wasn't Steven, but either way, she had to tell Seth. She couldn't let him continue working closely with a man who might be dangerous, who might have almost killed another deputy. She *had* to tell Seth, the sooner the better.

She just didn't know how she was going to manage.

She sighed so deeply that it made her shiver and, for just a moment, gave her a sense of lightness, of eased burdens, of peace. It was the night, of course. If days were peaceful up here in the mountains, nights were nothing less than heavenly. There were no lights to cast their reflections into the sky and block out the stars, no highways with traffic to break the night stillness, nothing man-made at all to disturb nature. The sounds were soft—crickets, the occasional rustles of wild creatures in the woods—and the scents—pine, flowers both wild and cultivated, clean, clear air—were soothing. Nighttime was a healing time. It was a time to relax, to rejuvenate, to refocus.

She was going to need a great many nights once Dillon was gone. A great deal of healing.

The door behind her opened, then closed again, so softly that if it weren't for the prickly little sensations racing down her spine, Ashley would have thought she'd imagined the sound. But it wasn't imagination. Without looking, she knew that Dillon had come out, knew that he was standing at the door, only a foot, maybe two, behind her. She knew that he, like her, needed the night's healing, too.

The boards creaked, alerting her that he had shifted. "Don't come out into the light," she said, her voice as quiet as the air.

The boards creaked again, then the door gave a faint groan as he leaned back against it. "Nice night."

"Hmm." She wrapped the ends of the shawl over her hands to warm her fingers, then tugged it tighter. "When I first considered moving here, I knew I'd be fine during the

day, but I wasn't sure about the nights. I thought they
would be so lonely. So scary.''

''Were they?''

''No.'' Gazing out over the untended fields, she smiled.
''There was a full moon when I moved in. I was a little edgy
and couldn't sleep, so I came out here, wrapped myself in
one of Granny's quilts and curled up in the rocker. It was
so bright, so clear and quiet. I could see easily all the way
to the woods. Everything was sharper, more intense—the
light, the smells, the air. I fell asleep there in the rocker and
didn't wake until dawn. After that, I was never afraid of the
night again.''

''Until I came.''

Finally she glanced over her shoulder at him. He was
even more in the shadows than she was. She could barely
make out the pale colors that were muslin in the quilt
wrapped around him. She couldn't make out his face at all.
''Until you came,'' she quietly agreed. ''Now, when you
leave, the nights *will* be lonely.''

''But not scary.''

She turned her back to him again. ''No, not scary.'' She
would have her fears; they just wouldn't be tied in any way
to the cycles of the sun, moon and stars. She would worry
about him, would wonder where he was and how he was
getting along and whether he ever thought about her. She
would be afraid that someday he would get caught, that
Bradley's men would track him down and finish the job
they'd started. She would spend the rest of her life worrying and wondering, and she would never have any answers, because she knew without asking that he would
never try to contact her. He would never let her know that
he was safe. Of course, if Bradley's men caught him, he
would never be able to let her know that he wasn't.

It would be hell not knowing. She thought she could let
him go, thought she could say goodbye to him and get on
with her life, if only she could know that he was all right.
That he'd found someplace safe to stop running. That he'd
settled into the sort of life he deserved to be living, a normal life, with a job and a home, with friends . . . and fam-

ily? Could she accept that he'd married someone else, had children with someone else, that he'd found someone else suitable for sharing his life when *she* wasn't?

She could, she thought with a thin smile. She might hate him for it, but at the same time, she would be grateful for knowing.

"Will going to Nashville be a problem for you?"

She swallowed over the lump in her throat. "No. The only person who keeps track of me around here is Seth, and he's too busy looking for you. I do a fair amount of traveling to shops and shows and to buy supplies, so no one will think twice about it."

"Can you get there and back in one day?"

"If Bessie and the weather cooperate."

"Maybe we shouldn't try for Nashville. Maybe we should go only as far as Knoxville or just some little place in Tennessee."

"Knoxville is too close. You've surely been in the news there. Nashville's big enough that they won't have much, if any, interest in Catlin news, not even if it involves a bank robbery."

He blew his breath out in a hollow sound. "I don't want you to drive that far in Bessie alone. What if she breaks down? What if it rains? I can't even give you the money for a motel room or gas."

"I've got a little money." She'd told him his first night here that she didn't have any money, not in the bank, not at all, but it had been a lie. Granted, her savings account in Bill Armstrong's bank was on the paltry side; no self-respecting bank robber would touch it. But like her granny before her, she kept a little stash here in the cabin, all the money she'd earned in the past couple of months, tucked away neatly in a round basket with a lid that she'd woven specifically for that purpose.

"Why don't you let me take Bessie? You can stay here where you're safe."

Her back still to him, she shook her head. "You wouldn't get past the roadblocks. Besides, your shoulder isn't healed yet. A few days working her gearshift will just make it worse.''

She knew from his silence that he knew she was right on both points; otherwise, he would have argued them with her. Instead, he stood there behind her, quiet and still.

A light breeze moved up the valley, rustling through the trees, making her shiver. "Want your jacket?" he asked.

She thought of the coats hanging on the wooden rack behind the door—some water-repellent, the others not, one long, most of them shorter, all of them chosen for function and not style. There was one, a heavy quilted parka in olive drab, that would feel wonderful right now. Even the black-and-blue nylon windbreaker would be warmer than the shawl, but she didn't ask for it or any of the others. "I'd rather share your quilt."

For a long time there was silence, then she heard a rush of breath and the rustle of fabric. "Come here."

It took only two steps to reach him. One arm was spread wide, the quilt falling like a cape toward the floor. She snuggled in, taking a place not at his side, as he clearly expected, but in front of him, the back of her body fitting nicely along the front of his. He hesitated a moment, then lowered his arm, drawing her closer, enfolding her in his embrace, both arms clasped around her waist.

Closing her eyes, Ashley breathed deeply and smelled spices, flowers and vanilla. The scent was warm, sweet and intoxicating, a heady contrast to the cold, clean smells of the night.

"I'm sorry I came here."

"I'm not."

"You'll be safe when I'm gone."

"I suppose I will." Safe. Lonely. Sad. But she would survive. She was strong. She'd made a satisfying life for herself alone before he'd come, and she would eventually manage to do so again once he was gone. She would get up early, have her tea out here in the rocker and spend her days in the workshop. She would still go to craft shows, resupply the shops with her goods and see Seth every Saturday.

It wouldn't be different at all...except that she would be missing Dillon every moment that she was awake.

"Will you ever tell Seth?"

"I don't know."

"Have you ever considered trying with him again?"

"Trying what?"

"Marriage. Trying to make it work this time."

She twisted just enough to get a faint glimpse of his face. "Would you like that? Would it make you feel better if you knew that Seth and I were married again, that I was living with him and sleeping with him?"

He scowled. "Yes. No. Oh, hell, forget I mentioned it."

With a private little smile, she turned forward again, clasped her hands over his and rested her head on his shoulder. "You could ask me to go with you."

"No, I couldn't."

"Why not?"

"Because you would say yes."

"Would that be so bad?"

"You need a home, Ash. You need to stay here, where your work is, where your roots are, where your heritage is. You belong here every bit as much as I don't."

"I could adapt." She said it quietly because she wasn't entirely sure it was true. He was right: she *did* belong here. This was her home, her life. This was who she was. But he was also wrong: *he* belonged here, too—or he could, if he would let himself. If he would trust her. If he would turn himself in, face his problems squarely and deal with them once and for all.

"Living with me wouldn't be fun or romantic or exciting. It would just be hard. You can't stay anyplace. You can't trust anyone. You can't do anything. All you can do is run, be scared and wish for something better."

"You don't sound too fond of the life-style."

"I hate it. And you'd hate it and you would hate me for making you live it."

She couldn't imagine anything that would truly make her hate him...but she could see herself simply stopping one day, no matter where they were or what they were doing, and saying, "I have to go home."

She drew a deep breath. "You know, you could always—"

Before she could finish, he laid his fingers over her mouth. "Don't say it. We had this discussion just this afternoon, and nothing's changed. I can't surrender, and you can't accept that, so let's forget it."

His fingers were warm, calloused, rough against the tender skin of her lips. She savored the touch for a moment before drawing his hand away, holding it tightly in hers and softly inviting, "Make me forget it."

He was still, barely breathing, as if he suspected that he was about to walk into a trap but couldn't avoid it. "How?"

"Kiss me."

"No way."

"You did it before, and I do believe you enjoyed it." In the tight cocoon of the quilt, she turned to face him and realized for the first time exactly how intimately close they were. "You did enjoy it, didn't you?"

"More than you can imagine."

She laughed. "Oh, Dillon, I can imagine plenty."

"Ash—" Whatever protest or argument he'd been about to offer died unsaid as he raised his hand to her. He touched her gently, so gently—her hair, her forehead, her cheek, her jaw. Then he found the words again. "It would be wrong."

She became as serious as he was. "We've both been alone a long time, Dillon. We've both been lonely. I admit that I would like for you to stay, that I can look ahead years from now and easily see the two of us together right here, but I know that's not going to happen. I know you're going to leave. I know that, if you have any control over it, I'll never see you again. I can accept that. What I can't accept is not being able to touch you, not being able to make love with you, not being allowed to have any part of you at all. That's all I'm asking for, Dillon. Until you leave, I just want to be a part of you."

He lowered his head until his forehead rested against hers. "It's only going to hurt," he whispered.

Her voice was just as soft and a lot shakier when she answered. "Saying goodbye is going to hurt, no matter what the circumstances. You can't make a commitment. You can't give me a future or make any promises or even give me any hope. At least give me this much." She had to stop to take a breath, to force air into her lungs and to banish— or at least try to—the tears from her voice. "Please, Dillon. Give me just this one night."

Closing his eyes, Dillon swore a silent curse.

One night. She made it sound like a generous gesture. *You can't give me anything else, so please do this for me. You can't stay with me, can't love me, can't marry me, can't give me a family, can't be here when I need you, can't live with me, can't grow old with me, can't die with me, but, hey, you can make love with me, so please give me that little bit of nothing.*

One night. Just one night. Maybe she would be satisfied with that. Maybe it would be enough for her. It would be enough to drive *him* crazy. Enough to haunt him for as long as he lived. Enough to guarantee that he would spend the rest of his miserable life longing for this place and this woman. Enough to kill him, little by little, every day that he wasn't here and every night that wasn't spent at her side.

He couldn't do it. He couldn't spend just one night with her and then spend hundreds—thousands—of nights without her. If he made love to her, he would never be able to leave her until they took him away in chains. He would be damned for wanting her.

And maybe even more damned for not having her. Wouldn't it be easier living among strangers, always alone, with the memory of one night to sustain him? Wouldn't it be better just once to ease the loneliness that sometimes threatened to destroy him? Wouldn't all those hard miles and all that hard living be more tolerable if he had one good, sweet, pure moment to carry him through?

One night doing the one thing he'd wanted desperately to do practically since the first time he'd seen her. Was that so much to ask? So much to need?

Ignoring the discomfort in his shoulder, he raised both hands to her face, cradling it in his palms. "Tell me to go to hell."

"Not unless you take me with you."

His smile was bitterly sad. "That's one of the things I'm afraid of."

Her responding smile was utterly sweet. "That's not going to happen. We're no different than a lot of couples out there, Dillon. They know that their relationships are likely to end sometime. We just happen to know when."

When. Tomorrow or the next day. Sunday seemed like a heartbeat away. If he hesitated, if he blinked, Friday would be gone, Saturday skipped over and Sunday would arrive.

Or it could be part of another lifetime. They could hold it at bay, if they moved slowly enough, if they tried hard enough, if they loved long enough.

"We can't have everything," she said softly. "We can't have much of anything. But does that mean we have to settle for nothing?"

He'd been settling all his life, it seemed. Settling for whatever affection he could have. Settling for the low expectations everyone except his grandfather had saddled him with. Settling for a second-class life as a first-class failure. Now she was offering him exactly what he wanted—not for as long as he wanted, but for a time. For a day or two—and that was a day or two more than he'd ever thought he would have.

He would be a damned fool to agree.

But he would be a fool to turn her down.

"Just promise me one thing."

He sensed rather than saw her sweet, satisfied smile. "What's that?"

"That you won't regret this." He could live with almost anything; but not her regret. Not knowing that, later, she might wish this night had never happened. Not knowing that she might be sorry she had asked him to kiss her, sorry she had shared such intimacies with him.

"Not as long as I live."

Still holding her with one arm, he reached behind him and opened the door with the other, then backed inside, drawing her along with him. He took a moment to secure the door before letting the quilt slide to the floor, taking her shawl with it. She was wearing a denim skirt, another long one that came almost to her ankles, buttoned, belted and buckled at the waist over a plain cotton shirt. He wondered what she was wearing underneath that shirt—a bra or nothing at all—then realized that in a moment he would find out. He would unfasten every one of those buttons, slide the shirt off her shoulders and down her arms and see her, touch her, kiss her, stroke her. He would remove the skirt, too, and lay her down naked on the bed. He would memorize the feel of her skin against his fingertips, would commit to memory forever the taste of her and all the different scents of her. He would arouse her, satisfy her, then do it again. And again.

Just thinking about it aroused *him*.

She reached for the big metal buckle at her waist, but he stayed her hands. "I want to undress you."

Her only response was a soft smile, then she turned and took a circuitous route to the bed, shutting off the lights as she went. Only the glow from the fireplace lit the room as she kicked off her shoes, turned down the covers, then waited, hands folded demurely together, for him to join her.

As he approached her, he tried to think of a single reason why he shouldn't do this, a single argument that could stop him, but his brain was incapable of cooperating. He *wanted* this, wanted *her*, more than he'd ever wanted anything in his life, wanted her so badly that he was willing to suffer for it later. Right or wrong, good or bad, sweet passion or intolerable pain, he had to do this. *Had* to. He just might die if he didn't.

Sliding his arm free of the sling, he lifted the fabric over his head and tossed it on the night table, then reached for her, hooking his fingers around her belt, using it to pull her to him. She didn't hesitate or hang back but came willingly, right up to him. "I've waited all my life for a woman like you."

She started to respond, then thought better of it and simply smiled instead. What had she been about to say? he wondered. That she'd waited all her life for *him?* Or maybe that she would wait the *rest* of her life for him? What a waste that would be, because she would be waiting for nothing. Once he left here, he could never come back.

Unless he did as she asked. Turned himself in. Went to prison. Served his time. One day in the distant future—if he lived long enough—they would let him go and he could come back here. *If* she waited. *If* she still wanted him. Hell, he wouldn't even have to wait that long to see her. They had visiting days in prison; a lot of them even made arrangements for conjugal visits. Ashley could take her chances on the road with Bessie every month or two or three, get herself all prettied up and drop in at the prison for a few hours' stilted conversation and a desperate fumble and grope behind bars. Wouldn't that be a terrific offer to make to a woman like her?

He would rather never see her again than see her in a shameful place like that.

Shaking away the grim thoughts, he unfastened the big brass buckle, then drew the belt from its loops and laid it on the night table atop his sling. Next he pulled her shirt free of the denim skirt, the cotton gliding smoothly along her skin. The shirt was white, a nice contrast to the pale golden hue of her skin, and the style was masculine, copied from a man's dress shirt, emphasizing the very decidedly feminine curve of her breasts and the narrowness of her waist. The buttons opened easily; in only a moment the two sides of the shirt were separated, revealing a strip of soft bare skin all the way down to her waist.

He had the answer to his question. She was naked underneath the shirt.

Now he owed her an answer that he couldn't give last night. Sliding his fingers over that strip of skin, he brought his hands to her throat, then her face. "You're a beautiful woman, Ash, more beautiful than any woman I've ever known.''

Her smile was bright, teasing and just the slightest bit unsteady. ''More beautiful than Pris?''

''I told you—Pris is pretty. You—you make a man feel weak. You're the strongest woman I've ever known, but just looking at you makes me want to protect you. You're sweet and lovely and delicate and tough, and you take my breath away.''

Leaning forward, she kissed him. There was nothing tentative or hesitant about it. Her mouth connected with his; her tongue stroked inside. He was feeling little shocks all through his body when, as quickly as she'd begun, she ended the kiss. ''You could have told me that last night when I asked.''

''Last night?'' He buried his hands in her hair, feeling it settle cool and silky around his fingers. ''When I was lying in bed praying that you would quit tempting and tormenting me while I still had some small measure of willpower left? When I was seriously considering using the handcuffs on myself because *maybe,* just maybe, they would keep me away from you?''

''Tempting and tormenting...'' Vague bewilderment was replaced by shameless satisfaction. ''You mean when I put your hand on my breast.''

''I mean when you sat in front of the fire and brushed your hair. The way you looked. The way you moved. Even the way you breathed.'' He chuckled softly. ''You were seducing me then, and you didn't even know it.''

''I'm trying to seduce you now, but you don't seem to know it.''

He sobered. ''I know, Ash. God help me, I know.'' Sliding his hands down, he caught the shirt and guided it along her arms until it was free and fell to the floor, a puddle of bright white on the dark woven rug. *Beautiful.* He hated to overuse the word, but he couldn't think of any other to describe the way she looked standing there, her hair mussed, naked to the waist, the firelight gleaming on her skin. So beautiful.

He reached out, almost touched her but not quite, his hand hovering only a fraction of an inch from her breast. "You know, don't you," he began, his voice so hoarse that it scratched his throat, "that this is going to destroy me."

The certainty in his voice made Ashley's heart ache. She longed to protect him, to draw him close, to hold him tight and keep him safe for the rest of their lives. All she did, though, was touch him, brushing her fingers just barely across his jaw. "Maybe not," she whispered. "Maybe it will heal us both."

For a moment he stood there, his hand less than a breath away, then he touched her. Her nipple hardened instantly, with no more than his light caress, and the ache around her heart seeped out in every direction, making her tremble. She wanted to let her head fall, to close her eyes and lose herself in the sweet sensations he was creating, but even more she wanted to look at him while he touched her. They would have so little together—tonight, maybe tomorrow, maybe even, if she was very lucky and fate was feeling kindly, tomorrow night. She wanted to remember every detail about every moment. She wanted to see every expression that crossed his face and softened his dark eyes. The desire. The need. The hunger. The pain. She wanted always, for as long as she lived, to remember his face.

With gentle touches, he guided her to the bed, laid her down on her grandmother's Double Wedding Ring quilt, then joined her there. Supporting himself on his left arm, with his right hand he stroked her, tender caresses that, because of the stiffness and pain in his shoulder, should have been awkward and clumsy but were nothing less than exquisite. They spread heat through her body, made her breasts swell and her nipples ache, stirred a desire deep in her belly that was unfamiliar in its intensity. The acts were nothing new—Seth had touched her, and so had the only other man in her life—but the results . . . They were different. Stunning. Breathstealing.

"Your skin is so soft," he murmured.

Her smile trembled. "Aloe and evening primrose oil."

"You smell so sweet."

"Honeysuckle." Now her voice was trembling, too, and her breathing had grown unsteady.

He ducked his head, placing kisses between her breasts, then breathed deeply. "Chamomile," he disagreed. "Every time I take a bath, I reach for the honeysuckle because it smells like you, but I always put it back because smelling like you would surely drive me insane. Now you've switched to chamomile and that will also drive me crazy."

Raising her hand to stroke his hair, she shook her head dazedly from side to side. "No, it would relax you. The scent of chamomile brings tranquility."

"I've been many things since the minute I walked into your clearing, but, honey, tranquil isn't one of them."

His teeth closed around her nipple in a tender bite, bringing a gasp of sharp pleasure from her and, at the same time, a low groan from him. He suckled her breast, drawing hard on her nipple, and her muscles twitched and tightened. Lower, his leg was hooked over hers, his hardness pressing against her thigh. Heavy denim separated them—her skirt, his jeans—but she could feel the heat, the length, of him. She could feel that simple, strong evidence of his need, and it made her greedy. It made her throb.

His kisses moved from one breast to the other, then across her ribs, lower, slower, until the skirt blocked his way. She watched as he slid down on the bed, finding the hem of the skirt, then working his way up, unfastening each button, pushing the fabric aside, frequently diverting his attention to a light touch across her thigh or her hip or drawing his fingers, just the very tips, across the pale cotton of her panties in an achingly intimate caress.

At last he opened the final button. Rising to his knees, he pulled the denim out from underneath her, dropped it over the side of the bed, then removed her last bit of clothing, following his progress with a trail of damp kisses—on her stomach, her hip, her thigh, the inside of her knee and all the way down her calf. Sitting back, for a moment he simply looked at her, and in the heartbeat and ragged breaths that filled her ears, she thought she heard him murmur one soft, gratifying word. "Beautiful."

She reached for him, both arms stretching out. "Please, Dillon..."

Grasping the hem of his sweatshirt, he started to strip it off, but stopped halfway through the motion. His expression was a mix of pain, impatience and embarrassment as she sat up and pushed his hands away. "Let me." But she didn't go straight to the task. She glided her hands underneath the fabric, bunching it, then bent to kiss his chest, bruises, scrapes and all, pausing only briefly to flick her tongue across his nipple, wondering if her mouth felt as heart-weakeningly good to him as his mouth had felt on her body.

Reaching his shoulders, she eased his left arm free of the shirt, then carefully worked it over his head and off his other arm. The dressing on his right shoulder was a reminder that his arm couldn't support even a fraction of his weight, that his bruised ribs, though much improved, also required special consideration. But that was all right. Though there was something tremendously appealing about lying underneath him—her body sheltering his while his, in turn, sheltered hers, his weight pressing against her as they moved together, arms and legs entwined—the options were terribly erotic, too. It didn't matter *how* they did it. All that mattered was that they did.

Advancing on her knees, she nudged him toward the edge of the bed. "Stand up," she whispered, her hands seeking and finding the button, then the zipper, of his faded jeans. Her fingers were suddenly clumsy, resulting in a great deal of fumbling that made him suck in his breath, then groan aloud.

"Ash..." There was a note of warning in his voice. "Don't play games or you're going to make me—" He groaned again as she opened his jeans and slid one hand inside. The muscles across his belly quivered as she explored lower, finding his arousal with a feathery light caress. Suddenly he grabbed her wrist, but he didn't pull her hand away. Instead, he pressed her palm hard against him. "Now, Ash."

Yes. *Now*. She freed her hand, and together they removed the last of his clothing, then he joined her on the bed again, and again he hesitated. "I don't know if I can..."

"*We* can," she whispered. Hands on his shoulders, she gently pushed him onto his back, then bent low for a kiss. His mouth was hot, his tongue bold. His hands, moving in heated caresses, were even bolder, rubbing her breasts, across her stomach, in hot, steady strokes between her thighs.

"Take me inside you, Ash." His effort to retain some bit of control tightened his jaw, making his voice thick and raw, and beaded sweat across his forehead. "I want to be inside you...."

She moved into place above him, seeking, guiding, sinking, taking him exactly where he wanted to be, where she needed him to be. He filled her, stretched her, made her feel more whole than she ever had before. He made her feel stronger, more alive, more womanly, more beautiful. For the first time in her life she *felt* beautiful, because of this incredibly beautiful man.

This incredibly beautiful and deeply loved man.

She closed her eyes on that last part. She had plenty of time ahead of her to think about loving him and losing him and living alone. Countless hours, endless nights. Tonight she wanted to focus on *this,* on the physical, on their bodies joined together, on the hunger and the arousal, the need, the sensation, the pleasure, the throbbing, the burning. She wanted to feel it all, wanted to make it all a part of her, a treasured memory that she could take out and relive when she had to make it through another lonely night.

His hands were on her thighs, moving restlessly, silently urging her to move, and she did, settling into an easy rhythm, taking him deeper, harder, feeding his arousal stroke by stroke, making him hotter, until, with harsh breathing and a harsher groan, he stiffened, went motionless for an instant, then filled her. She didn't stop, though, didn't give him a chance to catch his breath, didn't wait for the overload of sensation to become manageable, but continued thrusting against him, withdrawing, sheathing him

again within her body. As he stroked her breasts, her
thighs, any part of her that he could reach, he whispered
soft words, erotic sounds, coaxing her, tempting her, encouraging her. Unable to resist the pure, sweet pleasure a
moment longer, she gave in to it, too, and through it all, her
gaze was locked on his face.

His sweet, beautiful and very much beloved face.

"It *was* Russell Bradley."

Dillon hadn't been sure before he spoke that Ashley was
awake; she lay so still in his arms. But the instant she understood his words, the muscles all up and down her body
tightened, and he knew she was totally alert and waiting for
more. With a weary sigh, he told her everything.

"I was surprised when Russ offered me a job. I hadn't
seen him in years. We lost touch when he joined the navy
after high school and just happened to run into each other
when he was visiting Atlanta. We'd grown up together, but
you couldn't tell it by looking at us. He was wearing an expensive suit and gold jewelry, driving a seventy-thousand-
dollar import and having meetings at his convenience with
corporate CEOs, and I was strictly blue jeans, blue-collar.
I was working as a mechanic—not exactly a high-tech, fast-
track, big-money career. It was probably my tenth job in
ten years, and I was barely getting by, so when he called a
couple of weeks later and offered me a job in Asheville, I
took it. I moved there, settled in, learned the business—"

Ashley rolled onto her side, her head pillowed on his
arm. "Met Pris."

Without looking, he heard the lighthearted teasing in her
voice. If nothing else, the past few hours had at least convinced her that he didn't find her lacking compared to his
old girlfriend. "And met Pris. For the first time in my life,
things seemed to be coming together. I was making good
money, I liked my job, I had a nice place to live and a
good—"

He broke off for a moment, rubbing the soft underside
of her breast as he considered his next word. Just yesterday he'd insisted that he didn't have relationships, only af-

fairs, sometimes only anonymous one-night encounters, but that wasn't entirely true. It certainly wasn't true of Pris. He hadn't been in love with her and didn't think he ever would have loved her, but he had liked and respected her. What they'd had wasn't exactly a romance—Ashley was very possibly the only romance meant for his life—but it had been more than an affair.

"I had a good relationship with Pris," he said at last, and Ashley patted his stomach.

"That wasn't so hard to say, was it?" she gently teased. "Next time we'll work on a harder phrase, something like 'I trust you.'"

Or maybe one like *I love you,* he thought grimly. Resolutely drawing back from even the idea, he picked up the threads of his tale again. "My life was stable, routine and perfectly normal...until the Catlin job came up."

"When did Bradley tell you that he intended to rob the bank?"

"That night last April after I'd already done it." He sighed again, hating this story, wishing he didn't have to tell it to her. But she deserved this much. After everything she'd given him, everything she'd done for him, she deserved to know the truth. "I know now that Russell had never intended for me to get so good at my job. I was supposed to just learn the basics. I *wasn't* supposed to become so familiar with the systems that I could recognize a problem. The problem with the one we were installing in the First American Bank and Trust of Catlin was that it wasn't sufficient to meet the bank's needs. Any fool who knew anything about alarm systems could bypass that particular system. There's not a bank in the country with such an inadequate security setup."

"You told your boss that, and he said—"

"'Prove it. Prove to me that it can be done. Show me how it can be done.' So I did. I made very detailed notes, just as he asked."

"The notes that were found in your room at the boarding house."

He nodded, his chin bumping the top of her head. "I can't believe I was such an idiot. I've been a screwup all my life, but this was particularly stupid, even for me."

Ashley pulled out of his arms and sat up, turning on the bed to face him. He liked that she was all soft from their lovemaking, especially liked that she was still naked but made no effort to hide herself from him. She sat unself-consciously, her back straight, her legs tucked beneath her. "Come on, Dillon, don't be so hard on yourself. You were following your boss's orders. With ten jobs in ten years, maybe this comes as a surprise to you—" she smiled to take the sting from her words "—but that's what employees are supposed to do."

"Not when following orders leads to a crime."

Her smile faded and her expression grew serious and intent. "Your notes didn't convince him, right? So you asked, 'What do I have to do to prove this?' and he said, 'Break in and bring me proof. Bring me...'" She fell silent, no doubt replaying one of the previous days' conversations in her head, finding the little bit of information she wanted. "'Bring me five thousand dollars to prove that you were in the vault. If you can do that, we'll upgrade the system and fix the problem.'"

He nodded. That was exactly what he'd done. They had settled on that Wednesday evening for no particular reason except that the job had been finished that morning. The other techs had already returned to Asheville; only Dillon had remained behind. He had waited for the bank to close that evening, had gone to the café for dinner and had taken a leisurely walk around town, thinking all kinds of idiot thoughts, like what a nice little town Catlin was. Small-town America, Ashley had called it. A perfect place to settle down, if you could find a job that paid a living wage, and raise a family. He'd been thinking about Pris and how nice it would be to see her again, to make love to her again. About his job, how much he liked what he was doing, how good he had turned out to be at it and how grateful he was to Russell for giving him the chance.

Grateful. He gave a derisive snort at the memory.

''Russ said he would clear it with Bill Armstrong. A day or two later, he gave me the go-ahead. I made sure everyone had left the bank for the day, then I did exactly what I had told Russell I would. I circumvented the system, including the security cameras, let myself into the vault and took the five thousand dollars. I drove back to Asheville, where he was waiting for me in his office, and I gave him the money. I didn't stop at the boarding house to pick up my stuff. I knew that, as soon as Russ saw that I was right, we would be going back to work at the bank again, so I figured why bother.''

''What happened?'' she asked when he didn't immediately go on.

''Armstrong was supposed to be at the meeting with Russ, but he wasn't. He was in Catlin. In the bank. Russ called him, told him that I was there with five thousand of the bank's dollars, told him to go ahead as planned and take the rest of the money, then notify the sheriff that the bank had been robbed.''

She was silent and still for a long time. Had he lost her with that last part? Had she been willing to believe everything he'd said until he'd implicated Bill Armstrong? She had known Armstrong all her life. Along with her ex-husband's family, the Armstrongs made up the upper class of Catlin society. It was one thing for her to believe that Russell Bradley, a complete stranger, was involved in the robbery. It was another altogether for Dillon to ask her to believe that a man she knew and probably considered a friend was also involved.

He waited uneasily for her response, for skepticism, a denial, an accusation that he was lying. When it finally came, it was better than he could have hoped for, provided he had been able to hope at all.

''So Bill Armstrong robbed his own bank,'' she murmured. ''I always thought he was an insufferably arrogant man. So he's a crook, too. He and Bradley set you up.''

He reached for her, pulling her down beside him again. ''Hell, yes, darlin', they set me up. I made it so easy for them.''

"Why did you run? Why didn't you stay and tell your story then? Seth would have listened. He would have investigated your claims right along with theirs. Running just made you look guilty."

"Stay and tell Seth my story? You think it would have been that simple?" Even though she was entirely serious, he laughed anyway. "And what would I have said? 'Yes, Sheriff Benedict, I *am* the world's biggest loser. I can't hold a job *or* a woman, I've spent most of my life in one sort of trouble or another and I have an arrest record going back to when I was nine years old. And, yes, Bill Armstrong and Russell Bradley *are* upstanding citizens and highly respected businessmen, but I'm telling you the truth when I say that *they* robbed the bank, not me. *I* only broke in— *they* took the money.' And you think he would have believed me? You think he wouldn't have slapped the handcuffs on me and sent me off to prison as quickly as he could?"

"He would have looked into it," she insisted stuburnly. "When you disappeared, it was only natural for everyone to think you'd taken all that money. But if you'd had any faith in the system . . ."

He interrupted her with a quieting touch. "It's easy for you to talk about having faith in the system. You've never been in trouble. People have always liked and respected you. If you said something was so, they would believe you." He stared up at the rafters and the dried herbs hanging there. "When I was nine, one of my father's sons— Alex, the one whose name I share—cornered me on the playground at school and beat the tar out of me. When the principal broke it up, Alex said it was my fault. He said I had started it, that he had only defended himself. Keep in mind he was three years older than me, five or six inches taller and a good twenty pounds heavier. The extent of his injuries was a tear in his shirt. My shirt was torn, too. I also had a black eye, a bloody nose, two teeth knocked out, a busted lip and more bruises, bleeding and swelling than you can imagine. Do you want to guess who the principal believed? Who got suspended from school? Whose mother had to pay practically a week's salary to replace the little bastard's shirt?''

She didn't say anything. She just turned onto her side to face him, wrapped her arms around him and held him tightly. It was such a simple gesture, just an embrace, nothing more, but it made his chest grow tight and stirred a longing that left him feeling empty inside.

Closing his eyes, he breathed deeply and smelled her scents combined with his own. "We've lived different lives, Ash," he said quietly. "I've always had to prove myself. No one but my grandfather ever had much faith in me, and I learned not to have faith in anyone else. Yes, running made me look guilty, but I didn't see that I had any choice. In my experience, cops, more than anyone else, need proof, and all the proof, all the evidence in the bank robbery, pointed to me. Maybe Seth would have been different. Maybe he would have listened. Maybe he even would have looked for proof, but these are two intelligent men. I doubt they left even the smallest clue to implicate themselves.''

"You're an intelligent man, too." Her voice was muffled against his chest.

"No, I'm not. But I'm smart enough to know when I've been beaten. If I thought there was a chance that I could clear my name and stay out of prison, I'd go into town tomorrow and tell Seth everything. But there's no chance at all that Russ and Bill Armstrong are going to let me do that. If I try, I'm dead.''

Tilting her head back, she stared at him in the dim light. "And if you don't try, then what? You live the rest of your life as a fugitive. That is, assuming that they don't track you down and kill you anyway. You can't let them win, Dillon. You can't—''

Twisting toward her, he cut off her argument with a kiss. She made a frustrated sound that quickly turned into a soft sigh of submission. When at last he gave her a chance to catch her breath, she sighed again. "You're a wicked man, Dillon, trying to distract me like that.''

"Like what?" He kissed her again, quickly, hungrily. "This?" He cupped her breast in his palm, teasing her nipple until it was hard and swollen. "Or like this?" Ducking his head, he drew his tongue across it, slowly, hard, creating an unbearably pleasurable friction. "Or maybe like this?" His caresses and kisses moved lower on her body, across her ribs, spanning her waist, following the curve of her hip. He settled between her legs, bracing himself on one arm while, with his free hand, he treated her to a series of lazy, intimate caresses that made her back arch, the muscles in her thighs straining.

"Dillon..." Her voice was barely a whisper, harsh and throaty. Erotic.

"Do you find this distracting?" He slipped one finger inside her, then another, feeling her heat and the dampness that had come from both her own body and his. Her body clenched and tightened, and she tried once more to speak, but the sound faded into a gasp, then a low, husky moan.

You can't let them win, she'd said, but she was wrong. He couldn't do anything *but* let them win. He couldn't do anything but leave, try to stay alive and hope that his leaving kept *her* alive. He couldn't do anything but sacrifice the rest of his life, all those years that he could have spent here with her.

Except for *this*. Tonight he could bring her pleasure. He could make love with her. He could forget about Bradley and Armstrong, could put them out of his mind and give her a few hours of normalcy, of intimacy, of love, and he could pray that it would be enough. For her.

And for him.

Chapter 9

Ashley woke up early Saturday morning, momentarily disoriented until she realized the weight across her ribs was Dillon's arm and remembered why she was in her own bed and not on a pallet on the floor. Twisting onto her side, she faced him, watching him sleep, committing every detail of his face to memory. The relaxed line of his mouth. The graceful curve of his lashes. The way his hair fell across his forehead. The shadow of his beard across his jaw. It made him look sinister, she'd told him earlier, but she knew now that she'd been wrong. *Wicked* was a much better word, much more accurate. Yes, indeed, he looked incredibly wicked unshaven.

Raising her hand, she drew one fingertip lightly across his lips. His muscles twitched and, without waking, he brushed her away, then turned his head to the other side. Blowing out her breath in a heavy sigh, she eased from the bed, dressing quickly in the clothing she'd discarded the night before. She added logs to the fire, put a pot of water on the stove to boil, then put on socks and shoes. Five minutes later, wearing her parka and carrying a mug of hot tea, she slipped silently out the door and made herself comfortable in the rocker on the porch.

The sun wasn't up yet, though the eastern sky was already lightening. Once the sun rose high, it would burn off the mists and heat the air to a comfortably warm spring temperature. It would finish the job of drying out the land ... and Bessie's distributor. Unless Ashley's prayers were answered and the rains returned, there was little doubt that the van would be ready to go as early as this afternoon, ready to start Dillon on a journey that would take him out of her life.

She wasn't sure she was ready for that.

She felt like such a liar. She had told him right here on the porch last night that she understood that he would leave her, that she accepted the fact that she would never see him again. She had promised that she wouldn't ask for anything else beyond those few hours in her bed—no commitment, no future.

This morning her heart couldn't understand why he had to leave her; her soul couldn't accept never seeing him again. This morning, more than anything else in the world, she *needed* a commitment from him and a future with him. And she knew only one way to get them: if he turned himself in.

Or if *she* turned him in.

Drawing her feet onto the seat of the rocker, she tucked her skirt around her bare legs, then wrapped both hands around the mug for warmth. She could do it—could find some excuse for going into town today, could talk to Seth, could repeat everything Dillon had told her last night. Seth was no fan of Dillon's, but at the same time, he was no fan of Bill Armstrong's, either. He hadn't liked the banker before the robbery and liked him even less now. He'd taken a lot of grief from Armstrong about his department's inability to locate Dillon. If he had even the faintest suspicion that Armstrong had been ragging him about a crime that *he* had committed, Seth would certainly investigate, and he wouldn't stop until he either found evidence to support his suspicions or was positive beyond a doubt that Armstrong wasn't guilty.

Ashley could plant those seeds of suspicion.

If she dared. If she was willing to face the risks. If she was ready to accept responsibility for possibly sending Dillon to prison. If she told Seth, and he was unable to find any evidence implicating Bradley and Armstrong—evidence Dillon insisted would be too well protected to be discovered—then Dillon would remain the one and only suspect. Seth might not arrest him immediately, might wait until the investigation was complete and the other men cleared, but he would never allow Dillon to escape again.

But if she told Seth and he *was* able to put together a case against the other men... The rewards could be rich. Dillon could stay in Catlin. He could make a home and a life for himself right here. She could take that long look years ahead and see the two of them, living, working and raising a family together.

But what if *he* didn't share the same vision? What if she deceived him, turned him in, helped him clear his name and get the charges against him dropped and he still wanted to leave her? What if he returned to Asheville and to Pris or went home to Atlanta or headed out west anyway to try to put to rest memories of the worst time of his life?

He had never hinted or indicated in any way that he wanted to stay with her. Even last night when they'd made love, the closest he'd come to a declaration of emotion had been right after he'd removed her shirt. *You're sweet and lovely and delicate and tough, and you take my breath away.* As sweet as the sentiment was, it was a long way from *I love you.*

So those were her options. She could help him escape, thereby putting his life in danger, and never see him again. She could turn him in, and he might go to prison or he might be cleared of any wrongdoing. In that case, maybe he would stay with her, love her and never leave her. Maybe he would hate her for risking his freedom and betraying his trust, would leave her and never forgive her. Maybe he would be grateful for her help but would leave her anyway because, as he'd pointed out, she wasn't his kind of woman.

Every outcome but one would break her heart, but there was only one she couldn't live with. She couldn't watch him take off again, damned to a shadowy existence, unable to trust anyone, unable to let down his guard even for a moment, always knowing that there were people looking for him who wanted him dead. He was an innocent man, and he deserved to live like one. He deserved a home, a wife, a family, a job. He deserved to live his life with dignity. The only way he could have those things was to stop running, to stand up to Russell Bradley and Bill Armstrong, to trust in Seth and the justice system to clear his name. Surrendering was the best action he could take, whether he believed it or not.

Besides, she *had* to tell Seth about Steven Vickers.

A few feet away, the door creaked as it opened, but wisely Dillon didn't step out. She could see him—mussed hair, a lot of bare skin, a sleepy, contented look—through the wedge of the open door. "You're up early," he said in greeting.

Summoning a smile from all the worry inside her, she let her shoes hit the floor with a thump, then got to her feet. Just in case there were curious eyes that she couldn't see, she didn't speak until she was in the doorway, her back to the world. "Good morning." After closing the door behind her, she set the tea down, shrugged out of her parka, then moved into his embrace. He smelled of heat, soft sheets and herbs, and he felt . . .

Her smile against his chest was just a little sad. He felt like the other half of her.

With his hands in her hair, he tilted her head back and studied her face, his eyes dark and intense, his expression thoughtful. After one moment and then another, she shifted uncomfortably and asked, "What are you looking for?"

"Regrets."

"Do you see any?"

"No. I don't think I do."

With a smug smile, she cupped her palms to his cheeks, then leaned forward for a kiss. "That's because I don't have any. Listen, Dillon..." Her smile quivered before disappearing. "I need to go into town."

He went utterly still for a moment, then, reaching up and catching hold of her wrists, he pulled her hands from his face and clasped them tightly in his. "Why?"

"To get some money from the automatic teller. To let Seth know that I'm okay so he doesn't come up here to see. To find out where the roadblocks are and how many there are."

He wanted to say no. She could see it in his eyes. No arguments, no discussions, no leaving, no way. But clearly struggling with that desire, instead he offered a cautious response. "You can get the money tomorrow on our—our way out of town." His falter was slight, barely noticeable—but *she* noticed. "The roadblocks don't matter, and if Seth comes up here, you'll just have to keep him outside, then send him on his way. You did it the other day. You can do it again."

"The bank, you may recall, is directly across the street from the sheriff's department," she gently reminded him. "I would really prefer to not park out front there and leave you hiding in the van while I get money from the machine. You're right, I probably can distract Seth if he comes up here again, but I don't want to take any chances. And, sweetheart, the roadblocks *do* matter. They're the biggest obstacle to your getting out of here safely."

He continued to look at her, his gaze still searching her face, but it wasn't regrets he was looking for this time. He was seeking some sign that he could trust her, and it made her heart ache to know that, if he offered his trust, she would simply turn around and betray it. Would it make a difference to him that the end result would, with God's blessing, be his freedom? Would he care that she was only doing what she believed in her soul to be right for him? She hoped so. She prayed so.

When he released her and turned away, she felt his rejection more strongly than ever before. She didn't move but

simply stood there, staring down at the floor, a welcome
numbness slowly filtering through her. Then, from across
the room, with his back to her, he finally spoke, and she
understood that it wasn't *her* he'd turned away from but
himself. He'd sworn to never again do what he was about
to do, and he wasn't happy that he was doing it now. He
wasn't convinced that he wasn't making the biggest mistake of his life.

Neither was she.

"All right," he said, his voice quiet, self-reproachful and
tentatively—very tentatively—trusting. "When do you
want to go?"

"What about the key?"

Ashley looked up from the shoe that she was tying and
grinned. "I'll take a quick look through the weeds, but if I
don't find it, it's no big deal."

Dillon's scowl deepened in proportion to her grin. "No
big deal? How are you going to drive Bessie without keys?"

"I'll hot-wire it."

"You know how to do that," he said skeptically.

She replied with such innocence that he couldn't help
grinning, too. "Of course. Doesn't everyone?"

"*I* don't. Let me guess. Seth taught you."

"No. My granny. She was always losing her keys." The
smile grew brighter until just looking at her made him hurt.
He'd never known anyone with a smile like that. He wished
he could capture it on film, for all those future nights when
he would need some way to connect with her, when he
would need something more than cold, distant memories to
hold close. But he'd seen no sign of a camera, and it didn't
matter anyway, because no flat, two-dimensional photograph could ever do her justice.

Besides, he would never forget.

"Your granny must have been a resourceful woman," he
said quietly. "You take after her."

The compliment pleased her far more than it should
have, but he understood. She felt the same things for her
grandmother that he felt for his grandfather, and he

couldn't think of any greater compliment in the world than being compared favorably to Jacob Boone.

She gave her shoelaces one last tug, then stood up. She had changed into a dress after this morning's bath, a cotton print with short, fluttery sleeves and a shaped neckline that curved above her breasts before dipping low in the center to reveal just a hint of cleavage. It was loose, flowing and thoroughly feminine...even with the ragg-wool socks and moss green hiking boots she wore. She looked beautiful.

"Dressing up for Seth?" he asked, making no effort to camouflage the jealousy in his voice.

"Dressing up for *you,*" she replied, coming around the table to take his hand.

"I'd rather you *un*dress for me."

For a moment she looked so serious, so wistful. He wondered if she was thinking about tomorrow, when she would take him to Nashville, or if she was considering all the time they couldn't have together, all the things they couldn't do together. Then the moment passed, and she shook off the somber mood and smiled. It wasn't a very good smile, more than a little on the sad side. "Maybe when I get back," she said quietly. Leaning forward, she pressed a kiss to one cheek, then the other, finally reaching his mouth.

Long before he was ready for it to end, she drew away and started toward the door. There she paused and looked back at him. "Dillon..."

He waited for her to go on. She fumbled with the doorknob, moved her purse from one arm to the other, met his gaze, then looked away a half-dozen times. At last, with a deep breath, she went on. "Stay away from the windows and lock the door behind me. I'll try not to take too long. Is there anything special you'd like from town?"

Disappointed because that *wasn't* what she'd started to say, he shook his head. He watched as she walked out, closing the door behind her, then did exactly what she'd warned him against. He went to the nearest window, stood off to one side and lifted the sheet there just enough to see out.

With such easy grace, she crossed the clearing to the patch of weeds, where only a moment's search yielded her keys. He liked the way she moved. Whether she was cooking or washing dishes, weaving baskets, nursing his wounds, brushing her hair or simply walking ... He was fascinated by it all. He was fascinated by *her*.

He was afraid he was in love with her.

She climbed into the van, and through the glass he heard the engine crank and sputter before catching. It was badly in need of a tune-up. Given the time, the parts and the proper tools, he could have it running like new—or at least more smoothly—in no time. But he didn't have the parts or the proper tools, and he damned sure didn't have the time.

Letting the sheet fall as she turned the van in a tight circle in the clearing, he locked the door, then went to the chair where she did her needlework at night and slumped down, his feet stretched out in front of him.

Yes, he was in love with her. He wished he could deny it, wished he could write the feelings off as a peculiar mix of lust, gratitude and affection, but he would only be lying to himself. Granted, for his age he had little experience with loving or being loved, but he knew it for what it was. He could identify it by its very absence the better part of his life.

How many times in his life had he thought that maybe *this* would be the time he would fall in love? *This* would be a relationship, not an affair. *This* would be forever and always. Every new relationship had always held the possibilities; every new woman had always held the promise. But after a date or two or maybe three, he had always realized that it wasn't the right time or the right woman. He had even started to wonder if maybe there was nothing wrong with his timing or his choice of women, if maybe the problem was with *him*. Maybe, he'd thought, he just wasn't meant to fall in love.

Apparently he'd been wrong.

Blowing out a sigh, he reached into the basket next to the chair for her needlework. The fabric was white, rolled tight around the two long bars of the frame that held it. She had finished less than half of the scene, and the sections she'd done weren't always adjacent, but there was enough to get the general picture. It was a mountain scene, looking out across green valleys that rose into treetopped peaks, then dipped low into more distant valleys, with houses tucked here and there, fields being tilled, cattle grazing, kids playing. Clouds filled the blue sky, and high above, a brilliantly colored hot-air balloon drifted over the tallest peak. Like everything else she did, it was neat, impressive and beautifully done. She was an incredibly talented woman.

And he was going to miss her when he was gone, more than he had ever missed anyone, even his grandfather.

His finger hovering a trace above the fabric, he followed a line of trees from end to end, careful not to touch the stitches or the canvas. The shadings of green were so subtle that he couldn't actually tell where one color gave way to another, but he could easily see the depths and dimensions they created.

It was appropriate that she was putting so much time and energy into a mountain scene. He had meant it last night when he'd insisted that she belonged there on her granny's farm at the top of the mountain. Try as he might, he couldn't imagine her in any city, not even Raleigh, where he knew she'd once lived. She was as inextricably bound to this land and this place as Jacob had been to *his* land. The old man had been born on his farm, and he had died there. Sometimes—most of the time—it had been a real struggle for him to keep things going, but he'd never given up. He couldn't have, because losing his land would have meant losing a part of himself. Without it he would have withered away and died.

All his life Dillon had wanted to belong to something—or someone—that way. "Be careful what you wish for," the old saying went, "because you just might get it." Well, now that he had his wish, now that he'd found both a place and a woman he could belong to, he no longer wanted it. Ash-

ley and her damned farm complicated things. They made
him want to stay. They made him want to take his chances,
face up to his troubles and try to make a life for himself
here. But facing up to his troubles meant one of only two
things, and he was neither ready to die nor willing to go to
prison. That meant he had to get out, had to head west
where no one knew him. Leaving Ashley behind meant his
life wouldn't be worth living.

But it beat the alternative. Staying meant he wouldn't
even have a life to live.

I love you.

That was what Ashley had been about to say when she'd
stopped on her way out of the cabin. She had come within
a deep breath of making a declaration to Dillon that
couldn't be taken back. A vow that he might have appreciated at the time, but that probably wouldn't have meant
anything to him later, after he found out what she'd done
in town. He would hate her once he understood that she'd
turned him in, and he wouldn't believe anything she'd ever
said. He wouldn't trust her again.

He would *never* love her.

Maybe she should forget her plan. Maybe she should do
exactly what she'd told him she would, then go back home.
Fix dinner. Make love. Plan for the trip to Nashville. Say
goodbye. Forever.

Forever. She was only twenty-nine years old. She couldn't
even comprehend how long *forever* would be. She couldn't
begin to understand what it would be like living *forever*
alone, with unbearable loneliness, intolerable sorrow and
the emptiness of never knowing where Dillon was, what he
was doing or if he was even alive.

Only twenty-nine years old, and incredibly selfish. Her
future, or lack of, wasn't the issue. It was *his* future at risk,
his very *life* in danger. If he didn't mind living the rest of it
as a fugitive, what right did she have to interfere? Taking
him in and nursing him didn't give her that right. Making
love with him last night didn't. Even falling in love with him
didn't.

But he *did* mind living as a fugitive. He hated it, he'd told her last night. He was a good man who deserved a better fate than he'd been dealt. All he wanted was a normal life, and clearing his name could give him that. Even if he chose not to spend that life with her, she still wanted him to have it.

Scowling, she pulled into a parking space in front of the courthouse. Seth's Blazer was parked in the sheriff's reserved spot to her left. She hadn't been sure she would find him in the office this afternoon, but the dispatcher always knew how to reach him. She would have tracked him down if necessary.

Climbing out of the van, she slammed the door and turned not toward the courthouse but across the street instead. If something went wrong—if Seth didn't believe her, if Dillon somehow got away again—she wanted him to have enough money to get by until he was out of the area.

As soon as she'd withdrawn the daily limit from her savings account, she tucked the cash into her bag, then crossed the street once more. The courthouse, built of native stone, was closed on weekends, but there was a small side entrance that led to the sheriff's department on the first floor. She hurried up the steps, passing a state trooper who held the door for her.

Seth was alone, as she'd hoped. The dispatcher, who doubled as receptionist, desk sergeant and surrogate mother, sent her on back before returning her attention to the magazine in front of her.

When she walked unannounced into the small office at the back, her ex-husband was studying a large map that filled the available wall space between the filing cabinets and the window. Entire areas around her place had been marked off—as searched and done with, she fervently hoped. The last thing she needed was for a search party to show up at the cabin this afternoon while she was away. Practically everyone out there had known her all of her life; when they saw that her van was gone and that the padlock that secured the door when she left was also gone, most of them wouldn't think twice about letting themselves into the cabin to search it. And when the door wouldn't open because Dillon had locked it from the inside...

She grimly shook away the thought. "Hey, Seth."

He glanced over his shoulder, then turned to face her. "What brings you into town?"

"I needed some groceries." If it wasn't exactly the truth, it wasn't a lie, either. She *had* stopped at the grocery store and stocked up on milk, eggs and fresh bananas. She had also splurged on the best steaks in the whole meat department, a bottle of the finest wine the store had to offer—which, unfortunately, wasn't particularly fine—and one of Mary Lou's special German chocolate cakes in the bakery. If tonight *was* her last night with Dillon, she wanted it to be special, from the dinner straight through to the lovemaking. "You look tired."

"Twenty-hour workdays will do that to you." He gestured toward the chair in front of his desk as he sat down in the one behind it. "Everything okay up at your place?"

"Yeah." She rested her hands on the back of the wooden chair, but she couldn't bring herself to sit. She wanted to pace, but she couldn't do that, either, for lack of room.

Whatever she did in the next few minutes—pumping Seth for information about the roadblocks so she could help his prisoner escape or betraying Dillon's trust—was going to be very wrong. She wished she could just say goodbye and leave, but that would be wrong, too. So, drawing a deep breath, she chose the wrong that just might, with any luck, come closest to being right. "How is Tom?"

Seth's expression darkened. "Still the same. I'm worried about him, Ashley. I don't suppose you have any remedies that the doctors over there at Duke don't know about."

Her smile came and went. "I'm afraid comas are a little out of my field. Have you seen him?"

"I haven't had time. I've been staying here coordinating this blasted search." He gestured toward the map. "Do you have any idea how long it takes to search *one* acre of land up there? In places you could walk within five feet of a person and never know he was there."

"You think he's still in the county."

"He was hurt, and the weather's been terrible. He couldn't have gone too far." He shrugged. "I don't know. Maybe he's dead. Maybe we won't find his body until summer, when the hikers are out in force. Maybe we'll never find it."

She knotted her fingers together and fixed her gaze on her knuckles, turning shades of white, purple and red. "He's not dead."

"If his injuries from the crash didn't kill him, the lack of food coupled with exposure—" Abruptly he broke off. She knew he was staring at her by the heat of guilt that was spreading through her. "How do you know that, Ashley? How do you know he's not dead?"

Suddenly the idea of sitting seemed much more appealing. In fact, she was pretty sure her legs were going to give way if she didn't take her weight off them immediately. Sliding into the chair, she moistened her lips, then finally met Seth's gaze. "If I tell you, do you promise to hear me out before you do anything? And do you promise not to tell anyone else, at least not right away? And promise to keep your deputies out of it. If you need to bring someone else in, let it be a trooper or someone from the State Bureau of Investigation, but nobody local."

"Ashley—"

"Do you promise?"

"*No.* Now, what the hell's going on here? How do you know that Boone's not dead? Have you seen him? Have you talked to him? Did you—" He stared at her a moment longer, then closed his eyes in an expression of dismay. "My God, Ashley, you've been taking care of him, haven't you? *Haven't you?*"

The shout made her jump, made her muscles tighten and her stomach knot. In the years they'd been married, in all the years they'd known each other, Seth had never raised his voice to her. Even when he was angry, he'd always controlled it so carefully, had always spoken in an even, calm voice. The fact that he was yelling now didn't bode well for

Dillon's immediate future—or hers. "He was hurt, Seth, and half-dead. What was I supposed to do?"

"Let the son of a bitch die!" he shouted, then automatically checked his voice. "You could have gotten in your van, driven into town and told me—or is that too complicated for you?"

His sarcasm stung, and in response her voice sounded pouty. "It was raining. Bessie doesn't run in the rain. You know that."

He started to speak—more advice from the male point of view regarding the unreliability of her transportation?—then made a dismissive gesture. "Is he at the cabin?"

She didn't answer. He didn't need her answer.

"How long has he been there?"

Again she said nothing.

"Was he there when I came up to tell you that he'd escaped?"

Guiltily she dropped her gaze to the desk top, to a bulletin featuring a photograph of Dillon. She reached for it, holding it in unsteady hands, studying the picture. It was recent, taken by the Sylvan County Sheriff's Department, she guessed. He looked grim, tough...and afraid. She had seen the grimness and toughness herself that first night, but she had missed the fear, blinded to it by her own. "Can I have this?"

"What do you want with a picture?" Seth asked derisively. "You've got the real thing hidden up there at your cabin." But he didn't protest when she folded the paper carefully so the photo was intact and slid it inside her purse. "Take the bulletin and give me some answers. Is he at the cabin?"

"Yes."

He shoved his chair back from the desk so hard that it banged off the back wall. Quickly Ashley stood up and moved in front of him as he came around the desk. "Please, Seth, you have to listen to me. You have to hear me out."

"I'll listen *after* he's locked up in my jail. Now, move out of my way or I'll move you—right into the cell next to his."

She didn't budge. "If you bring him in," she said, her tone intense, her words deliberate, "one of your deputies will try to kill him."

Shaking his head, he muttered a curse. "Come on, Ashley, you don't believe that. Yes, the men are mad as hell at what he did to Tommy, but—"

"I'm not talking about Tom—and just for the record, Dillon didn't shoot him." She drew a fortifying breath. "I'm talking about the deputy who did."

He stared down at her for a long time, his breathing loud and measured, then slowly returned to his chair. She didn't sit down right away, though, but remained where she blocked his exit from the room. "I'm listening. Start talking."

"Which would you like to hear first? How the bank was robbed? Or how he escaped?" The look he was giving her hardened, lending his eyes a cold gleam. Clearing her throat, she didn't wait for him to voice his obvious preference. "Tom and Dillon were ambushed at Sadler's Pass. The car went off the road and into the ravine. They were both injured, but..."

Seth's expression was skeptical. "Ambushed," he repeated dryly.

"There was a van blocking the road and three men who were shooting at them. One of those men shot Tom." Going on quickly before he could show any more doubt, she added, "It was a black van. Presumably the men would have gone down into the ravine to make certain they were dead, but a woman with kids stopped. She called for help on her car phone."

He considered her thoughtfully for a moment, and she suspected that her last comments had struck a chord. She would bet that they *had* received a call about the accident from a woman with children, that the woman *had* reported a black van and three men in the area. Still, he sounded far from convinced when he spoke again. "This is *his* story."

She nodded.

"And you believe him."

Another nod.

"Why?"

Because instinct had told her early on that Dillon wasn't guilty. Because even when she'd been his hostage, he hadn't hurt her, hadn't wanted her to be afraid, had been quick to reassure her that she would be all right. Because when he had been soaked, freezing and suffering from his injuries and exposure, he had been more concerned with *her* wet clothing, with whether or not *she* was warm and comfortable. Because handcuffing her that first night had filled him with shame. Because she'd started trusting him practically from the start. Because she'd started falling in love with him soon after.

"Because his story of being ambushed, considered along with everything else, makes sense," she said at last. "Because all of his injuries weren't caused by the accident. Because, like Tom, he had been shot. In the back, Seth. Because..." She glanced hesitantly at the door, seeing through the glass that no one but the dispatcher was in the outer room, that she was still absorbed in her magazine, but she lowered her voice anyway. "Because I think it was Steven Vickers who shot him."

She told Seth everything—how Dillon had gotten the job with Bradley Electronics, how he had discovered the problems with the bank's system and pointed them out to his boss, how Russell Bradley had challenged him to prove his assessment by breaking into the bank, how Bradley and Bill Armstrong had then used *his* break-in to cover up their own. When she finished, she sat back quietly in her seat and waited for him to speak.

When he finally did, his expression was drained, his voice weary. If he was still angry, she couldn't tell. "When did he show up at the cabin?"

"About five o'clock Tuesday."

"So he was there when I came by the next morning."

She nodded.

"Why didn't you tell me?"

"Because he was standing right inside the door with Tom's gun."

That piqued his interest. "Tom was shot with a nine millimeter. We think it was his own gun."

"All of your deputies carry nine millimeters, don't they? Including Steven Vickers."

Looking pained, he didn't comment on that. Of everything she'd said this afternoon, that, she knew, was probably the hardest for him to accept. He had hired Steven himself, had trained him and fathered him along. It had to hurt to even consider the possibility that *his* officer had been bought off by the bad guys, that one of his own men had tried to kill an unarmed prisoner, that in the process he had almost killed one of his fellow deputies.

After a moment he shook his head. "Ashley, this is crazy. Steven's a cop. We've known him all of his life. He almost married your sister, for God's sake. How can you believe that he's part of this?"

"I don't blame you for not wanting to hear this, and I don't expect you to believe it. Just consider the possibility, Seth. Look into it—not because I'm asking you to, not because it might keep Dillon alive, but because *if* it's true, Steven has to be stopped. He has to be punished."

"It's *not* true. None of it is true. It can't be."

"Then who shot Dillon?" she asked gently.

"Maybe Tom did. Maybe Boone tried to escape after the accident, and Tom shot him." But she could see that he wasn't impressed with his own theory. Tom had suffered serious head trauma in the crash; Dillon had injuries of his own, both from the wreck and from his confinement in the Sylvan County Jail. Tom was taller, much heavier and far more muscular than Dillon. How likely was it that the badly injured deputy had shot his prisoner in the back, lost his gun to the wounded man and was then shot himself?

Not very.

"How is Boone now?"

"He'll be fine."

After another silence, he grudgingly asked, "You believe this guy?"

"Yes."

"Everything? You believe he thought he was just doing his job when he broke into the bank? That Bill Armstrong—bank president, former mayor, school board member, county commissioner—was behind the robbery of his own bank?"

Ashley stood up and paced off the length of the room, five feet, maybe six, then retraced her steps, passing her chair and ending up in front of the window. There was a small parking lot out back, enclosed with an eight-foot-tall chain-link fence and secured with a wide gate. The occasional impounded car went into the lot, and when prisoners were brought into the jail, the deputy parked out back, then brought them through a narrow door only a few feet from this office.

Right now the only vehicle in the lot was a Crown Victoria, old and much used even before its tumble into a ravine. The front left door was missing, and every window was either shattered or missing altogether. She couldn't identify a single body part that hadn't been scraped, crumpled or accordioned; the roof had been flattened until it rested mere inches above the door frames. The only way the back doors could be opened was with a crowbar, which meant Dillon must have escaped through the window. Lucky for him he was so lean. If he'd been bigger, taller or heavier, he wouldn't have been able to wriggle through that small space. He would have been forced to stay there and wait for Seth and his men to arrive. And if his luck were bad enough and Steven Vickers had been the first deputy on the scene...

Sighing, she turned her back on the badly damaged car and faced Seth. "You sound just like him. That's the reason he took off a year ago. He didn't think anyone would believe him. Armstrong and Bradley are good citizens, and he's..."

"A punk."

His response weighed down her shoulders and made her sigh again. "Maybe he was right. Maybe you would have been too bigoted and narrow-minded to listen to him.

Maybe you would have taken the easy way out and locked him up without ever considering other suspects. Maybe you would have been so eager to solve Catlin County's biggest crime ever that you wouldn't have cared that you were sending an innocent man to prison.''

"That's not fair, Ashley."

She smiled sadly. "Life *isn't* fair. Ask Dillon."

For a long time he sat silent, toying with a pencil on his desk. Finally he tossed it onto the desk pad, sat back and met her gaze. "What is it you want from me?"

"I want you to talk to him. To listen to him. To prove—"

"Or disprove."

She acknowledged his interruption with a nod. "To prove or disprove what he says. And I want you to let him stay at my cabin until you have proof one way or the other. I don't want him locked up here. I don't want him where somebody can get to him.''

"Why are you doing this? What difference does it make to you?''

Ignoring his questions, she moved away from the window. "Give me enough time to get home and talk to him, to tell him that you're coming. Thirty minutes should be plenty. And please don't tell anyone anything, especially Steven.'' She walked to the door, then turned back and finally answered those two questions. "I'm doing this because it's the only thing I *can* do. Proving his innocence makes all the difference... *He* makes all the difference in the world to me.'' She slid her purse strap over her shoulder and opened the door, then stopped once more. "Thank you, Seth.''

The first hour and a half Ashley was gone passed at a relatively normal pace. Dillon knew it would take her close to thirty minutes to make the fifteen-mile drive down winding, narrow roads and another half hour to return. Figure another thirty minutes to get her money and talk to Seth, and she should be on her way home. Hell, she should *be* home by now, he thought with a scowl. She'd been gone at least two hours, maybe two and a half.

Maybe she'd had trouble with the van. Maybe she'd needed time to track down Seth. Maybe she had stopped at the store or gotten delayed by friends or acquaintances.

Or maybe she wasn't coming back.

Maybe she had gone to see Seth, all right, to tell him where his missing prisoner could be found.

No. He couldn't let himself start thinking that way. He trusted her. He *did*. There could be any number of innocent reasons why this trip was taking so long. He didn't have to automatically suspect the not-so-innocent ones. Ashley deserved better than that.

He stopped his restless prowling in front of the fireplace. The fire was out, the ashes cold, sending a pungent smoky scent into the room. He had let the flames die soon after Ashley left. It was such a sunny, warm day outside. But inside, with the door closed and all the windows covered, it was gloomy and uncomfortably cool. Maybe he should build another fire to warm the place before she returned.

Or maybe they could warm each other in bed instead.

With a sigh, he settled his gaze and his attention on the mantel, where primitive pots shared space with carved boxes and one tall round basket. He picked up one box and lifted the lid to reveal a half-dozen metal buttons inside. Silver thimbles, some looking fairly old, nestled in the next box, and two thin gold bands sat on a piece of fluffy cotton in the third. Wedding rings. Hers and Seth's, or maybe her grandparents'? Feeling guilty and more than a little foolish, he picked up the larger of the two and slid it easily onto his finger. It definitely wasn't Seth's, he decided. Sheriff Benedict was a big man with big hands. This ring might fit his little finger, but definitely none of the others.

For a time he stared at his hand. Even in the cabin's gloom, the gold somehow gathered enough light to gleam brightly against the dark bronze of his finger. He'd never worn a ring of any sort, not once in his entire thirty-four years, but this one felt comfortable. Familiar. Right.

But it *wasn't* right. He wasn't anyone's husband and wasn't likely to ever be.

Returning the ring to the box and replacing the lid, he picked up the tall basket. Most of her baskets were woven with thin, flat reed or narrow bundles of sweetgrass, but this was made from some sort of vine, with a flat, round lid. Lifting the lid by its round wooden knob, he looked inside and grinned. She didn't have any money at all, she'd insisted, but she had lied. The basket was filled with bills, a few fifties and twenties but mostly tens, fives and ones, some rolled together, others crumpled and dropped in. He wasn't surprised that she kept a little cache of money around the cabin; it sounded like something she would do, exactly like something her granny would have done.

Hearing the uneven sputter of the van's engine chugging up the hill, he put the lid back on and the basket back where it belonged and went to the front window to look out. A tremendous feeling washed over him—relief mixed with shame. He shouldn't have doubted her. She'd given him no reason to think that she would betray him, and he regretted the lack of faith. Better than anyone else in his life, though, she would understand where the doubt had come from.

She climbed out of the van and slammed the door, then circled to the other side, taking a grocery sack and a small cooler from the back. He would like to go out to meet her, to greet her, but he went no farther than the door, opening the lock, staying safely out of sight of any prying eyes.

"How did it go?" he asked the moment she was inside.

"Okay." She didn't stop but went straight to the kitchen, setting her load on the counter there. Potatoes and a bottle of garlic powder spilled out of the bag, rolling until the back-splash stopped them. "I picked up a few things for dinner tonight."

"You saw Seth?"

"Yes," came her muffled answer as she opened the refrigerator and ducked behind the door to unload the cooler.

"Everything's on for tomorrow?"

Straightening, she closed the refrigerator, set the cooler on the counter and removed a cake from the bag, setting it aside out of the way. She finished unloading the remaining items, gathering them neatly on the counter, before finally facing him. "You really want to leave tomorrow, don't you?"

He studied her face in the yellow glow of the overhead light. She looked so serious, so unhappy, so... So filled with regret. Feeling an odd little quiver inside, he cautiously answered. "I don't *want* to leave at all, Ash. Don't you know that? But I have to. If I want to stay alive, if I want to keep you alive, I *have* to go."

"No, you don't. You don't have to go anywhere. If you stay, we can work things out. We can—"

He laid his fingers over her mouth. "No more arguments, please."

Last night she had let him stop her, had let him distract her. Not so this afternoon. She pushed his hand away. "*Would* you stay if you could? If you woke up in the morning and the bank-robbery charges were gone, if Russell Bradley and Bill Armstrong had disappeared, if you were a free man, would you stay here?"

His grin was crooked and felt phony. It *was* phony. There was nothing amusing about her question, nothing worth smiling about. She was talking about the one thing he wanted most in the world—to stay here with her. The one thing that he could never have, because the bank-robbery charges weren't going to be dropped, and Russell and Armstrong weren't going to disappear from his life. He was never going to be a free man again.

"Honey, you wouldn't be able to get rid of me," he murmured.

She considered his answer for a moment, seemed to grow a little unhappier, then flatly announced, "I told Seth where you were."

Dillon stared at her, certain that he must have misunderstood. But the words remained between them, emotionless and blunt, and her expression confirmed them. He took a step away from her, then another, not stopping until the table was at his back. "You...told...Seth...."

At last her grimness and regret gave way to other feelings—to fear and anxiety, remorse and sorrow. "I had to, Dillon. Can't you see that he'll help us? That he'll protect you? That he'll prove your innocence so that you can stay?"

He'd never felt such numbness. It was almost as if he were outside looking in, watching this little scene unfold between two other people...except for the sharp little ache of betrayal that was rapidly growing in his chest. "You told Seth," he murmured again, then his voice sharpened. "*What* did you tell him?"

"Everything."

She didn't elaborate; she didn't need to. She had waited until she'd gotten all the details herself and then gone running off to repeat it all to her precious Seth. She had played Dillon for a fool, had made him believe in her, had coaxed him and seduced him....

A sickening shudder rippled through him. Oh, God, was that what last night had been about? Seducing him into trusting her, into opening up and letting down his guard? All her talk about wanting him, about having just one night together, about not having a chance for a commitment or a future but settling for just one little bit of intimacy... Had it all been lies, all part of her plan to get away from the cabin alone this afternoon? Had there been any truth at all in anything she'd said or done in the past five days?

"He's coming up here to talk to you," she said uneasily. "He's going to let you stay here at the cabin while he checks out your story. He just needs to hear it from you."

He didn't believe her. He wasn't sure he could ever believe her again.

"I—I asked him to give me thirty minutes so I could talk to you, so I could make you understand...." Her voice quavered. "Dillon, you *have* to understand. This is *right*. It's best—"

"Right for whom?" he interrupted. "For Seth, who gets to singlehandedly capture the armed-and-dangerous bank robber? For you? This earns you points with him, doesn't it? Are you willing to settle for his gratitude, or are you hoping to get something more from him? Hey, maybe he'll sleep with you—he could go a long way toward easing that loneliness you were talking about last night, couldn't he? Maybe he'll be so grateful that he'll even let you back into his life."

Her eyes bright with unshed tears, she responded with more dignity than he deserved. "Right for *you,* Dillon. You haven't done anything wrong, beyond trusting the wrong people, and—"

He interrupted her again with an angry, mocking laugh. "Damned right, sweetheart. Obviously I haven't learned my lesson yet. I trusted *you.*"

"You haven't done anything wrong," she repeated, becoming more agitated, "and Seth can prove it. Now that he knows who to investigate, he can clear your name. You'll be able to stay here. You can have all the things you want—a job, a home, a family, a place to belong."

"With *you?*" he asked, his voice menacingly soft. "You think I would stay here with you? You think I would trust you? You think I would still want you?" He wanted to find some satisfaction in the hurt that flashed through her eyes, but he couldn't feel anything except his own hurt. Anger. Betrayal.

Her hand trembling, she reached out to him. "Dillon, I love—"

He moved away so abruptly that the centerpiece of dried flowers in a pottery vase fell to its side and rolled onto the floor, the vase breaking with a hollow thunk. Detouring to the bed to pick up his shoes and socks, he went to the fireplace, sat down on the hearth and slipped his arm free of the sling, then began the task of putting on his socks, working quickly even though it sent sharp needles of pain through his shoulder.

He'd never been so clumsy—knocking the flowers over, fumbling with his socks, with his shoes and the laces. It was because his hands—his entire body—was shaking. Because he didn't want her to touch him. Because he couldn't let her say those words. He couldn't let her tempt him, torment him. He couldn't listen to any more of her lies.

He had thought when he'd come here that he knew all there was to know about betrayal, that his mother, his father, Russell Bradley and others had taught him everything. But he'd been wrong. They had never taught him how badly it could hurt. They had made him feel unwanted and unimportant, stupid, foolish and expendable, like a nuisance best dealt with harshly or an embarrassment best dealt with not at all. But they had never made him feel so lost, so hopeless, so disillusioned or so achingly sorrowful.

He felt all those things and worse as he tied his second shoe, then stood up.

Ashley stood up, too, from the floor where she'd knelt to pick up the vase. Her hands filled with chunks of pottery, she faced him. "You can't leave," she pleaded. "Seth is on his way up here right now. The mountains around here are still filled with search parties. You can't take the van, you don't know your way through the forest, and your shoulder isn't healed enough to risk that kind of travel. Please, Dillon, please wait."

"Wait for good ol' Seth to lock me up?" He made a derisive sound as he retrieved the handcuffs and keys from underneath the middle sofa cushion, then fished Deputy Coughlin's pistol from the bottom of a basket filled with bits of fabric left over from other projects and no doubt intended for one of her quilts. He tucked it into the waistband of his jeans, then started for the door. On the way he paused, the table between them. "You know, if any woman in the world could have persuaded me that she was worth going to prison for twenty-five years, it would have been you. I could have convinced myself that giving up half my life was more than a reasonable price to pay for spending the rest of it with you. But I would have been so wrong."

"Dillon..." Once more she reached out. This time he didn't jerk away. He stared at her hand for a moment, so strong and delicate, then deliberately turned his back on her. He refused to hear the soft, anguished cry she gave as he crossed the few yards to the door, refused to wonder if the tears that had filled her eyes earlier were spilling over now, refused to even consider how much she might be hurting. With each step he forced himself to concentrate on the hard, cold facts. She had lied to him. She had turned him over to the authorities, knowing that he would rather die than go to prison. She had betrayed him.

This was one betrayal he feared he might never get over.

Taking a deep breath, he unfastened the lock he had automatically secured when she had returned from town. He didn't want to do this, didn't want to head back out into the rugged mountains, didn't want to leave the cabin where, for the first time in his life, he'd felt a sense of belonging. But it wasn't the cabin that had given him that feeling of home, but rather Ashley, who had misled him, who was helping to send him to prison, who hadn't thought twice about risking *his* life and *his* freedom on the remote chance that she might gain what *she* wanted.

He hesitated before opening the door, aware that there was something he needed to say. *I'm sorry,* maybe, because he certainly was. He was sorry he had trusted her, sorry he had given her the chance to let him down, sorry that he'd made love with her and sorry that he'd fallen in love with her. Or he could try *Thank you.* For taking him in, for nursing him, for making him trust her, for seducing him into a moment of sheer idiocy, for reminding him once again of Russell's lesson—*Never trust anyone*—and for sending him to prison. Yeah, thanks for nothing.

I love you. Not *loved,* not past tense, not over and done with, but right now and in the future—with his luck, probably forever. But telling her now would serve no purpose but to underscore the futility of it. *Damn you* served no purpose, either, except possibly to vent a little of his anger.

Apparently he was wrong. There *wasn't* anything he needed to say. He simply needed to open the door and walk out of her life.

His fingers closed around the knob, and he twisted it, pulling the door open at the same time. He didn't take a

single step, though, because the barrel of a pistol identical
to the one secured in his waistband was pointed right between his eyes. He drew a small breath but otherwise didn't
move so much as a muscle as Sheriff Benedict softly asked,
"Going somewhere, Boone?"

Feeling lower than he'd ever felt before, Dillon exhaled.
"Yeah," he answered just as softly. "Straight to jail." Then
he followed the sheriff's glance to Ashley, still standing
beside the table, her hands clenched tightly around the
shards of pottery, and he silently amended his response.

Straight to hell.

Chapter 10

"Where's the gun?"

Ashley watched as Dillon lifted his shoulders in the slightest of shrugs. "In my waistband."

"Get it, Ashley," Seth commanded, his own gun never wavering.

She remained motionless for a moment, unwilling to get so close, all too painfully aware that Dillon certainly didn't want her so close. But she had to cooperate, had to do whatever Seth said; otherwise, he might decide that in her custody wasn't the best place for his prisoner to be. Dropping the hardened clay on the table, she moved around between the two men, awkwardly lifting the hem of the sweatshirt Dillon wore, and pulled the pistol free. The entire time—only a moment, maybe a lifetime—he watched her with such an unforgiving gaze. When she moved away after handing the gun by its grips to Seth, she could actually feel it the instant she stepped out of his line of sight.

Seth came into the cabin, closing the door behind him before gesturing for Dillon to sit down at the table. He claimed the chair at a right angle for himself and directed

Ashley to sit at the opposite end. "Ashley says you have a story to tell."

Dillon shifted his gaze slowly to hers, making her shiver. "Ashley lies," he replied sardonically.

"She says that breaking into the vault at the bank was part of a test of the new security system, authorized by your boss and the bank president." Seth waited a moment, but when Dillon offered no response, he went on. "She also says you didn't shoot my deputy."

Finally Dillon looked at him. "You've got the gun. Check the ballistics."

"While you're at it," Ashley added, "check Steven Vickers's, too." When Seth sent an annoyed glance her way, she simply shrugged, then watched as he picked up Dillon's—or rather Tom's—gun. He removed the clip, unloaded it, then pulled back the slide and ejected a single cartridge that hit the table, bounced, then rolled toward Dillon.

"I'll do that," he said grimly, glancing first at her, then at Dillon. "There are fifteen rounds here—one in the chamber, fourteen in the clip. That's the max this model will hold."

"Which shoots down—pardon the pun—your theory that Dillon shot Tom after Tom shot him, each firing the same gun," Ashley replied. Unless, of course, he believed that Dillon had just happened to be carrying with him a couple of shells of the exact type the sheriff's department used and had reloaded the pistol. She felt a tremendous sense of relief. All it would take to get Seth seriously started on a new investigation was an inconsistency or two like this. Now he knew that there had to be a second gun involved and—with no evidence to suggest that Tom carried a second pistol—also a second man. Now he wouldn't stop until he found out who shot his deputy...thereby proving that Dillon didn't.

Gathering the bullets, Seth reloaded the clip, pushed it back into place in the pistol, then looked at her. "How about making some tea? We've got some talking to do."

Without hesitation, she went into the kitchen and put water on to boil. Behind her Seth began asking Dillon questions and, judging from the time he was taking, probably making notes, too. She had been so sure of his ability to clear Dillon's name, but she had no idea how he would go about it. She supposed his first act would be to run ballistics tests on both the pistol Dillon had taken from Tom and whatever weapons Steven Vickers had, along with checking phone and financial records of everyone involved. She seriously doubted that Russell Bradley and Bill Armstrong had risked robbing the bank of nearly half a million dollars so that they could tuck the money away someplace safe for use in their retirement years. Surely they had spent at least some of it—part of it, maybe, to pay off the men who had tried to kill Dillon last week.

Of course, once the ballistics tests proved that it was Steven Vickers who had shot Tom, that would make things so much easier. The past day or two had proved that she didn't really know Steven at all, but she didn't imagine he would be willing to go to prison for the rest of his life—or to face death, if Tom didn't recover—without giving up his accomplices. Once he knew he'd been caught, *all* the money in Armstrong's bank wouldn't be enough to buy his silence.

Unless Dillon was wrong, and the bullet that had hit Tom hadn't come from the black-haired man in the Wildcats letter jacket. There had been three men, all of them shooting; Tom had lost control of the patrol car, and Dillon must have been scared as hell. Could he really have seen which one of the three had been responsible for Tom's injury?

As the water came to a boil, she added a half-dozen orange pekoe and black tea bags, along with a bag of mint tea, then set the pot aside to steep. Seth would be so grateful that she wasn't giving him chamomile, elderberry or ginger tea that he would forget he was one of those rare Southerners who didn't like iced tea, and Dillon... He didn't like her herbal teas, either—god-awful, he'd called them—and he wouldn't like this any better. Right now there probably wasn't a single thing associated with her that he did like, except the fact that he would soon be free to leave her.

This morning she had thought chances were good that he would understand why she had betrayed his trust, that he would recognize the benefits as far outweighing the risks, that he would forgive her. Now she doubted that that was ever going to happen. She was going to have to live with his anger and hatred and without him.

But she had known the risks and had taken them anyway. She had no one to blame but herself—and Russell Bradley and Bill Armstrong, damn them.

She had to admit, though, that faced with the same decision, knowing what she knew now, she would take the same action again. Her living alone wasn't important. Dillon living free was.

When the tea was ready, she filled two glasses with ice and tea, placed them on a tray along with honey, sugar and spoons and carried it to the table. Immediately she retreated to the kitchen once more, busying herself with unnecessary cleaning and with preparations for a special dinner that she wasn't sure she could eat, before finally deciding to bake. She was on her third batch of oatmeal muffins when Seth called her name.

When she turned, he gestured for her to go outside with him. She picked up a paper bag holding the first two dozen muffins, then followed him out. He was standing at the top of the steps, staring across the fields, when she joined him.

"You're an idiot," he announced, sliding his arm around her waist and drawing her close to his side.

"I know."

"You live way up here where no woman should live alone. You eke out a living with crafts that require a ton of work for very little return. You don't have a telephone or any way to call for help if something happens. Now you go and fall in love with a wanted fugitive—and then you turn him in to the sheriff. You just can't do things the easy way, can you?"

She rested her head against his chest. "I never said I was in love. . . ."

His chuckle interrupted her. "You forget, I've known you all your life. You've never speeded, never gotten a parking ticket, never even cheated on your taxes. Yet here you are, breaking every law in the book to protect a wanted felon. There's got to be some explanation for it."

"I was his hostage," she murmured in her own defense.

"So he told me. And how long did that last? Twenty-four hours? Twelve? However long it took you to decide that a handcuffed prisoner who gets shot in the back while in police custody is deserving of your protection?" He paused, but she made no effort to answer. "Besides, honey, I saw you look at him. You never looked at me that way, not even on our wedding day."

Her eyes got teary, her voice thick. "It doesn't matter. He's never going to forgive me for this."

"He trusted you, and you let him down. You can't expect him to see past that right away to the fact that you had good reasons for betraying his trust. But he'll get over it someday. He'll come around and you'll be here waiting."

"I don't want to wait for someday. I've already waited all my life." She wiped away a tear that had slipped free, then sniffed. "Can you help him, Seth? Can you prove that he's not guilty of taking all that money?"

His shrug reverberated through her. "I think so. If it's worth anything, I believe him. We know at least two shots were fired up at Sadler's Pass—the one that took out Tom and the one that got Boone—and neither of them came from Tom's gun. And he's right about the woman who called in the accident. She did have two kids with her, and they did report seeing a black van with three men who left as soon as they arrived. Then there's the photo. While you were moping in the kitchen, I showed him some photographs from our files, including one of Steven out of uniform. Boone identified him as the man up at the pass."

"So what will you do now?"

He grinned down at her. "I've got so many things to do that I hardly know where to start. I'm going to do as you asked and leave him here for the time being...unless you've changed your mind. If you have, I can jail him over in the next county, where he would be safe."

Wondering if he'd made the same offer to Dillon, she shook her head. He probably hadn't. As much as Dillon hated the idea of going to jail, she was pretty sure he hated the idea of staying there with her even more. If Seth had given him the option, he would be leaving with him.

"Are there still search parties up here?"

"Maybe." Catching the chastising look she sent his way, he shrugged. "I'm coordinating the search for my department, the state police and SBI. As far we're concerned, this area has been cleared. But there are lots of private citizens out there looking, too, and most of them probably know that the Briggs brothers tracked Boone to the bluff out back." Releasing her, he leaned against the porch railing and faced her. "How is it they managed to miss his tracks right here?"

"Luck. A lot of rain. My own big feet. So you think some of them might be around."

He nodded. "Armstrong's reward still stands, you know, and every hunter and local boy who knows these hills could put that ten grand to good use. You be careful. Citizens don't operate under the same constraints we do. Some of these boys will be quicker to use deadly force than a cop. Stay inside and keep those sheets over the windows."

"We will."

"I warned Boone about trying to escape again. I also warned him about you." Grinning again, he lifted his hand to brush over her hair. "I told him that if he harmed one hair on your pretty little head, he would have to answer to me. I figured it was too late to warn him about breaking your heart."

"Gee, thanks," she said, hoping her dry tone concealed the ache in her throat. "You're such a good friend."

"It's just part of the job." Bending, he pressed a kiss to her forehead, then took the bag of muffins. "The Catlin County Sheriff's Department thanks you. Stay inside. Stay locked up. I'll be back tomorrow."

She waited until his Blazer disappeared in the trees below before reluctantly returning to the cabin. Dillon was lying on the couch, an open book resting on his stomach, but he wasn't reading. His gaze was fixed and distant. After a moment's hesitation, she crossed the room and sat down in the armchair, right on the edge of the seat. "I'm sorry," she ventured.

The look he gave her was cold and damning. "Not half as sorry as I am."

She clasped her hands together in her lap. "I—I don't know if he told you, but Seth believes you."

"And that's what matters to you, isn't it? Your precious Seth."

"No, Dillon, *you* matter. You're *all* that matters."

"Oh, that's right." He tapped the heel of his hand against his forehead as if remembering some great truth. "You *love* me. You love me so much that you can't wait to see me in prison."

Tears welling again, she had to clear her throat to speak and even then managed only a whisper. A plea. "Dillon, please don't do this. I only did what I thought was best—"

He sat up, swinging his feet to the floor, dropping the book, facing her with an intimidating scowl. "Who gave you the right to decide what's best for *me?*" he demanded. "We spent a few days together. We had sex twice. You think that entitles you to destroy my life?"

Aching inside and seeking only to ease the pain, she gave him a sorrowful smile. "You're the world's biggest loser, Dillon," she said softly. "You don't need me to destroy your life. You've been doing a fine job of that on your own."

With that, she stood up, went into the bathroom and closed the door. Sliding to the floor, she hid her face in her arms and, for what she swore would be the first and last time for Dillon, she cried.

Dinnertime came and went without notice. Ashley made no offer to cook. If he was hungry, Dillon was capable of fixing his own meal, but he tended to lose his appetite when things went really wrong.

He couldn't imagine anything being more wrong than his life was tonight.

You're the world's biggest loser, Dillon. They were his own words, but that didn't make hearing them in Ashley's voice any easier to bear. Neither did knowing that he deserved that insult and any other she might offer.

He'd thought the past eleven months had been miserable, but he was learning a whole new meaning for the word this evening. He should have insisted that Seth take him to jail. He would much rather take his chances with Vickers and the rest of them than spend one more silent, awkward, painful hour with Ashley.

It was time for bed. Earlier this afternoon, he'd had such plans for tonight. He'd intended to spend the entire evening making love with her, resting only when their bodies demanded it, saying the longest, sweetest, most intense goodbye anyone had ever said.

Instead, they hadn't spoken since she'd shut herself away in the bathroom.

Rising from the sofa, he walked past her chair, where she'd spent the past two hours working on her cross-stitch, and to the bed. He turned down the covers, removed his sling and shut off the lamp. After kicking off his shoes, he sat on the bed to remove his socks and sweatshirt.

That done, for a moment he simply sat there. He was more tired tonight than he could remember ever being, but it wasn't a physical fatigue. He would welcome that; he could crawl into bed, close his eyes and sleep until it was gone, until his body was well rested. No, this was a spiritual weariness, and all the rest in the world couldn't heal it.

But Ashley could.

There should be something shameful about wanting her after what she'd done, but he couldn't produce the shame. All he felt was the wanting. The need. The loss.

And the betrayal. It was still there, a painful emptiness centered somewhere in his middle, a place that throbbed at odd moments, that ached with the knowledge that she had lied to him, had misled and deceived him. It hurt in ways he had never experienced with an intensity that he hoped to never again experience.

But all the anger, all the hurt, all the disillusionment didn't change the facts.

He needed her companionship, her support and her faith. He needed to hold on to her. He needed to touch her, to draw strength from her. He needed to love her.

He *did* love her—although this evening a person would have trouble seeing it in the way he'd treated her.

Across the room, she put her needlework away, turned out the lamp and gathered an armful of quilts from the wooden stand. He watched as she spread them in front of the fireplace, each one adding its cushioning to the braided rug there. When she was done, she went into the bathroom, closing the door quietly behind her.

Dillon stood up and unfastened his jeans. Instead of pulling them off, though, he left the bedside and went to her pallet. Picking up each quilt, he folded them as carefully as she'd laid them out, stacking them over the arm of the couch. He was shaking out the next to the last when the bathroom door opened again. She came a half-dozen feet into the room before seeing him and stopping short.

She was wearing her nightgown and holding the wooden-handled brush in one hand. Ready to torment him, he thought, swallowing hard. That was all he needed—Ashley in that barely-there gown sitting in front of the fire brushing her long blond hair—to bring him to his knees. To make him beg for mercy, for relief, for sweet, swift death.

He folded the quilt in half one last time, added it to the pile, then bent to pick up the last one. Instead of folding it, though, he wrapped his hands tightly in the fabric. "I can't—" His voice was harsh, hoarse, the words unintelligible. After clearing his throat, he tried again. "I can't do this, Ash."

She remained exactly where she was. "Do what?"

"Waste our time like this. In another day or two, the sheriff is going to take me in. He's going to lock me up, and I promise you, there's not a judge in North Carolina who will let me out on bail, not after last week's escape and last year's flight. This may be the last time we have together for a hell of a long time, and I can't spend it being angry.''

"Seth isn't going to arrest you."

"When he can't find evidence against Russell and Armstrong, he'll have no choice. I'm still the only one who's been charged. I'm still the only one they can take to trial. Someone has to pay—"

"But it won't be you."

His smile was a poor effort. "I wish I shared your faith." But he didn't. He just couldn't believe that, after a life-time of things going wrong, now when he was in the worst predicament of all, fate was going to work in his favor.

"You're not nine years old anymore," she argued, "and Seth isn't a grade-school principal. This isn't two little boys pointing fingers at each other, saying '*I* didn't do it, *he* did it.' We're talking about points of law, Dillon. Evidence. *Proof*."

"And what if Seth doesn't find evidence that the others are involved? What if he doesn't find proof that I was framed? *I* go to trial. *I* go to prison."

At last she came a few steps closer. "The evidence ex-ists—unless Bradley and Armstrong committed the perfect crime. Do you honestly believe they're that smart, that good?"

"Maybe they're that lucky, because I'm sure as hell not." The words came easily—it was an old habit, putting him-self down—but the moment he heard them, he wasn't so sure they were true. In the past five days, his luck had been pretty extraordinary. Three men had tried to kill him, but his only injury was as minor as a gunshot wound could be. The car he'd been riding in had rolled side over side into a deep ravine, ending up a bent and twisted wreck, but he had walked away from it. He could have easily died of expo-sure from the rain and the cold, but he'd found shelter. He could have been captured by one of the search parties, could have gotten hopelessly lost, could have stumbled onto a cabin owned by an unsociable, gun-toting hermit who didn't like strangers, especially those wanted by the law.

All things considered, he had been lucky the past week, and Ashley was the best luck of all.

"You really think this will all work out?" he asked hesitantly.

She nodded.

It was a gamble. If she was wrong, if Seth couldn't find any evidence linking Armstrong and Russell to the robbery, Dillon would surely go to jail. But if she was right... If she was right, he could have everything he'd ever wanted. He could stay here. Marry her. Have a family—children, grandchildren. Grow old. Be happy. Belong.

Blowing his breath out, he folded the last quilt and set it aside. "Do you realize—if Seth does find proof—what you're getting into? You're going to be stuck with me for a long time."

For the first time all evening, the tension that had kept her stiff and remote disappeared, and she slowly smiled. "It could never be long enough."

"You'll have to marry me."

"I guess I will."

"You deserve better."

Shaking her head, she closed the distance between them. "I've never known anyone better than you, Dillon. I've never loved anyone better."

All he had to do was reach out, lay his hands on her shoulders and pull, and she was in his arms, her soft body snug against his. He lowered his head, pressing his cheek against her hair, and closed his eyes, remaining that way for a long time, savoring the feel of her, the scent, the touch. After a while, though, he shifted until his forehead was resting against hers, until all he could see were her clear blue eyes. "If you're wrong..."

"I'm not wrong," she whispered.

"If you are, it'll kill me, Ash. Leaving here, leaving you, being locked up..."

"I'm *not* wrong," she repeated fiercely. "Trust me, Dillon. Trust Seth. Trust yourself. And pray."

"Oh, darlin', I've been praying since the first moment I saw you."

"For what?" Her voice was husky, teasing, enticing. "That God would deliver you from me?"

He chuckled. "Some part of me knew you were dangerous from the start."

"*You* were the one with the gun."

"And you were the one with the eyes of an angel, a gentle touch, more kindness than I knew what to do with and the loveliest breasts...."

Leaning back in the circle of his arms, she frowned at him. "You didn't see my breasts that first night."

"I got a glimpse when you were changing clothes, and it was enough to give me fantasies." Cupping her face between his palms, he stared hard into her eyes. "I do love you, Ash," he whispered. "Whatever happens... remember that."

Her eyes drifted shut as he bent his head to kiss her. It was a brief kiss, gentle, sweet, then he released her and backed away. It took her a moment to react, another moment to open her eyes, yet another to focus a decidedly bewildered look on him. By then he was already undressed and sliding underneath the covers that blanketed her bed.

"What...?"

"Don't let me interfere with your routine," he replied with a gesture.

She glanced down at the brush in her hand as if she'd never seen it before, then, damnably slowly she smiled. She sat cross-legged on the rug where her bed had so recently been made and unmade, turned slightly toward him and began drawing the brush through her hair with slow, steady motions.

Tempting and tormenting. Last night that was how he had described watching her brush her hair two nights before. Tonight it was no less of either. It made his body hard and his spirit weak. It heated his blood and sent a tremble through his hands. It was tantalizing, teasing and pure, sweet torture.

Gazing into the fire, she began talking, her voice soft, hypnotic. "I picked up this habit from my grandmother. Every night she sat right here and brushed her hair. Those were the only times I ever saw it down. Right up until her death, the first thing she did every morning was put it up in a bun, and the last thing she did every night was sit here and brush it out." She sighed contentedly. "She was a good woman. She believed in hard work, family, God and love. She always said she could tell all she needed to know about a person just by looking into his eyes. She would have looked into your eyes and seen your soul."

As Ashley certainly must have done, Dillon thought, to find anything in him worth loving.

"She was a wonderful woman—beautiful. Tough. Resilient. My grandfather used to say that she had a kind heart, a strong back and a good head on her shoulders—a major compliment from a man of few words like him. Her life wasn't easy. They never had much, and they struggled for what they did have, and three of their eight children died before their second birthdays. But she had this tremendous faith, and she never lost it, not when her babies died, not when her kids grew up and moved away, not even when my grandfather died." She smiled dreamily. "I adored her. I admired her. I wanted to *be* her when I grew up."

"I think you succeeded," he murmured. "You're a beautiful woman. You're tough, kind, strong, smart, and you have this amazing faith."

She flashed him a smile that made his breath catch in his chest. "You think it's amazing that I have faith in you. It isn't. I knew the very first night that you weren't some desperate, cold-blooded criminal."

He was starting to feel pretty desperate now, but there was definitely nothing cold about his blood. He was hot enough to burn. Still, he resisted leaving the bed and joining her on the rug, and he stopped himself from calling her over to him on the bed. "If you knew," he began, his voice thick and raspy, "then why were you afraid of me?"

"I did think you were dangerous," she admitted, then grinned. "Turned out I was right. You *are* dangerous... and wicked... and handsome... and sexy." Leaning forward, she laid the brush on the stone hearth, then gracefully got to her feet, unfolding, rising, stretching. Backlit by the fire, she came to him slowly, each movement fluid and smooth, pulling her gown over her head as she walked, dropping it to the floor.

Dillon had the presence of mind—just barely—to kick off the covers, which heated his already feverishly hot skin and did nothing to conceal his arousal. When she reached the bed, she didn't stop, didn't hesitate or fumble, but placed one knee on the mattress, moved over him, sank down and so smoothly, so easily took him inside her. Her body was fiery hot, tight, greedily drawing him deeper, until he could offer no more, until she could accept no more.

Resting her hands on the mattress, she leaned over him. There was no denying that she was aroused—her nipples were hard, her skin moist, her body where it held him damp—but her eyes were clear, true blue. Not hazy, not dazed, but sharp, piercing, honest. "I love you, Dillon, and I'm sorry I hurt you. I'm sorry I gave you reason to doubt me. I'm sorry I couldn't treat your trust with the respect and honor it deserved. But it'll never happen again, I swear to you."

He lightly stroked her hair. "You did what you thought—what might prove to be—best for both of us." He drew a breath that smelled of her unique scents. "I'm sorry, too. I said some things...."

"You were entitled."

He shifted underneath her and felt her body move with him, adjusting, tightening. It sent a shiver up his spine. "One thing I said, that giving up half my life is a reasonable price to pay for spending the rest of it with you... That's true. If I have to go to prison—"

"You won't."

"But if I have to..." He broke off, unable to go on. The enormity of what he wanted to ask, the arrogance of believing he might deserve it, stopped him cold.

But Ashley apparently found it neither enormous nor arrogant. Bending lower, she pressed her mouth against his, rubbing, tasting, then drew back only enough to give the answer he needed to hear. "I'll be here for you, Dillon," she whispered. "Always and forever."

Chapter 11

He brought the subject up again late the next morning. Ashley was standing at the counter, spreading thick slices of bread with garlic butter, and Dillon was a few feet away, sharpening a paring knife—the closest she could come to a steak knife—on a whetstone with slow, even strokes when abruptly he said, "What I asked for last night..."

She gave him a sidelong smile. "What would that be? As I recall, we both asked for a number of things last night...and got them, too."

Clearly uncomfortable, he turned to look out the window, lifting the curtain just a bit. "If I get convicted... About waiting." After a moment of silence, he faced her again. "I wouldn't ask that of you. Twenty-five years is a hell of a long time. It's your entire life."

"Not quite," she said dryly. "You don't even know how old I am, do you?"

"You're young," he said with a grin. "You'll always be young. That's all I need to know."

"For the record, I'm twenty-nine. And also for the record...this is my home, Dillon. This is where I'll be living in five years, in twenty years, in twenty-five years. This is where I'll be if you're here with me, and this is where you'll find me if you're not."

He started to touch her hair, but drew his hand back before he did. "You're a beautiful young woman, Ash. It's easy to say you'll wait now. But what about a few months or a few years from now? What about when you get lonely? What about when you get tired of living alone?"

"For starters, I'm young, yes, but you're the only man who's ever called me beautiful." She softened the remark with a smile, then went on. "I don't get lonely for just anyone. There are times I miss my parents, times I miss Seth. I *always* miss my granny. But those longings aren't interchangeable. Seeing Seth doesn't make me miss my folks any less. Seeing *anyone* wouldn't make me miss you any less. Living with someone else wouldn't make up for not living with you."

"You would be wasting your life—"

She stopped him with a chastening look. "Why are we even discussing this? Let's wait and see what happens. Even if Seth can't find enough evidence to arrest Armstrong and Bradley, he'll find enough to make you look less guilty. He'll create a reasonable doubt. We'll get a good lawyer, and we'll take our chances. Whatever happens, we'll deal with it—both of us, Dillon. You and me. Together."

Rising onto her toes, she pressed a kiss to his mouth, then turned her attention back to the steak, wine and German chocolate cake she was fixing for lunch. Since this was the first bottle of wine she'd ever bought, she had bought a corkscrew, too, but it was nowhere in sight. Talking more to herself than to Dillon—"I know I bought it . . . I'm sure the clerk put it in the bag....now where could it be?"—she did a quick search of the kitchen, then sighed. "It must have fallen out of the bag in Bessie," she decided.

"I'll check—"

She stopped Dillon before he'd taken even one step. "Remember what Seth said. You stay inside."

"He told us both to stay inside."

"Yes, but I live here. No one would be surprised to see me out there. You, on the other hand . . ." Patting his arm, she stepped into her old beat-up loafers, then left the cabin.

It was a beautiful day—bright, sunny, a slight chill in the air but not too uncomfortable. The air smelled of spring, of pines and wildflowers, of budding trees and shrubs. She loved spring and early summer in the mountains, loved the colors, the fragrances, the sounds. Birds' songs competed with streams tumbling over rocks and down cliffs and breezes rustling through the leaves, and the blossoms— redbud, dogwood, apple tree, honeysuckle, azalea and rhododendron—were heavenly. The next few months were a wonderful time to be living exactly where she was living.

She only hoped that Dillon could share them with her.

She hurried down the steps and across the bare ground to the van, opening the passenger door, leaning inside for a quick look. Sure enough, the corkscrew was lying on the floor, one corner of its cardboard package caught underneath the rubber mat. She pulled it free and was preparing to back out of the van and straighten when suddenly a face appeared through the driver's window opposite her. Her startled cry died unvoiced as she stared at Steven Vickers. He was wearing the green baseball cap of the Catlin County Sheriff's Department, but instead of his uniform jacket, he wore a Catlin High letter jacket.

And he was holding a gun.

Before she recovered enough from her shock to react, a hand closed around her mouth from behind, and powerful arms pulled her away from the van. She caught a glimpse of the man who held her reflected in Bessie's window, but he was a stranger. So was the man behind Steven and the fourth man approaching from behind the cabin. But the last man, bringing up the rear, was no stranger. She knew Bill Armstrong well. She had gone to school with his youngest daughter, entrusted her savings to him and been turned down by him for a loan when she had first returned to Catlin.

Everything Dillon had said was true. If she hadn't already believed him, this would have convinced her beyond a doubt.

Dillon. Oh, God, Dillon. They had come here to kill him, just as he'd predicted they would, and he had no way to defend himself because Seth had taken the gun yesterday. If he died, it would be her fault for confiding in Seth, her fault for convincing Dillon to stay, her fault for not getting up early this morning and sneaking him out of the county as they had planned. If he died, she would never forgive herself . . . but if he died, she realized with a chill, she was going to die, too. There was no way these men might let her live to testify against them.

Armstrong stopped in front of her, his expression harsh and cold. She had always thought he was a pompous and phony old goat, but this morning she realized that it wasn't arrogance in his eyes. It was evil, chilling, narrowly focused. "Is he in the cabin?"

She made no effort to reply with her mouth covered; after a moment's wait, he impatiently gestured for the man who was holding her to move his hand. "You bastard," she said softly.

"I'm not interested in your view of my character, dear. Is Boone in the cabin?"

She said nothing.

"Call him out." It was the fourth man who'd spoken, drawing her attention to him. Like the others, he was dressed casually, in jeans and a jacket, a hunting rifle cradled in his arms, but he didn't look like the others. His jeans were pressed, his jacket expensive leather, his hiking boots top-of-the-line. He was young, about Dillon's age, but he was far more polished, more elegant, more like Bill Armstrong.

So this was Russell Bradley, Dillon's old friend, former boss and betrayer. She couldn't imagine any two people less likely to be friends than these two. She couldn't imagine anyone less deserving of Dillon's friendship than this man.

"Call him out," he repeated, his voice soft, lacking all traces of his Georgia upbringing. When she still didn't respond, he shrugged, and the man holding her twisted her arm behind her back, forcing her wrist toward her shoulder. This time she couldn't control the cry as sharp little fingers of pain stroked through her arm, up into her shoulder and down her back.

Steven Vickers moved around the van, holding his pistol firmly in both hands. "Boone!" he shouted. "Dillon Boone!"

Inside the cabin, Dillon was leaning on the counter, idly waiting for Ashley to return, when his name echoed through the windows. His muscles went taut, and cold chills swept over him as he acknowledged in an instant that Seth Benedict was supposed to be the only one who knew he was here and that definitely wasn't Seth's voice. Moving to the nearest window, he raised the sheet a few inches, and his heart stopped beating in his chest.

Bradley, Armstrong, Vickers and the other two men from Sadler's Pass. God help him—God help Ashley—they were in trouble. They were dead.

His gaze lingered for a moment on Ashley. She looked frightened and in pain from the way the big son of a bitch was bending her arm, but other than that, she seemed unharmed. She wouldn't stay that way long, though...unless he figured out a way to help her.

As Vickers yelled his name again, Dillon let the sheet fall and gave the cabin a sweeping look. Seth had taken the deputy's gun, and Ashley didn't have one of her own, not that it would help if she did; he had never fired a gun in his life and wasn't about to start when she was standing between him and his target. The deadliest weapon available was the paring knife on the counter. Muttering a prayer of thanks that he was left-handed and still had full use of that hand, he slid the knife out of sight into the sling, then started toward the door. There he saw the walking stick, long, solid wood, hard wood. He hefted it, decided it could surely do some damage, then let it slide through his fingers until he was gripping it near the top. Taking a deep breath, he opened the door and, leaning on the stick, he feigned a slight limp as he walked across the porch to the top of the steps.

Russell smiled the big, friendly smile he used to hide his black soul. "You're a hard man to find, Dillon. We figured you were dead somewhere out there in the forest until some of Steven's trackers finally picked up your trail again this morning. We never suspected that it might lead straight to Sheriff Benedict's lovely ex-wife."

A dozen agitated thoughts were racing through Dillon's mind as he listened. Where were the trackers now? Had Vickers sent them back home or deeper into forest to search for further tracks that didn't exist? If they'd gone back home, would they tell the sheriff what they'd discovered or trust Vickers to do it? How could he ever have trusted Russell, and did he get Ashley into this mess?

His fingers clutching the hickory stick tightly, he breathed deeply to make sure his voice was steady—to make sure he didn't plead—when he spoke. "You don't want to hurt Mrs. Benedict," he said, not shaky, not intense, just a quiet, careless warning, "because if you do, Sheriff Benedict will kill you."

"Sheriff Benedict won't have any reason to believe that it was us," Armstrong said.

"He knows everything. We had a long talk yesterday. Right now he's investigating each of you—" he gestured toward the three men in front, then made brief eye contact with each of the others "—and it won't take him long to find out who *you* are."

"All he knows is what you've told him," Russell contended. "He won't find anything to implicate us in either the robbery or the tragic events here."

Dillon shrugged. "He's got the gun I took from the deputy. Tests will prove that I didn't shoot him. The same tests done on *his* gun," he continued with a nod toward Vickers, "will prove that *he* did."

Vickers held up his pistol, a nine-millimeter semiautomatic identical to the one Dillon had taken off Coughlin. "You're right, Boone. Tests *will* prove that this gun was used to shoot Tommy. They'll also prove that Ashley was killed with the same gun. Then, presumably distraught over all that you'd done and over the prospect of spending the rest of your life—or dying—in prison, you turned the gun on yourself.''

"Seth won't buy that," she said scornfully. "How are you going to convince him that Dillon got hold of your gun when you *presumably* haven't seen him in almost a year?''

Vickers's grin faded, and his eyes turned cold as he looked at her. "Then we'll just have to take care of Seth, too.''

And that would leave them in the clear, Dillon acknowledged grimly. Not knowing who else might be part of Russell's scheme, Seth had proposed conducting his investigation quietly, completely on his own, at least in the beginning. If Vickers killed him and destroyed his notes, the only other person who could possibly speak out was Tom Coughlin...who had suffered serious head injuries... who was in a coma...whose recall of the shooting—provided he survived—could be easily discounted.

He and Ashley were screwed. He couldn't even try to bargain to save her life, because Russell held all the cards. Dillon had nothing to offer.

"Come on down here," Russell ordered.

Still using the stick as a cane, he slowly made his way down the steps. At the bottom, he stopped. "You people are crazy. You're willing to kill four people, two of them cops, for a lousy half-million dollars? That's nothing. It's certainly not worth dying for.''

"But that's the beauty of our plan," his old friend—his dearest enemy—replied. "*We're* not the ones who are going to die. And we never could have done it without you, Dillon. I knew the day I saw you in Atlanta that you would be perfect for it. You had never accomplished anything. You'd been in trouble all your life. You were a failure, a screwup. Yet you were smart enough to do what we needed you to do, trusting enough to not suspect what was up and honest enough to not rip us off. You were a perfect pawn.''

The truth of his words settled bitterly on Dillon's shoulders. So it had been an even more elaborate setup than he had suspected. From the very beginning, before Russell had even offered him the job, it had all been part of their plan. If only he hadn't lost that last job in Atlanta... If he hadn't accepted Russell's offer, if he'd had something or someone to keep him in Georgia, he could have avoided this entire nightmare. He never would have met Ashley, probably never would have known what it was like to love anyone the way he loved her, but at least he wouldn't be standing here preparing to die. He wouldn't be at such a damnable loss to think of a way to prevent *her* from dying.

She was looking at him, her face pale, her eyes bigger and bluer than ever. He wished he could hold her one last time, wished he could tell her how sorry he was and how very much he loved her. Then she smiled, just a faint little curving of her mouth, and he knew that she knew. She understood.

"Let's hurry up and get this done with," Armstrong snapped. "We've all got better places to be and better things to do."

Vickers stepped forward. "We've got to make it look like he killed her, then killed himself. Darrin, go inside and find her car keys. We'll say she saw a chance to escape, and he stopped her."

Ashley couldn't stand by silently while two people she'd known all her life planned the best way to murder her. "Right," she said sarcastically. "I was in town alone for two hours yesterday afternoon, but this morning I decide to escape. You guys are idiots. You think Seth or anyone else with a brain will believe that?"

Russell Bradley turned to look at her. His gaze was measuring, derisive and just a little bored. He was a far more dangerous man than she'd first thought, she realized. He truly had no qualms about murdering two innocent people, one a stranger, one whom he'd grown up with, whom he had considered a friend. He had no heart, no soul. "This whole incident will be quite a trauma for the county of Catlin," he explained patiently. "One deputy comatose and in critical condition, the sheriff dead, his unfortunate former wife murdered by the same cold-blooded killer who then ended his own life... Everyone will be in shock. They'll believe whatever they're told."

"You underestimate my friends and neighbors," she said coolly, but she wasn't sure she believed it. Three deaths and Tommy Coughlin near death... *Why* it happened could easily forestall any questions about *how,* and with Bill Armstrong—former mayor, everyone's banker and everyone's friend—there to smooth the cover story over, the *how* might very well never be asked.

"What do you think?" Steven joined them as the man named Darrin came out of the house with her keys in hand. "Ashley out here and Boone inside?"

"Sounds reasonable," Bradley replied. "Take care of him first. Be sure you make it look self-inflicted."

Ashley's heart rate tripled. "Bill, you *can't* do this," she pleaded. "You can't let them do this! You have your money. Please, Dillon will leave. That's what he was planning to do anyway. He'll leave the state and he'll never come back."

Armstrong looked at her without even a hint of remorse. "It's too late to bargain, Ashley. It was too late the minute he got arrested over in Mossville. Go on, Steven."

Switching the pistol to his other hand, Steven took hold of Dillon's arm as Darrin moved in on the other side. Terrified, trembling, barely able to breathe, she took a step forward before the other stranger blocked her way with his arm. "Dillon!"

He smiled at her, an accepting sort of smile that was underlaid with sorrow. "It's all right, Ash. Everything will be all right."

Tears blocking her throat, she watched, silently praying—pleading, screaming—for him to do *something* as he climbed the first step, the second, then the third. He stopped there, fumbled, then swung around, bringing the hickory stick crashing against the side of Steven's head. As the deputy staggered back, then fell, the stick continued its powerful arc, slamming into Darrin's arm, sending him to his knees and his gun flying through the air.

Ashley reacted instinctively, ducking underneath her guard's outstretched arm, diving for the pistol where it landed in a patch of yellow jasmine. The commotion of a struggle sounded behind her as the man came after her, grabbing her ankle just as her fingers closed around the rubber grips of the pistol, just as she rolled onto her back, clutching the pistol in both hands, pointing it only inches from his heart. It made him freeze where he was.

She had always thought that she was absolutely incapable of using a gun for self-defense; she had told Dillon as much his first night here. She would never shoot to protect her property and had doubted that she could do it to protect her life.

Well, she had been wrong. If she had any idea what to do to make this gun fire—if there was a safety, if it was on, if the hammer had to be cocked or if she could simply pull the trigger—she would do it. She would kill this man, and Russell Bradley and Bill Armstrong and the others. She would kill them and be glad to do it.

The sound of a gunshot boomed, making her jump. Scrambling to her feet, she risked a look at Dillon, who was standing at the bottom of the steps, his left arm around Russell Bradley's shoulders, holding the other man in front of him. The sun glinted off the newly sharpened blade of the knife he held at Bradley's throat. Steven Vickers lay unconscious on the ground, and the other man, Darrin, was sitting a few feet away, bent over in pain, cradling his right arm to his chest. Bill Armstrong had raised his rifle, taking aim on Dillon and Bradley, but he wasn't the one who had fired. It was either Seth, standing at the rear of the van, or one of the men with him.

Without waiting for an order, Armstrong threw his gun to the ground. "Thank God you got here in time, Sheriff. We tracked Boone to Ashley's cabin, and when we tried to take him into custody, he disarmed your deputy and his friend. He probably would have killed us all if you hadn't come."

Seth moved forward. "Your luck's run out, Bill. Dub Collins didn't like being cut out of the capture. He figured that he tracked the guy, so he deserved credit for catching him. To ensure that he got it, he came straight to my office when you sent him away." Slowly, his gaze shifted. "Ashley, you okay?"

"Yeah, I'm fine."

Turning toward his backup without taking his eyes off the men, Seth said, "Handcuff them all and read 'em their rights. Start with Mr. Armstrong."

"Wait one minute, Benedict—"

One of the men—an SBI agent, Ashley thought—stepped in front of Armstrong. He was a big man, backed up by a big gun. "Put your hands on the roof of the van," he ordered in a voice that demanded compliance. As the banker obeyed, another of the men took the pistol from Ashley and led the stranger away.

She started toward Dillon, but Seth, his attention already locked on him, stopped her a few feet away. "He's not worth killing, you know," he said quietly.

Dillon remained motionless. His fingers were wrapped so tightly around the wooden handle of the knife that his knuckles were white, and his breathing was audible, slow and measured. "That's what he was going to do to us," he replied, his voice just as quiet. "They were going to shoot Ashley in the back, to make it look as if she tried to escape and I killed her, then killed myself." He smiled faintly. "They were going to kill you, too."

Bradley wet his lips nervously. "Come on, Dillon, please don't do this. I've got a family—a wife, kids. Please don't . . . I'll tell them everything, I'll tell them how we set you up for the robbery, just please, *please,* don't kill me."

Seth glanced down at Ashley and, in a tense voice, murmured, "You could jump in here any time."

Her gaze stayed on the two men in front of them. "Frankly I think cutting his throat is too easy, too quick. I'd rather see him suffer." Then she sighed. "All right." Brushing Seth's hand aside, she approached Dillon. Pain etched thin lines around his eyes and mouth. In the condition he was in, the blows he had struck with her walking stick had probably hurt him almost as much as they'd hurt the two men. "I chose hickory for that stick," she began softly, "because my granny used to tell me that it was a good, strong wood for clubbing varmints that got too aggressive. Somehow I don't think she ever expected it to be used on varmints of this sort."

His gaze, very faintly amused, met hers, and she studied him for a long moment before giving him a knowing smile. "You aren't going to hurt him. You're a better man than that. You're a better man than he could ever be." She hesitated a moment, then reached for the knife. For just an instant, his grip tightened, then he let her pull it away.

He released Bradley, who moved away so quickly that he stumbled into Seth's arms, then Dillon tenderly touched her cheek. "I would have killed him if they had hurt you."

"I know, because *I* would have killed them if they had hurt *you*." She drew a deep, shaky breath. "I almost got us killed, and I am so sorry. If I hadn't gone to Seth, if I had taken you to Nashville this morning—"

He stopped her with a shake of his head. "I don't think I would have gone. I don't think I could have left you." At last he pulled her into his arms, holding her tight.

Clinging to him, Ashley was just starting to get comfortable, to get over the delayed shakes and to begin to think about the future ahead of them, when Seth cleared his throat and, with such reluctance, said, "I hate to intrude...."

Without giving up one degree of their closeness, Ashley and Dillon both looked at him.

"I know you didn't rob the bank, Dillon—or at least it happened the way you said—but . . . there's still the matter of the charges against you. We can get them dropped, but it may take a little time. These men are going to jail for trying to kill you guys and for trying to kill Tommy, but beyond the one comment that Bradley made, I don't have anything yet to tie them to the robbery."

She stared at him. "What are you saying, Seth?"

Before he could answer, Dillon did, with a soft, resigned sigh. "He's saying that he has to arrest me."

Panic began growing dead center in her chest. "*No.* Seth, you can't do that. You know he's not guilty."

She tried to pull away, but Dillon held her tighter. "Ash. Listen to me, Ash." He waited until she'd stopped her struggle, until she was focused on him. "It's okay. He's just doing his job. Honey, you were right. We've got to get this cleared up. We don't have much of a future with this hanging over me, and I want—I *want* that future. Fifty years from now I want a bunch of blond-haired, blue-eyed grandkids and great-grandkids hearing stories about how their granny once helped an escaped prisoner hide from the police and how she saved their grandfather's life. I want them to know why hickory makes good walking sticks. I want them to know how to bake bread and make quilts, how to weave baskets and weave dreams. I want it all, Ash, and it starts with this. With clearing my name."

Tears filling her eyes, she turned once more to Seth, pleading with him. "You left him here yesterday. Why can't you do it today?"

"Because yesterday no one knew he was here but me," he replied miserably. "Today a lot of people know and a lot more are going to find out. I'm sorry, Ashley, but until the charges are dropped, I have no choice."

Dillon brushed her hair back. "It won't be so bad. You can get a lot of work done to make up for this past week, and when I come back, I'll be a free man, Ash, and..." He tilted her face up, dried her tears and gave her the sweetest promise she'd ever heard. "I'll be back to stay."

The dirt road climbed and twisted through the hills, passing trailers, log cabins and farmhouses. The pastures were lush and green, the fields newly planted or being prepared for planting. It was a warm April day, the kind of lazy day when wading in a creek or walking barefoot down a dirt road beckoned, when lying in the grass and watching butterflies, birds and clouds seemed a perfectly productive way to pass the time.

It was a perfect day, Dillon thought, gazing out the side window of the Blazer, for going home.

"You should have let me tell Ashley that you were being released today."

He glanced at Seth. The sheriff had called him yesterday afternoon to tell him that the robbery charges against him had been dropped, that the same charges were being added to the attempted-murder charges Russell, Armstrong and the others were facing. It had taken Seth three weeks, some serious investigating and, Dillon suspected, a fair amount of arguing with the district attorney to convince him to dismiss the charges. A statement from Deputy Coughlin— conscious and alert, although a long way from recovered—had been a major help.

Dillon had spent those three weeks in a jail a hundred and fifty miles from Catlin. Until the investigation was completed, until they were certain that Vickers had been the only deputy working for Bradley, Seth had thought he would be safer elsewhere. Dillon had appreciated the precautions, but it certainly would have been easier being in Catlin, where Ashley could have visited. As it was, he hadn't seen her since that Sunday morning, when he had told her he loved her, kissed her goodbye and left her in tears on the porch.

She had wanted to make the three-hour drive to visit him—Seth had even offered to bring her—but Dillon had refused. He hadn't wanted her to see him in jail, locked up like a dangerous animal. Somewhere along the way being free had become more important to him; being free when he next saw her had seemed tremendously important.

He'd had one other motive behind his refusal. They hadn't known each other long—only six days. Six frightening, intense, emotional days. He'd known that time, quiet and peace couldn't change the way he felt about her; nothing ever could. But he'd wanted to give her a chance to see if the same was true for her. Once her life had returned to normal, once the danger was gone, once she fell back into her usual routine, would she still feel the same? Would she still want him? Would she still love him?

Soon he would find out.

With a sigh, he finally responded to Seth's comment. "I wanted to surprise her."

"What are your plans now? You going to marry her?"

"If she'll have me."

"I don't think you have to worry about that," Seth said dryly. "What about work?"

He turned to the window again. "Her grandfather was a farmer. So was mine. I grew up on his farm. I think I'd like to give that a try."

"If that doesn't work out, I'm going to be hiring a new deputy soon."

Dillon gave him a sharp look, then laughed. "Right. With my background, I'd make a perfect cop."

After a moment Seth chuckled, too. "At least you'd bring a different perspective to the job." Taking his foot from the accelerator, he shifted down and turned into Ashley's narrow, winding driveway.

"Stop here," Dillon said abruptly. "I'll walk the rest of the way."

Without comment Seth brought the truck to a stop. Dillon climbed out, then reached in the back for the small nylon bag that contained his meager possessions. In jail he'd worn a prisoner's uniform, and Seth had brought him a set of new clothes this morning, so his old jeans and Ashley's sweatshirt were in the bag, along with the toiletries the sheriff had provided. He started to close the door but hesitated. "Thanks, Seth."

"For what?"

"Getting me out. Not locking me up in the first place. Not using these three weeks to convince Ash that she was making a big mistake. She listens to you, you know."

"Maybe...but she loves you." After a moment he leaned across the seat and extended his hand. Dillon shook it. "Be good to her."

With a nod, he closed the door, slung the bag over his shoulder and set off up the hill. The cabin came into sight first, looking much as it had for the past eighty or a hundred years. Bessie was parked out front, as pathetically ugly as ever, and the door to the workshop was propped open to

let in the warm afternoon air. No doubt that was where he
would find Ashley, weaving a basket or dipping candles,
molding soap or stirring up her sweet-scented potpourri.
That was where he would find his welcome, if there was
one. If Seth was right.

That was where he would find his future.

He crossed the clearing and stepped onto the stoop, then
into the doorway, his tennis shoes making no noise on the
weathered wood. The bright lights were on inside, and the
worktable was clean except for a spool of thread, a pair of
scissors and an assortment of needles and pins. The loom
sat neglected, and the quilt frame, a quilt stretched across
the bars, was un—

His startled gaze moved swiftly back to the frame and its
quilt. It was unbleached muslin with an intricate pattern
worked in browns, yellows and golds, old, heavily used and
very much treasured. It was his grandmother's quilt.

He'd thought it had been lost forever.

A soft hum from that side of the room drew him through
the doorway and closer to the frame. He saw her feet first,
bare, slender, delicate, then a flash of leg, mostly covered
by a long chambray skirt. Seeking courage and praying for
the best, he stopped beside the frame and crouched down
so he was closer to her level.

She was sitting on the floor underneath the frame, her
head tilted back, using an impossibly small needle to replace old stitches on the back that had finally given way.
For a moment she was totally unaware of him, then her
humming gradually faded and her stitches slowed until the
needle was barely moving. Finally she looked at him. Her
hands dropped to her lap, and she simply looked.

God help him, she was beautiful, with the kind of beauty
that made him ache just to see it. Looking at her made him
feel weak. It made him feel humble. And it made him so
grateful.

Her smile came slowly, starting in her eyes and making
its way to her mouth, lighting her entire face, lighting his
entire life. She didn't move toward him, though. She simply sat there and smiled that smile.

"How—" His voice was husky and quavered. "How did you find my grandmother's quilt?"

"I have them all. And the Bible. And the photographs." Her voice was as sweet and unconsciously seductive as he'd remembered in his dreams every night for the past three weeks. "I drove in to Asheville one day and looked up your old girlfriend. When the landlord cleared out your apartment, Pris persuaded him to give them to her. She knew they were important to you. She knew you would want them back."

He drew his finger along the pattern where it folded over the wood frame. "I can't believe you did that, that you went to so much trouble. . . ."

"It wasn't any trouble," she whispered. "I was just repairing a few places on this one. I wanted to have it ready for you when you came back." Her gaze darted away, then back again. "You *are* back, aren't you?" she asked hesitantly. "You aren't leaving?"

He shook his head solemnly. "When Seth arrested me, I told you then that when I came back, it would be to stay."

On hearing that, she gave him the sort of welcome that he'd been dreaming about for weeks, launching herself out from beneath the wooden frame, throwing herself into his arms with enough force to make him tumble backward and take her with him. Laughing through tears, she covered his face with kisses. "I've missed you so much," she whispered. "I've been waiting and hoping and praying . . . Oh, Dillon, I love you."

Cradling her face in his palms, he kissed her, tasted her, savored her. She was so sweet, so special, so familiar—a part of his very soul. That was only fair, he supposed, since she already owned his heart.

Needing air, he ended the kiss—no, not ended, but interrupted, since he would pick up where he'd left off in a minute—and pushed her back so he could memorize every tiny detail of her expression. If he ever needed in the years ahead to know what pure joy was, he could recall this moment . . . or he could simply look at her face or his own.

"How long would it take your family to get here from California?"

"For something special?"

"A wedding."

"Less than twenty-four hours."

He feigned disappointment. "That soon, huh? I kind of had plans for the next twenty-four hours... and the next... and the next... and they don't include anyone but you and me."

She smiled delightedly. "Of course, if we told them to come next week, they wouldn't show up early."

He returned to the kiss, then rolled her onto her back on the floor and leaned over her, resting his head on his right hand, using his left to unfasten the top button of her white blouse. "Next week," he murmured. "That should be enough time." He opened the next button, then the third, before a sudden intensity swept over him. "I love you, Ash."

She grew serious for a moment, then her expression softened and warmed. "I know. Oh, by the way, Pris gave me a message for you. She said to tell you that she wishes you the best."

He thought of all the things he had in his life now. The cabin. The farm. A place to belong. A bright future. The promise of children and grandchildren, of years of passion and years of pleasure. And Ashley. Beautiful Ashley who had taken him into her home and her heart, healed his body and his spirit, saved his life and his soul. She had undone all the harsh lessons of his past and taught him the tender lessons of love. She was every wish and every dream he'd ever had, all rolled into one. She was his life.

"I *have* the very best," he whispered before he kissed her once again. "I have *you*."

*   *   *   *   *